REAPING INDEPENDENCE

a novel

by Jeffrey Messineo

ISBN: 979-8-9871924-0-5

Swift Media
Laguna Hills, California

To all those who would read a book
And say, "I'd like to do that."
Well, maybe you can, and I think you should.

Prologue

Maktub

Her first memory was from before she was born. Strangely, she could see and hear, feel, understand, a world she knew nothing of. She moved through beaded doorways and sensed orange lights; she flew within another's sphere and knew it to be true. Ya, in utero. The roar and the churn of liquids flowing through her body and of her host was constant. She didn't know it then, but this was the clearest she would understand her mother. The last she remembered of her.

She picked up her tab, she hadn't quite figured out the language. The sprytes were always bringing her snippets and feelings like morsels of a wonderful chocolate chip cookie but she didn't know how to handle the visits. Didn't even know what they were for a very long time. Still didn't, really.

She had heard the story of a poet. When this poet worked the fields, on occasion she would hear poems like thunder in the hills. The poet would run like hell to get paper and pen to write the poem down but didn't always make it. Sometimes she caught them by the tail and reeled them back in. Of course, getting the poem back to front. The same storyteller was sure she passed a host story from her to another with a kiss. Stories are funny that way.

To be sensitive to what all the world has to offer has been a gift to a certain few throughout the ages and many have suffered for the privilege. It's a tricky bunch, these receptive ones. Throughout time some have encouraged prayers, meditation, even climbing through a trap door to the attic to reach the spirits. The truth is the only ones who must do this, use trickery, are the slightly touched and the charlatans. Our sprytes, our daemon, are just as happy to come see us on the couch. They become part of our processes and, often, not in ways we expect.

There are those who attempt to reach that great beyond through drugs, alcohol, weed - some cannot break through without that sort of aid, but that need is the result of one of two things:

1. They are diluted, or deluded, whether through family influence or disposition. The magic, their ear, isn't much in them.

2. They hear all the daemon too well and are just trying to quiet those daemons down.

The sad fact is: if one doesn't handle contact well, or, somehow, they use their given talent combined with their hard-earned skill to become well-known, the sprytes, the daemon, get over excited and can overwhelm that particular human.

It is known that one man suffered from this very affliction. He had too many daemons then too few. He had stopped listening. He attempted to tell these spirits what to do, ordered them around, and that put him in a bind, strong-willed as they are. He was transported to a place of total silence and darkness. There is talk of deep depression feeling like being swallowed completely in a black hole of oppression. For some, that was simply the emptiness after the sprytes had left. But daemon never leave - you just stop listening. When the man couldn't stand his perceived silence anymore, he withdrew from our world by departing off a very high, very lonely bay bridge.

All these things Kwynn knew in her bones, flowed in her marrow, but not in her conscience. It had not been named. Just as the baseball player gifted with a lightning bolt for an arm or the genius that understands time and space on a different plane from the rest of us, one just is. You just are. And once you know, you still just are.

Maktub, the ancient Arabic word: It is written. Is it? If so, it has happened. It will happen. Agency and choice. Fate or free will.

Most of us block out the daemon rather than accept them as they are and for what they offer as helpers. In this case: To find answers and to tell a story.

The story of a hero. A story that has been told many, many times before and even heard by a few. The story of a girl, of once-a-boy, of a missing father, of a world that has fallen out of balance, out of power.

We begin with a traveler. Then a warrior. And a watcher.

These people are not, each, as you imagine them in folklore of olde. They are part of our world as it is now, or was, or soon will be. As it has been and always will be, except for one thing and, don't worry, I think you'll know it when you see it.

Friday

.bookish

Friday, 2029/08/03 05:53:00

Motes dallied and glowed from the breaking sun throughout the intimate bookstore as the rays shone and cut the spine of each neatly shelved book; light and dark stacked and repeated in perfect, uneven columns.

Kwynn, sitting at a desk, picked up her computer tablet, her tab, and imagined all the different pieces of this program. She moved the pieces around in her mind working for an understanding of a puzzle for which she didn't know the shape or rules. The answer had to be right in front of her. In her deepest tendrils there was a tickle at the edge of touch.

She sat at the heart of a small independent shop with a few thousand square feet spread before her, the walls stacked floor to ceiling with the book-filled shelves. The sections had a mix of tall stacks in history and fiction, science and art, that allowed the patrons to hide and browse. The children's section was low and open. Here, the children could see the books or tumble over the orange and green beanbag chairs.

Things were going to change today but a new beginning did not mean her past was erased. Quite the opposite, as we all do, Kwynn carried all that came before into all that came next.

She refocused her energy back to her tab setup and the holographic simulation refocused around her. The violet glow encircled Kwynn in darkness mimicking her short purple hair tinged in black. Despite the risk, Kwynn wouldn't ignore the persistent, ever present, drive. Mrs. Bridwell's warnings were part of her quotidian existence, yet, here she was back in the holograms on her last day at the bookshop attacking the firewall. It was as much a part of who she was as the arced stripes in her nails or the bumps on her kneecaps.

She heard the silence.

No.

Some bare hum. Silence. Hum.

Silence. In. Beats.

The immersive technology had unnerved her once. These holos were a whole other place, truly another plane of existence, even if the projections were right in front and around her at the desk of the shop. In this other world, she bumped up against the gates of TheRanch again and again to get to this kernel in the program. She needed to gain entry to TheRanch, a place out in the ether from which she was forbidden. She imagined herself like John Henry fighting against the machine. John Henry who drove his drill with a hammer in a dank railroad tunnel so long ago. Humans would beat machines even if it killed us. The difference: Kwynn wasn't going to die of exhaustion swiping and coding in an attempt to beat this firewall but, truth be told, there were those who were sure to take a different view of the incursions.

Kwynn reset her mind with a deep stomach breath for a state of relaxed concentration and flickered in the glow outside the virtual gates. With three years on this quest, she was on the verge of a win. Every time a new algorithm came out-and-around on the web, she tried the thing out here. Each time she was confident it would be the one. Each time it wasn't.

No one showed up, yet, to stop her despite what she always heard from the Bridwells. They were wonderful but Kwynn could never balance the Bridwells' support for all the tech with the warnings against her network adventures. Regardless, none of the algos she used to attempt the break-in were worth the disk space they cost. She had a new 4096 bit-hash algorithm cycling right now in another attempt to crack the code. These cryptographic hash functions were security algorithms developed out in the world and grew exponentially.

TLDR; The cryptic security breaks down to big brains and big boxes, the biggest brains and boxes in the world, all fighting to keep each other outside, or inside, their respective networks or the computers themselves. Geniuses built the systems and, right now, she can't break the code. Kwynn just couldn't solve the puzzle. She loved riddles and puzzles. Since she could remember, Kwynn ate through the puzzle books like the candy her dad gave her while he worked on this very program. It's true, not long ago her dad built this system.

Hold on, the motion in the hologram stopped and the script finished to nothing. Nada. Ok, same as it ever was.

Kwynn stretched and rubbed her eyes with her knuckles. She wiped a crunchy boog from the corner of her eye; flicked.

Fine. She had no right to the place. Her father was long gone. Beyond the loss when she was fifteen, Kwynn took the death as not very dramatic. Even alive, the issue was his unending focus elsewhere and always. Hacking into this place wouldn't fill the hole inside her but she clung to the effort like a prayer. The habit itself helped Kwynn feel closer to him. So, each night at the end of the marathon hack session, she tried a new personal combination on the pass code like a kiss on the forehead of the bastard. She didn't know why she tried so hard to connect to a dead man's legacy but, at this point, she had nothing else.

The password field blinked the cursor at her like a challenge. The same challenge every time. Entering symbols in the password prompt, Kwynn imagined throwing rocks in a water-filled hollow hewn from stone. Her query would plunk then sink. Nothing.

Kwynn tried a combination of Gibson (baseball not guitar), numbers (his phone number - her birthday) and her middle name randomly replacing all letters and spaces with numbers and symbols. Nothing happened. Her entries all bounced off the gates of the firewall. The prompt stalled, hung up in the violet tinged gloam. Not an entire failure but she had no response from the system either, simply darkness.

A ray of sunlight rose beyond a clump of bougainvillea outside and poked Kwynn right in the eye from past her interface. She refocused her vision and measured her surroundings, her body, to morning. She worried for a second if she'd be able to pull these all-nighters soon.

Kwynn registered movement somewhere back in the globe-glow of her holo. Ha! Something actually happened then a hum, but she floated in stasis, an in-between space. There was something else. Kwynn's inner alarms blared. Thump. Her adrenaline shot. The blood in her jugulars juiced past her ears.

"Oh, this is really bad."

Kwynn lost her anchor and thrashed through the wave of a storm. Lightning flashed on the purple horizon and electricity snapped. Void and shadow overtook her and placed her nowhere.

Her consciousness zoomed anew to the here and now. The holos flashed like a solar flare, squeee-ed then the tab shut down and the holo projections disappeared. The tab immediately began a reboot. All the previously open holo windows flew in front of her like magician's doves. A must of dust hit Kwynn and she glanced over her shoulder. The dust could only be the deep purple-velvet curtain separating back-of-store from front. Kwynn closed her tab.

Now, standing with the light eating curtain over her shoulder was Sunshine, as she liked to be called. Kwynn still called her Mrs. Bridwell. In any case, Sunshine held a single purple balloon.

"OK, Kwynn, summer class finished. You got the report in?"

"I did."

"Congratulations. Then it is graduation day!"

"Nope, just Thursday."

"Oh, child. You should celebrate your successes. College is still a big deal," Sunshine said handing her the balloon.

Kwynn nodded and said, "What can I do?" None of it felt like much. Kwynn watched the balloon float to the ceiling.

Sunshine did the same, "O.K. Have it your way."

Mrs. Bridwell walked over and picked up the mail

splayed at the foot of the still locked entry and said, “Your ride will be here shortly.”

The Bridwells set up a chance to work on a music video with some friends of theirs in L.A.

“Um, okay.” Kwynn said this as if she had something better to do. “When?”

“An hour or so.”

“What?” She actually didn’t have anything better to do but she’d been working to be prepared, mentally, to take off like this.

But Mrs. Bridwell knew Kwynn better than she knew herself, “Those shoots are short and this one’s coming up. You’ve done all you can here for now. It’ll be great.”

"Sunshine!” Mr. Bridwell said from the backroom. “Somethings wrong with the website!"

“Tell the webiste,” Sunshine said as she looked at Kwynn with a flourish.

"Webiste?" Kwynn squinted in pain.

"Ya, you’re a graduate web girl, website developer, it's all too long. This is French sounding, more distinguished: Webiste. Or Webbist, like a chemist. Biologist. Webbist."

"Why not coder?"

"Oh, you're more than that."

"What's wrong with ‘coder’?" Kwynn itched the bridge of her nose and re-activated the comp on the desk.

“Nothing. It's just a tool in your belt.” Sunshine ducked in the back.

While the OS on the store computer booted, Kwynn rose and straightened the small stack of leather and cloth bound books on the corner of the desk. The front desk which doubled as a workstation for the website, marketing, accounting, graphics, and first-person shooters everyone played when no one was supposed to be looking. Kwynn itched a tickle on her neck and went to type but a spider rested its spindly legs across her hand.

“Ah!” She knocked the pile of books to the ground as she bounced backwards against the chair and wiped her hands and head of the imagined spiderwebs.

“Are you ok?” Sunshine poked her head from behind

the curtain.

"Just a spider."

"Like eight thousand legs of a thousand spiders crawling up your arm?"

"You're not helping," Kwynn said as she ran her fingers through her hair and scratched her scalp with her nail tips in an attempt to end the tickle.

"You know some cultures believe spiders spin the web of fate."

"Mmhmm. And others think they are the tricksters messing with us," Kwynn turned her attention back to the desk.

"Get to work," said Sunshine and disappeared to the back.

The comp projected the holo and Kwynn scribbled her pass code in the spinning orb of light. The system logged Kwynn in and rotated to reveal a multi-colored work area. The space was filled with thousands of organized files and directories. When she selected a file, Kwynn chose with an interface of clearly formatted text that interacted with a rotating representation of either the code, style or imagery that made up the web application.

She studied the bits of code as they scrolled by like floating slices of light in front of her. There had been some sort of hack to the webstore and not the fix kind of hack, the break kind of hack where unexpected links appeared at the bottom of pages. Kwynn opened and scrolled files but couldn't quite find the source. One digit out of place on one page would break the entire thing. These types of hacks made crooks no more than a couple bucks per website, why would they even waste their time? Because if you get enough drops it fills a bucket.

She flicked and scanned, rushing through lists of thousands of files and could find nothing out of whack.

"Sunshine!" Kwynn said this time.

Sunshine wrapped the velvet curtain behind her ear as she popped her head out.

"I can't find the problems," Kwynn said.

"OK, you need to look past the problems and simple

solutions to the core of the issue," Sunshine said.

"Can't I just go to the back-up?"

"No, those things freeze our system. As a matter of fact, those backups are worse than the problem itself. Take a sec, what's wrong?"

"There's a script somewhere inserting those bullshit ads."

"Step outside the issue. See from the new vantage point. Then you can achieve a solution."

"I hate these things."

"You must be more than your problems, Kwynn."

"Well, I hate them," Kwynn said.

"Hate is a strong word. So is love."

"I'm not going to pretend I love this crap."

"Be careful: What you pretend to be is often who we become," Sunshine said as she checked her watch, unlocked the front door and disappeared behind the curtain again.

Kwynn gave a sideways glance, stopped and gathered herself. She opened the Operating System shell and did a search of the site directory.

"Got you." The search found the unwelcome code much faster than her eyes could. The nefarious ad strings and website redirects were tucked at the bottom of a functions page in a plug-in, inserted into the theme and dropped into a hidden directory. She cross referenced the modified dates of additional files matching the hack date and wiped her hands of the problem. Next.

Kwynn had a minute and with the trip coming up, she didn't know when she'd be able to mess around with getting into TheRanch. She was close. She knew she was close. She tapped her tablet alive, and the windows flew in front of her. Kwynn swayed and swiped through the hundreds of projected tabs and windows from before. Mr. and Mrs. Bridwell appeared before her. Kwynn actively ignored their presence.

"What're you doing?" Mr. Bridwell said.

"Nothing," Kwynn said and put the tab to sleep.

"Really?!" the Mr. said, moving to Kwynn's side, tapping the tab awake.

"No," Kwynn said. "Well, sort of. It did something."

"So, what did you find?" he asked adjusting to see.

"They found you, didn't they?" the Mrs. said.

"No. Ya. Maybe."

"Well, you better get out," Sunshine, the Mrs., said moving toward Kwynn to look at the holos despite herself.

"I'm wiping my trail," Kwynn said.

"Too late for that, kid," he said. "Contact is enough."

Kwynn blinked long, tapped her tab to sleep. The holos fluttered and blanked. Kwynn stuffed the tab in her bag. After all they had done for her, she didn't want to leave them with problems or on bad terms.

"You can't blame her," Mr. said to his Mrs.

"The hell I can't," Mrs. said looking between the two. Then, mostly to herself, "All this time. She's on her way to start out in LA. I don't want her exposed."

"She almost got in!" he said.

Sunshine: straight mouth, lips tight, no words.

"Kwynn, she's right," Mr. said, still tumbling it through his prodigious mind, always weighing the chess moves. "You gotta lay low."

"And you gotta catch on with that job. You're ride's already out back. Two guys and a truck."

"We propped the proverbial door open, you gotta do the rest."

"You gotta let it be," Mrs. said. She patted Kwynn on the shoulder. Her way of letting her know it would be alright. "Go on out back."

Mr. Bridwell said as he hugged her, "You'll be safer out there anyway. It's time." Though Kwynn never saw it with her own eyes, Mr. Bridwell had adventure behind those glasses.

Movement outside the shop window caught their attention. Two men in suits of some sort of dark green deep inside black, like seaweed, flickered in the daylight past the book's stacks through the front window.

The entry's hanging cowbell announced the suits. The standard issue agents raised their hands in appeasement but not their eyes. Their eyes were all business.

"Kwynn, we just want to talk."

Mr. walked straight at them. He moved with a speed and determination Kwynn had never seen from him. He of the plaid shirt and oxford sweater. And taser?

Mrs. swiped the purple velvet curtain and pushed Kwynn into the storeroom away from the commotion. A jolt and two successive thumps bumped up front.

"Got your bag?" she said as they walked past the boxes, through the metal back door into the alley exposing her to the blinding Arizona sun.

Sunshine grabbed her shoulders, looked deep in Kwynn's eyes, "Have a great trip," and slammed the door.

A cube truck idled in the alley.

A grim-faced dude, thin, jeans and t-shirt, kinda cute, stood on the ground, hands on his hips next to an open passenger door, "Get in. We gotta go." Bossy. Kinda short.

Kwynn walked past him without looking, put her foot on the step side and stopped. In the cab was a goofy, expectant smile glowing on the face of the big ass driver, "I'm Harley. That's James." Harley's arms were most people's thighs.

Kwynn did as she was told. She climbed past the first black grated step and Harley grinned even bigger, if that was possible, "You're bitch."

"But," she looked to the little stucco and wood strip mall store, back for the people who cared for her since losing her Dad. Silence.

"It's fine," James said behind her. "Are you coming or not?"

She looked at him on the ground over her shoulder, a little cross, climbed to the center of the cab and threw her bag behind the seat.

James hopped up, Harley popped the truck into gear and off they drove.

Glen

Friday, August 3, 2029, 11:20 a.m.

In the safety of the parking lot, Glen consciously felt the cool air-conditioning on him before he turned off his Wrecan company truck. He knew what was coming. He grabbed his things, exited and by the time he hit the fob to lock the truck, his body was covered in sweat. Not some humid sweat, this was baked oven sweat. Glen walked past the guard shack on his way into the Southern California Wrecan Power Center just north of Los Angeles, CA.

Reza, the guard, saw him, "Feels like Iraq, huh?"

"In spring," Glen said.

"Like home."

"Well, enjoy it. We have another week of it." Glen never slowed his gait, held up his sweating electrolyte filled sports drink as he passed the guard shack. They comfortably waved each other off.

He swiped his key-card to enter the shining three-story office building to a small anteroom. The entry wasn't fancy, just a guard desk and a metal detector. Glenn walked through the metal detector as the guards looked on then something occurred to one, "Back, again?"

"Yes, sir," Glen said and continued his way down a short hallway, flashed his key-card on another pad and entered the Power Center, a cool open room at least three stacked men high.

Glen settled into work at one of the consoles. The facing wall was stacked full of large screens lined edge to edge for maximum use of space. The panoramic view before him and his cohorts presented graphical representations of solar, hydro and wind electrical outputs. Other screens had lines and graphs of the production facilities in the natural gas, geothermal, nuclear, and single coal plants here. The engineers and project managers had half a dozen workstations, each with eight computer screens on their desks surrounding the worker. Every one of those screens tuned to the input, output, voltages and millions of other data points of the power grid in California and parts of Nevada.

Because of the heatwave, Glen worked a word processor on a modified version of a temporary rolling blackout plan. Really, it was below his pay grade but the more he prepared, the more concerned he became.

Maybe, that's why he was on it. Nothing new. All new.

As the temperatures rose, power consumption rose. The power companies increased power production but wouldn't, couldn't, meet demand of the millions of air conditioners, refrigerators, injection machines, grinders, phones, computers and a billion other electricity hungry machines we count on every day. Dominoes would fall if they didn't control consumption. West coast sized dominoes.

By definition 24/7/365 facilities don't run on typical 8-5 office culture, the shifts are staggered.

Prakash, his boss, was here on his day off, somewhere. Where the hell was he? It wasn't a question anymore. Glen continued to review and write these plans. He was confident it was time to implement controlled rolling blackouts. The Flex alert barely registered a blip in usage change and they should be ahead of this problem.

Not at his desk. *Rolling blackouts were the only way.* Not in the control room. He had a solid plan and schedule for the week as it was. *The 115+ degrees on the thermometers forced this.* He found Prakash in the break room.

"We gotta prepare the rolling blackouts," Glen said.

"Isn't that what you are doing?" Prakash said.

"It's hot. People crank the AC when it's hot, Prakash," Glen said. "Nobody does the 'lordy, lordy' Cat on a Hot Tin Roof thing until they're forced." Glen flailed his hand like a southern belle in the heat.

"We're the power company, Glen," Prakash said while he munched a hot dog he'd scored off the rolling warmer in the break room. "People depend on us."

"We force them. Those cranked AC's mean 20-30% increase in power demand. The stuff on the line won't keep up for a full week. Voluntary flex bleeped. Nobody changed. But this, this is going to be big."

"You know the channels. We're a public service," Prakash said. "Keep your plan ready."

"Oh, it's ready."

"Then go home," Prakash said as he left the room. He turned back around, "Wait, did you come back? Your shift ended three hours ago."

"I'm worried. I wanted to make sure we were prepared."

"Ya, me, too."

"I know why I'm here late," Glen said. "Why are you still here, boss?"

Prakash popped the last bite of hot dog in his mouth.

"I could only get these at the ballpark when the kids were little," he said with a smile and walked out of the break room.

Glen's poc-comp binged. His wife: Went to pick up. Out of meds up here, can you go down to Santa Monica?

He shot back a thumbs up and went back to the console to keep massaging how to stop a massive power failure. He'd get down to Santa Monica a little later.

Murray

Fri Aug 3 - about 8:15a

Murray cradled his camera with a forearm length lens as still as he could and clicked like hell. He made sure to stay behind and underneath the papery purple leaves of the bougainvillea bush. As long as he avoided the finger-length thorns on the branches it was a perfect hiding spot. Some gardener had trimmed the thing in a way that made a hollow beneath the bulk of the plant like the tube of a wave.

If he played this right these shots, combined with the pics he stole off her poc-comp, what you'd all call a phone, would buy that house in Costa Rica. He hated to do this but he had to do something. This one job could set him up for a long time in paradise. No more sneaking around looking for a shot of what we all got. Aren't we all naked under these clothes? Murray didn't know what the big deal was really, he just wanted to get paid and be done. What's that saying? What you do every day of your life is your life. Holy cow, whatta life.

As sleazy as it was, as a professional, he was quite proud of this one. Well, not of what he had to do but HOW he did it. This little singer literally, and I mean literally, never lifted her eyes from the phone except to perform on stage or in the studio. If her eyes didn't grace that screen, she was asleep. The problem, one of many, was she slept with that poc-comp in a tamper proof jam box. The thot never looked away except to call her mother and boyfriend. By the way, the boyfriend was another hot ticket off on location for two months in Prague. He played a vampire or werewolf, wizard? Whatever the 'gram hive mind was pushing to the teenies. It was all grist for the over hormonal youngsters' imaginations.

Our starlet was shooting this ad in Palm Springs for an out-of-market skin care line. It was a massive payday for her. Somehow her handlers thought ads done in foreign countries aren't seen in the home market. No brand dilution. Just $$$.

What Murray planned would dilute her brand plenty. Two lonely 20-somethings with comp-age tech can send some spectacularly revealing imagery, and vids, to each other. Talk about portraiture. He would make out, no doubt.

Back to his genius. The only way he could gain access to the poc-comp was to mimic the screen. She had to be looking away. This morning, like every morning at this time, she used the little device for one of those phone calls with her mom. She took her eyes off her screen only by holding it to her ear while she sauntered to her car and chatted.

Murray spoofed the devices unique MAC address and wireless information, did a quick copy of her drive to his tab and spun through the pictures she had up on the private-cloud-hash-protected-drive. The I.T. type screen-share-app he used was fool proof unless a mark was looking, then they'd see him clicking through their files and apps. In short, Murray stole her files most ingeniously and laid his hands on lots of pics grandma wouldn't want to see.

Even though it could take the little starlet down, Murray was ready to stop stressing rent and credit cards every month. He could never zero the debt and his rent never stopped. The combination of this little starlet and the heart throb was worth a fortune. The 'intimate' shots they shared back and forth told quite a story.

They were just kids but what did he care?

What right did people have to this stuff? They don't.

He just needed rent.

Murray clicked a few more pics of her topless in the hot tub. It was nothing she hadn't shown in her last video but he made sure to frame some leaves from the surrounding bushes in a few. The flora and fauna made people know they were unauthorized. The dip-shits at the gossip sites pay more that way.

"Three more clicks for good luck and that's enough."

As Murray extricated himself from the bougainvillea bushes, a thorn reached out and gouged the back of his neck. He wiped and found some blood mixed with sweat on his hand as he walked to his car. He popped the trunk to stow his gear and licked his hand to rub the sting out of his scratch.

"Whatta job."

Murray lumbered into the car. He turned on the auto-drive-it and told it to head home. He pulled out his tab and activated the holo with his privacy glasses. That bastard Willie sat in his brown chair in his brown office.

"Did you get 'em?" Willie said, not looking over from his other holos.

Murray squinted at him.

"Well?" Willie said and looked now, directly through him.

"mmmm," Murray said.

"What?"

"MMMMMMM."

"What, Murray?"

"All I got were some hot tub shots. Her security guy caught on to me," Murray lied. A lot of good a conscience does. "She never left the phone unless it was in the jam box."

"Murray."

"Trust me, what I got will pay rent this month," Murray said.

"Ya, ya, ya."

"They're on their way."

"Did you at least keep the leaves?" Willie said.

"Yes. I kept the leaves."

"Good. These need to feel stolen or we won't get anything. They want stolen moments."

"I know, Willie."

"Check back with me later." End transmission.

Asshole.

Murray pulled off the glasses as transmission resumed. He pushed them back on his face.

Willie still sat there in his shit hole chair in his shit hole office. "Check that. I changed my mind."

"Something better?"

"Get to L.A. now. There's a better one. And a package." End transmission.

Murray closed his tab.

"Asshole."

He glared at the console then Murray spun the viewer to

the Zillow pics of the cabana in Costa Rica while the car drove itself toward the I-10 to merge with the highway and work them towards Los Angeles.

Mariposa

Fri Aug 3 - 12p or so

Murray mindlessly swiped his pocket comp through post after post after post, closed his eyes and pushed out a long breath for patience. What time was it again? 12:04. Two more minutes and they would come out to recess. After the drive back from Palm Springs, his 6'4" frame screamed more than a support animal piglet smuggled onto a cross country flight. This sit at an elementary school tested the little patience he had left.

That idiot Willie's new task was convoluted but Murray wasn't paid to think. He pulled the unmoving butterfly off the dash. Murray inspected the delicate, cobalt sheathed carbon fiber wings of the nanobot for the twentieth time and read an imprint along the body: The Xerces. He set the thing back on the dash.

Murray wriggled in his crappy car seat, grabbed both the back of his head and chin and torqued. His neck cracked then he looked back to his pocket comp screen and searched Wikipedia: The Xerces blue butterfly (Extinct) was unique because of its color and habitat.

"Ya, being extinct may not be so unique."

At the turn of the last century, the San Francisco sand dunes in the Sunset District were occupied by the Xerces. Developers considered it better habitat for people, excavated the land and homes were built. Well, if a copy of an obscure blue butterfly did the trick, great. The elementary school Murray surveilled had a butterfly garden and he had a Xerces. Apparently, girl scouts needed projects and a drop in butterflies and bees had caught the imagination of the preteens.

The sweltering Los Angeles sun bounced off the dark, scratched windows of the school below. Murray blinked away the swimming light trails in his eyes when, finally, the bell rang. Not a moment later, the the door of focus swung open. A big group of kids escaped the classroom by foot followed by three in electric wheelchairs. He could finally see his mark. After double checking the image on his screen, he tapped the app controller on his comp and the blue Xerces butterfly lilted down to the playground.

Murray steered the nanobot toward his target, Elsa, who rolled over to the garden with two other little girls walking beside her. Each scanned the flowering bushes, sketchbooks and pencils in hand. Murray watched the entire playground pretty closely. He didn't need one of these other kids latching onto his bot.

A boy locked onto Elsa from the other side of the yard. This kid looked to be the bully in the class and proved it. As the Xerces slowly lilted toward Elsa, Murray was shocked and pleased when the boy ran across the yard at full tilt, jumped on her lap and bit her on the cheek hard.

Elsa screamed bloody murder as the girls swiped at the instigator. He ran full speed into the classroom with the girls, two aids and a teacher in tow.

"Perfect."

Murray piloted the butterfly gently onto the wheelchair battery while Elsa rolled toward the class alone. The staff chased the boy into the school. Elsa transferred to a smaller hand-propelled, sports-chair that was stationed next to the door and rolled to the playground with a wipe of her eye.

The notebook and pencil lay on the electric chair while the nanobot nestled safely out of sight and waited for recess to end and for Elsa to go home for the day.

.traveling_west

Friday, 2029/08/03 12:17:00

Kwynn sat side by side in the cab of the box truck rubbing shoulders while the sun relentlessly baked her through the windshield. This section of I-10 between Arizona and California was flat. Featureless rock and dirt squeezed the road to a point on the horizon and even at high speeds the driver could not hold the wheel for miles at a time.

No AC, Kwynn thought. The wind in the wide-open windows could almost convince her she wasn't bored. Check that.

"After we grabbed those shots, Milosz had us run up to shoot the Biltmore in Scottsdale," James said.

"Enough," Harley said. "Besides we didn't shoot, we hoofed the gear."

"The Biltmore was designed by Frank Lloyd Wright," James said. "Interestingly, he designed some sprite statues that were 20 feet tall. They were the focus of the night shots. Some brooding and magical high contrast."

Kwynn had seen them, the statues were nothing special. And boring. She was thankful the Bridwell's set this ride up and the crew had two guys from the second unit driving back to L.A. Kwynn hoped the Bridwells were alright. They had done so much for her as guardians over these last years since losing her Dad.

"Can we talk about anything else, James?" Harley said and brought Kwynn back to the conversation.

"Why?" James said.

It must be a couple hours on the road with his monologue about the second unit stuff. Kwynn looked at her poc-comp, pocket computer. It was a little past noon. Immediately after the poc-comp processed her face and opened, a push notification popped over the top of everything.

Astounding Act of Bravery. Watch the video! She clicked through unconsciously and stared at the news report intro before she realized what she was doing because another notification popped up.

Wrecan Co Most Valuable Company. Energy and Tech are the drivers. A series of graphic ads for recent best seller books cycled through.

"Wrecan bastards." She closed the vid and the announcements. "When will these marketing AI figure out the difference between bookseller and book buyer?"

Something else tickled in the back of her mind, an open space wriggled. The network service dropped her poc-comp, spun some lame ouroboros looking animation for a few seconds then the connection popped back. Her follower count on Twitter and Instagram spun up in front of her eyes. A bot must've found her interesting for some reason because all of her posts were getting likes and comments from way back. She closed the device and watched the sand, rock and scrub brush blur past until a sign post ahead broke the trance: 100 miles until the next gas station.

"We better top off," James said from the passenger seat.

Harley slowed then took the left from between the median. They were back to detail speed as sand sizzled under the tires. The dry crackling wind was warm and steady as the sweet, spicy smell of desert sage drifted in. It was a short welcome before the stench of hot bodies took back over.

The pocked road lead directly to the gas pumps. There was no differentiation between road and station; a two-pump job, with handles that couldn't be legal. There were none of those plastic parts just a nozzle and a trigger. James pulled the gas nozzle like a six gun, fired a few rounds and dropped it in the tank. Harley stood and stretched to relieve some kinks and took a look around.

Kwynn sidled away from the truck. She took a few steps to gravel then dust then sand. Dead sticks of sage brush stuck out of the soil like gnarled witch fingers. In the difficult heat of summer, nature forced the plants to protect themselves. The plants outward signs of life were hidden until the cooling off of autumn rain and longer nights allowed buds to form. She took a pic, considered posting then strolled over to study the straight line of the highway which mimicked the horizon. Something tickled in the back of her mind. A scratching appeared there that she knew but couldn't place.

A Text. Kwynn pulled out her phone to a poop emoji from James as he walked toward the building. She pocketed and scuffled to the mini mart.

Harley was out in the weeds crouched over a garter snake that must've eaten a mouse. The snake bulged mid-body with a swollen mass twice its width.

"Kwynn - check it out! This..." Harley was alone. Something else caught his attention.

Across the road was a light blue rusted Chevy step-side truck, parked half in the culvert. It smelled of gas and dirt even as he walked up. He wondered if a truck that old even had electronics in it beyond headlights and, maybe, a radio. The window was open so he leaned in. There was a metal dash, black plastic steering wheel, a few knobs and sideways slots for what must be the heater or fans. Some rug samples as floor mats and a Mexican blanket across the bench seat. Three dials for speed, oil and battery.

"Hmph, cool. RPM and an aftermarket shifter, too."

"And what do you want with that?"

Harley was startled by the big dude who limped his way, his red-blond hair dirty and scruffy with redder eyes ready to break his neck with a look.

"What'd you put under the hood?" Harley said.

"Who says I did?"

"I didn't. Just thought."

"All original but for the boring out."

"The odometer must've turned over a couple times."

Getting in with a little difficulty, "She ain't got 3500 miles on her. But I can fix her myself. New cars, you can't get your hands in and too many computers. Diagnostics, right?"

"It's a nice truck."

"It's mine," he said as he turned over the engine. He drove off without a glance as Harley watched him navigate the highway crossing just as an over-sized black SUV hauled ass past them.

Harley turned around to see Kwynn and James coming

back to the car. All of the lights fluttered, clicked off at the gas station inside and out then back on.

James scanned the lot and the road, "Harley, let's go!"

"Did the lights just flick off and on?" Kwynn said.

"I don't know," James said, stepped into the truck and started it. "Let's go!"

Harley opened the door and jumped in as James slowly rolled and checked the truck-stop in his rear-view mirror. "Lights are on."

.a_window_in_a_wall

Friday, 2029/08/03 15:27:00

The strangest thing to Kwynn was the machine-like silence. All the way from the highway she could appreciate the quiet precision. It wasn't quiet by any means. The wind howled through the sandy, rocky landscape but the propellers spun silently as sentinels queued up on watch. The behemoths spun few rotations, large swathing spins on dinosaur sized wings. Sparse between were medium sized turbines that seemed to spin twice as fast and smaller peppered turbines quickly spun like a school of sardines in the ocean. Spinning and darting while the big ones powerfully, languidly performed their duty. The turbines were placed in the valley and on the ridges; some very new and aerodynamic, others older and of metal but not too different from the wooden windmills we imagine on a Nebraska farm quietly grinding corn morning, evening, night and morning again.

"Those things must create a lot of power," Kwynn said mostly to herself.

Of course, it was James, "They do. In fact, just one of those makes enough power a year for over 400 houses."

James drove the box truck toward the afternoon sun while Kwynn bounced along with Harley on her other side. James slowed and exited to a smaller highway.

"Where are you going?" Kwynn said. "Don't we need to get this stuff back?"

"We do," Harley said.

"But we'll be late," Kwynn said.

Kwynn was told they needed to stop off in Joshua Tree to pick up some sort of jig. Fine. Who was she to argue.

They continued through a few more undulating miles of turbine encircled road until they turned through a sandstone and rock ridge into a valley of sorts with nopali cactus and Joshua trees. Dotted throughout were dark greenish scrub brush with white branches and lots of crushed tan granite sand. It was hot and smelled of heat, dust and green. Not a forest green, desert green. Light brown and green and yellow.

Eventually, they reached a dirt track running off the highway in a straight line toward two small buildings, an adobe house and a metal barn with bunches of some sort of structures she had no idea what.

The first thing she could make out was what looked like the side of a ramshackle, flap board hut with a window in the middle. As they drew closer, it turned out to be a single wall. Kwynn could look straight through the window to the desert beyond. Round pieces bordered the edges and were revealed to be machine cut logs. The 25-degree slant of the roof line held a long board extended with a metal rod suggesting a fulcrum. On one side was a 10-speed bicycle balanced near the edge of the roof, six feet worth of board in front of it. On the other, an upside down identical 10-speed stretched out the end of the board to unnecessarily balance the fulcrum.

"Who is this guy?" Kwynn asked.

"Well, he works here at this outdoor museum," Harley said.

"So, these things are art?"

"It makes you think, doesn't it?" Harley said.

"To be precise, all of this art is Noah Purifoy. He was an African American artist out of Watts and Joshua Tree," James said.

Harley glanced at James, "Our man is a cousin of his who tends the place and used to work with Milosz. He's a metalworker and has a jig they used to use when he was Milosz' camera operator."

"Here he is now," James said.

As they slowed to a stop an unshaven man met them. He had more gray than black in his hair with the walk of someone just starting the journey; all jaunt, no worries. He was holding some sort of steel and aluminum mount in his hands.

"I suppose you came for this," he said.

"We did - but could we grab a drink?" Harley said.

Kwynn jumped in, "We're fine - Don't worry. We gotta go."

"No, no, no. I thought you were rushed. If not," he said

and put the jig mount on the ground. "C'mon in."

"We are in a rush," Kwynn said as Jim and Harley exited the cab on each side ignoring her reticence.

Harley touched the contraption on the way by with his toe, "What is it?"

"Just some camera mount we tinkered out for a commercial. Milosz was still trying to show how ingenious he was then."

"Well, it seemed to work out," James said. Milosz, the DP they worked for, had parlayed regional car commercials into national ads eventually winning an Oscar for a sweeping epic a few years ago.

"I guess so," our guide said.

Kwynn walked past a flatbed trailer with a flat tire and a dozen folding chairs lined perfectly in a row looking not quite ready for a hay ride. As she chewed on what was going on with the trailer, she walked right to a low wall with a drinking fountain. A sign on the wall marked the drinking fountain 'White'. A toilet just below the height of the fountain and six feet to the right was marked 'Colored'.

"Want a drink," he said.

Kwynn stammered.

"Knock it off, Vin," Harley said. "She's brand new."

Vin laughed. James laughed.

Kwynn didn't know what to do.

Vin put his arm around her shoulder and they walked toward one of the squat wood and adobe houses covered in dust, "Some uncomfortable truths in Noah's art work, but, girl, you're going to have to lighten up if you want to stick."

Kwynn was fine with coded language in computers but coded art was a different story. These people were going to be a challenge to read.

Vin laid out four thick gold-colored glasses. Each one had a small pedestal as a base. These weren't wine glasses but not quite a water glass either. He pulled two yellow soda Jarritos bottles from the fridge. Popped the tops on the fridge side-mounted opener. Caps caught in a small bucket below.

He split the pair of soda bottles between the four glasses

just to the top of each. He poured with both the left and right hand at the same time. He did this all with the practiced timing and flow of a magician. Or a musician. An entertainer.

Kwynn was mesmerized. Vin picked his up and took a gulp.

And burped loud and long.

"Pineapple!" Vin said. "Sugar tastes so good in the heat."

Harley and James took a swig as Kwynn straggled then drank quickly realizing her thirst.

"Shouldn't we go?" she said.

"Relax," Harley said.

"Aren't we on the clock?" she said.

They all laughed. She didn't know what was so funny. They were on the clock.

"Listen, kid," Vin said. "You may be on the clock but you get a day rate. If it's 6 hours or 20 hours, it's the same. Don't you worry. They'll get their pound of flesh."

"Relax for a minute," Harley said.

"Says the guy with the job," Kwynn said.

"So, do you," James said.

"Not on this side of it," she said. "I still have to earn it."

"So, you say," James said.

"I do," she said.

"Ain't none of my business," Vin said as he tied a straw in a knot. "Seems you gotta get in the crew. Once you're there it's up to you. Don't want to run around like a nut but you don't wanna be caught sleepin' either."

"Isn't this magical," Harley said with a grin. "Vin offering up advice to the youngsters."

"C'mon," Vin said while gathering up the glasses. "I don't get to sit around on set all day talking anymore. I gotta get it in where I can. But, tell you what, it's all up to you."

"If it's up to me, I'd like to get going," Kwynn said.

"Then let's go," Harley said.

James agreed and Kwynn followed the three of them out.

"You tell Milosz to bring that back himself. Or, on second thought, keep that damn thing. I ain't got no room for it anyway," he said from the dusty drive in the heat of the bright but affectionate sun.

On their way out, Kwynn stared at the bicycle on top of the roof and wondered if we just force balance on whatever. We do. Giving us reason where there is none and narrative where there isn't. Or it's art. Kwynn pulled out her poc-comp to take a pic.

James got a text. He pulled out his device. Where are you? "Shit."

"What?" Harley said. "I felt mine vibrate, too."

"It's Phyllis wondering where we are," James said. Did you swing by Cucamonga on the way out of Joshua or something?

"I'm telling her we're passing Cucamonga now."

"Are we busted?" Kwynn said.

"We're on the errand they sent us on," James said. "These things take time. Don't worry, you'll still be a P.A."

"I'm not even a P.A., yet."

"Kwynn, it's your cover. Besides, you're assisting the production," Harley said. "And, if it matters to you, you have now attained the coveted Production Assistant title."

"That wouldn't be fair," Kwynn said. "People work hard for jobs like this."

James and Harley both laughed.

"Okay, how about Professional Bitch Boy?" James said.

"Girl," Kwynn said.

"Professional Bitch Girl," James said. "Hmmm... that doesn't have the same ring."

Harley said, "Well, there's gopher, driver..."

They pulled to the highway and waited to turn left, blinker flashing.

A black suburban sped straight towards them, took a quick right off the two-lane highway and kicked its tail into a slide. They slid to a stop just next to them; passenger to driver side, dust cloud swirling.

"Suits!" Harley punched it onto the highway in front of

an old station wagon and turned left. The suburban fish tailed a 180 and followed them.

The suits ran alongside the box truck on the wrong side of the road.

Harley, of course, had his window open (no AC) and the suburban lowered its smoked glass window.

An agent with glasses, crew cut and ear piece looked at him, "Stop!"

"No!"

"I said, Stop!"

"Nno!"

"Stop!"

"N.Nnno. - I won't stop."

Hom - BwaaaaH The black spy-mobile swerved around an eighteen-wheeler that pushed the pursuers on the shoulder in the sand. The suburban fishtailed and came back.

"Don't make us stop you!" the agent yelled and pulled his gun. "Stop!"

"No!"

Another car zigged as the suburban driver zigged then zagged as they zagged. The spy then stayed straight and the car swerved into the desert sand.

Just behind was a car carrier. The spies swerved losing that game of chicken and went nose deep into an airbag popping culvert.

"What'd you do?" Harley asked.

"I just looked around," Kwynn said.

"Who are you?" Harley said.

"Don't. We shouldn't know," James said.

"That's bull shit," Harley said. "That's the shoot first crew. They don't 'talk'. What's your story?"

"I..." Kwynn was cut off.

"No. That's the order," James said.

That was all there was to be said. Harley bit his lip and shook his head. The cab went quiet. While Kwynn sat and wondered what the big, fucking secret was. At least, what this part of it was.

"Are we gonna need to drop this film off?" Harley said.

“No, let’s get to Phyllis. I’m tired. We’ll do that shit tomorrow,” James said.

“Good,” Harley said. “I’m sick of driving already.”

It's hot

Friday, August 3, 2029, 3:48 p.m.

Glen looked out over the diamond sparkling Pacific Ocean from the cab of the company pickup. At the moment, he sat at a stop light. He never failed to marvel at the systems of stop lights, and presently, specifically, people at stop lights.

This was a long light on Ocean Boulevard at an intersection with alternating turns for cars and for people. The cars and people flowed and stopped. Red light. Green light. Each waited their turn then rushed across in a pack like pigeons lifting off at the park.

Even with his AC ripping full bore, the sun baked his face and left arm with dumb heat. What a god-awful hot day. They really were going to need to implement the rolling black outs.

The light changed and he did his part to race to the next red light. This wasn't the first time the Kaiser by their place was out of one of Elsa's meds so Glen had to come down to the larger Santa Monica pharmacy to fill it. No use getting mad over it, we're lucky we have them at all.

He turned in the driveway, parked and hustled in. It was his day off and if he didn't make it quick, he would drive a marathon in a car in the time it took one of those stud Kenyans to do on his feet. He needed to be quick.

He scooted in to the place, wound through some nicely cooled, cement corridors to find the pharmacy and grabbed a number. Glen swallowed his rush and took a seat. They called him immediately and he approached the window.

"Good afternoon. I have good news and bad news," said the technician.

"Ok."

"We have the meds."

"Good, if you'll..."

"But we only have a week's worth."

"We typically get a couple months' worth."

"Unfortunately, we're experiencing a shortage. Apparently, this particular immunotherapy was in a shipment that was in a container coming from Japan. The container, it went overboard."

"The entire shipment."

"Of that drug."

"And another is on its way?"

"That's what I heard."

"And it's not made here?"

"It's new. It's Japanese. We should be fine next week."

It's Friday, he'll be able to sneak out again and swing back down next week to pick them up. He took the mostly empty packet of meds and skedaddled to his truck which was 130 degrees inside. He turned on the engine, hit the AC and was blasted with hot, humid over-warmed old, conditioned air.

He hit the buttons and opened the windows to get some air moving as he pulled up to the driveway. There was an opening in traffic then he *firrrped* his brakes and bounced to a stop. A grown woman in a full work out get-up was engrossed in her poc-comp, eyes glued, headphones in. She didn't even look up at Glen's near collision with her. She walked on past and pushed the button at the corner and waited.

Glen just watched her then saw an opening and punched it, forgetting her as soon as he passed her.

.Paolo's

Friday, 2029/08/03 20:13:00

Kwynn entered what must have been a restaurant or nightclub. Glasses, silverware and china all chattered and clanked. Dragged chair legs echoed off the cool cement floor and bare brick walls.

In the corner a man in his thirties sat and watched from a group of small half-covered iron tables. The white tablecloths hung like gowns discarded. The man's black hair and t-shirt were stylish more than sloppy.

A grey-haired man walked through the back door. With his walk, it was the owner, Paolo. Next to him was a woman of similar age, Anabelle, who moved easily and powerfully as a dancer. She met Kwynn's eyes from across the restaurant, then, in a blink, both stood before her.

She (Anabelle): you know who she is.

Owner (Paolo): No.

She: She's come to play.

Owner: Ah.

She, finally to Kwynn: He's quite accomplished. He has played all over the world. He is mobbed in Europe.

Kwynn: Is this your place?

Owner: I'm just rebuilding. These four walls and exposed posts are just a start. I'm rebuilding it.

Kwynn sat at a two-top table as U2 played on the dais with Pete Seeger. Paolo, played the piano with them, then sat across from Kwynn.

Anabelle's there: It is the resistance. Like Paris. Fascists posters hung on the walls outside.

Suddenly in tears,

Kwynn was shocked

as an explosion rang out and

rapid gunfire followed.

Instinctively, she jumped toward the commotion and looked outside. A smug bald man on a balcony spewed and gesticulated to a cheering mass on the street below him. He finished a statement, crossed his arms and nodded approvingly.

Paolo: You can't see. You need glasses.

Kwynn shook her head and looked back to him: I'm fine.

Paolo: Take mine.

Kwynn: You aren't wearing any.

Paolo: Take them.

Kwynn looked at him and, he's the type that compelled you, cannot be denied, so she complied. Kwynn employed what she learned in acting: Don't act. Be. So, she reached to him and carefully removed glasses from his face.

Kwynn grinned. She looked up from the 'glasses', "They need cleaning."

Grabbing a napkin, she surrounded the would be glasses and frowned intently. She hoped to impress Paolo with her earnestness. Still standing, she cleaned a smudge from the lens.

Wiping once, then scrubbing hard in circles, erasing the smudge when - POP - black rimmed glasses appeared in her hand. Small doll sized, then - POP - full sized.

The shock was like an electric current through her mind. A bolt through her gray matter and skipped her heart a beat with a solid thump.

Kwynn: Have I willed this?

Paolo and Anabelle, they laughed and were very pleased.

Paolo: Yes, yes, I know as much.

Anabelle, smiled at him with a knowing smile. He had done it again, as he always had.

Dropping into the chair, Kwynn put on the glasses and it did seem clear. Clear that she knew this all along.

You have to force things into being with shear might and will. Creation is an act of brute strength not subtle beauty. An island formed by a volcano and a child born are not acts that come sweetly in the evening light. They pound and force their way into existence like a stallion running on the plain. Perhaps beautiful and majestic from the outside but a heart pounding, mouth frothing, lungs aching effort on the inside.

Paolo: Can you see now?

Kwynn: I can.

Paolo: You'll have to use it to perfect it. Really, to even be any good at it. Piano, for example, is my instrument and my tool but it takes use. You will have to come to terms to use it. You cannot falter in this journey. Truly, this is the only way. And use it. Power. Strength. Will. Meaning. Bring them to the light. And remember.

Kwynn: Remember what?

Paolo: You are not alone.

"Kwynn," James said and knocked her shoulder. "You should see this."

Her vision zoomed away from her mind's eye. She pulled her sight to right back in front of her. Her heart beat hard from the surprise of her magic trick. She rode in the truck still driving down the highway nothing but headlights, Harley at her shoulder. "All I see is darkness," she said.

"That's the point," James said. "It's L.A. and it's dark. Everywhere."

.arrival

Friday, 2029/08/03 22:45:00

"No data, no signal," Kwynn said as she, James and Harley pulled up to a large Santa Monica craftsman home set back from the edge of a cliff. The large surrounding homes reflected the light of the rising moon, overlooking an indistinct vastness.

"Weird. I have never seen this city so dark," James said.

"Especially out there. I can't see anything," Kwynn said. "What's that?"

"The ocean," Harley said.

James parked in the driveway. It was the type with two strips of concrete about the width of a car's carriage with grass in between. They got out of the truck, walked to the front porch and hit the ringer but, no power, no buzz, apparently.

"And how are we supposed to get her attention in the middle of the night without a doorbell or a phone?" Harley said.

"Where's her room?" said Kwynn.

"Around the back, upstairs," James said.

Harley reached down past some artsy bamboo into the river stones filling the planter, headed around back. He spied an old wood framed window upstairs. It looked to be a bedroom window and tossed the rock. Which went straight through the old pane.

"Don't make 'em like they used to?" Harley said.

"Actually, that window's probably older than the three us put together," Kwynn said.

The window didn't shatter or chink. The small plate glass was left looking like a shot from a Hitchcock movie, a black space opened in the reflection of the moon where the large shard fell out. Phyllis' face popped into view, scowled and disappeared. Presumably, she walked down to let them in.

They ran around to the front porch.

A moment later the front door swung open, "Jesus, the powers out but you still could've called - or knocked," Phyllis said. “I am waiting to hear if the shoot is still on. My guess: yes. They have their own power, obviously.”

She left the door open and walked back in the house, a space left where they were meant to follow.

This being her house, she navigated easily in the dark. Kwynn took the lead and they shuffled into the front room hoping not to break anything else.

A THRUMMMMM rushed from way out there to right here and in a whoosh the lights were back on. The hum of refrigerators and lights and electric boxes - computers pinged and rebooted - or devices pinged and ponged with the rush of information they must have been lacking. Texts, emails, app notifications. We all stopped where we were and pulled the devices out and gave them a look quickly.

“Yep, looks like the shoot is still on,” Kwynn said.

Phyllis walked back into the living room to see us head-tilted to our devices, and waited expectantly. She looked out the window. Looked at the kids. Looked out the window again. “You need to get that truck back,” she said.

“Ya,” said Harley.

“Did you drop the film off?”

“Not with the power out,” Harley said.

“Don’t worry, they’ll take it. Power or not. Besides power’s back.”

“I guess we should have taken it straight over.”

“I guess you should have.”

“We’ll take it tomorrow. FotoKem is closed in Hollywood.”

“Not in Burbank. They’re always open.”

“We can’t drive all the way over to FotoKem.”

“Take it now,” she said chasing them toward the door, zigzagging through the furniture they just bumped on the way in.

“That’s another hour and a half. We just drove six.”

“Go. All of you. And take that truck back while you’re at it. It can’t stay outside my house.”

They tumbled back out of the house to the driveway as Phyllis closed the door.

"Shouldn't we tell her about the suits in Joshua Tree?" Kwynn said to James and Harley while getting back in the truck cab.

"Nah, she'd just worry anyway," Harley said.

"Besides it's not new information, really," James said.

"Ok, then can't we crash at your place," Kwynn said. "And do this in the morning? She won't know."

"We better not," James said.

"Besides, we're staying here, too," Harley said.

"I thought you guys lived here in LA. Don't you have a place?"

James and Harley shared a look. "We're sort of between places."

They headed straight up Santa Monica Boulevard and passed the NUART theater with its big neon lights from another era, art deco with blue, red, white and orange in squares and streaks.

"Look at that place," Kwynn said.

"Yes, the NUART is a popular art house theater built in the early 1930's," James said.

"Is it still open?"

"Of course," James said. "As you can imagine, people around here believe in the spirit of movies. The flicker of film in the projector, the space between the frames. The places we fill in ourselves."

"They still come to theaters."

"They do."

They took an onramp to the 405 and headed North, turning east on the 101. They traveled to the Ventura Freeway to the 134 and hopped off at Buena Vista.

They took a few turns then parked in the small lot behind an open rod iron gate next to a squat, block square building. James hopped out, "I'll be right back."

"No way," Kwynn said. "This is my first film job. I gotta see this."

Harley got out with them and popped open the back of the box truck after unlocking the padlock. In the back were stacked boxes, all black with metal protected corners and side by side turn clip locks. One side of the inside of the truck had a built-in box floor to ceiling.

"What's with the white wall in the back?" Kwynn said.

"It's a dark room. It's where we change the film," James said. "If light touches the film, it's ruined. We change the film into and out of a magazine in the pitch dark."

"Some say, the light chases the spirits away."

"It's a chemical reaction," James said.

"Some say the chemicals hold the spirits in the film. The film captures a small part of them and records it forever. That's why film has more life than video. Why it feels more 'artistic' to those who care."

"Haven't you ever wondered why all the actors get face lifts all the time?"

"Sure, it's so they stay young looking."

"It's not the vanity, though of course it's some of that, but mostly it's because they lose a little bit of their soul every time they shoot a scene. The emotion, the spirit, it goes right into the film."

"That's crazy."

"Ever see a stage actor?"

"I don't know."

"Well, you take a look. They don't age the same."

"Is that why the Navajo didn't like their picture taken back in the 1800's?"

"That and the kicking them off their land thing," Harley said.

"Spoils go the victors," James said.

"That's not fair."

"Nobody said it was fair," James said. "It just is." He grabbed a 9x9x18 inch box, chinned the other two to the other two boxes. James set his on the ground, closed the truck back and locked it.

They, all three, walked to the front of the building, opened an aluminum and glass door with a security beep. Inside, the gray carpet was dirty and worn. Before them was a big receiving desk that was 60 years old if it was a day. Nobody was there.

They set the boxes on the counter and in walked a zombie worker. Not really a zombie but he was short and squat, just like the building, with dark bags under his eyes. He came to a stop and looked at them. James told them the production name and he printed a sheet on a dot matrix printer. He opened each box and pulled out multiple film cannisters taped tightly shut with colored, cloth tape, all with the production name and shoot date marked clearly. He noted the number of canisters in each box of film on the sheet, had James initial it and handed him the bottom triplicate copy without ever saying a word.

As soon as they were outside, Kwynn asked, "Is it always that quiet?"

"Ya, the lab guys don't have much to say. They're a quiet bunch," James said.

"It's locking in all those spirits," Harley said. "Their souls are tired."

"Sure, they are," said James. "Let's drop this truck off."

Luckily, they just had to drop it at the production office rather than go by the camera place.

Although the production office meant that they had to travel to West Hollywood. They cut back down Barham, which they told her was the proper way to get where they were going. All decent PA's on up knew that the best way to get from Burbank to Hollywood was Barham and to get through Hollywood was Fountain. Not the Blvd's of Sunset, Hollywood or Santa Monica.

The story goes like this: Bette Davis is on Johnny Carson millennia ago and he asks her, "For the young actors out there, what advice do you have for them on how to get to Hollywood?" She says, "Take Fountain."

No truer words were ever said.

Of course, Harley took Barham to Pico and Kwynn couldn't believe the Hollywood Bowl was right there. They passed just below the Magic Castle which seemed to carry some sort of golden glow up on the hill. Then he took her down Hollywood Blvd past old places like the Chinese theater with its cemented footsteps and hand-prints adjacent to miles of gold stars. Each a walk of fame. They may have seen a few night walkers. Some fulfilling their vice of music others in more traditional ways; all surely convinced that every night was Halloween.

They caught the very end of Fountain. But this was the scenic route. They crossed boy's town through West Hollywood until they reached a building straight out of the sci-fi tradition. Small and beautiful. Iron doors and plated glass. Iron chairs and spinning cloth ceiling fans inside. A large grey pool table in the middle and a brass cappuccino machine the size of a beetle, the VW kind, waiting, shining, when they knocked on the entrance.

The receptionist, a small man with flowing brown hair appeared followed by a small cocker spaniel with the same flowing brown hair. He flipped his hair dramatically when he saw who was waiting for him.

"Hi, boys!"

"Hey, Chadwick. Can you buzz us in?"

"I'll buzz you in anytime!" He flipped his hair again with a smile, picked up the phone, and proceeded to buzz. The gate to the side of the building opened and Harley ran back to the truck and pulled it into the gravel parking lot.

"Aren't you shooting tomorrow?" Chadwick said as he looked at a sheet behind the semi-circle, beautiful wooden reception counter.

"We are but we can't park the truck with all the camera equipment at our place," James said.

"Phyllis kicked you out even after the drive, didn't she?"

"Yup."

"Ha," Chadwick sort of laughed but more like flirted. "Who's your friend?"

"I'm Kwynn," she said and shook his hand. He held it a little too long. Chadwick looked at her then to James. Something passed between them that Kwynn couldn't quite make sense of.

"She's a new PA?" Chadwick said.

"Hmmm," James said.

Harley waved outside the door.

"Gotta go!" James said.

"See you next time," Chadwick said as he looked after them through the wall of windows.

Once they got up the block a bit, Kwynn asked, "He's a little forward, isn't he?"

"He's sweet," Harley said. "He's been gifted with an overactive imagination in a world of active imaginations."

"Ya," she said. "But his seems focused elsewhere."

"More like everywhere," James said.

"He don't mean nothing by it," Harley said. "I'll tell you this: he's good at his job."

They walked another block and hopped into a crunchy looking Honda Accord that sat in a walled parking lot. Harley took a left across a couple lanes and past a median onto Santa Monica Blvd. Kwynn's jaw dropped as they passed a huge grocery store, the Troubadour and Dantana's.

"You guys that's the Troubadour - I can hear the music!"

"It's your imagination. We're too early," James said.

"Is that Dantana's?! Can't we stop and look for stars!"

"Don't get too excited Kwynn. Every corner has old movie or music industry haunts," Harley said.

"You'll get used to it."

Kwynn had a lot to get used to. She also wanted to get back and get on her tab. She drummed her finger on her leg in the back seat spinning more ways to crack the code. Her nightly ritual was probably going to have to wait but she could still move pieces of the puzzle around in her head. Her brute force password attacks weren't working and she had a thought. It was possible that there were some weaknesses in the code, maybe she could exploit them like those idiots did with the webstore. It's really a direction she should have attacked much sooner but giving up really wasn't really in her nature, even if it was the wrong direction. Now, after further consideration, as much as she wanted to get into TheRanch, she wanted to crawl into bed more.

They pulled up to Phyllis' place and Kwynn led the way, took a look at the sky. The moon was always there, like a rock, while changing in its dependable phase. It shined in its imperceptibly moving place when all the light around her went out, "The half-moon got brighter with all those lights out."

James looked up standing at her shoulder, "That'd be a quarter moon but, it would, wouldn't it?"

Harley joined them, "Helps you understand the stories they told about the moon and the stars."

Kwynn and James nodded agreement. Where did she say that hide-a-key was, now?

Crypto

Fri Aug 3 - a quarter to 11

Murray stopped his car on the greenbelt side of a suburban street and wriggled in his seat under a partial moon in the dark of night. Velvet green lawns glowed under landscape lights while neutral colored commuter cars rested beneath uniformly painted stucco tract homes. He swiped on his tab through a few dozen beach front homes too agitated to dream about the cool ocean breeze.

One street over was a swatch of empty land filled with power lines and a small wood slat house perched in the middle. That house was the family home of his butterfly lover. The corner bedroom lit up there was rustling in there. Time for work. Murray activated a different program on his tab then clicked and swiped to a screen showing the tweenie room. Boy band posters and a poster of his singing starlet from this morning hung on the wall. Of course, she was a fan. He grimaced at his part in the wicked celebrity culture and, with the mic activated, he heard something interesting going on in the hallway. Rent won't pay itself. He articulated the tiny camera lens toward the room door.

On the screen were two subjects in the hallway. A silhouetted discussion between Elsa's parents.

"I'm taking this to the district if I have to," the Mom said. "That boy has terrorized Elsa since school began. He has to be moved. He's a menace. She isn't safe."

"It's the scorpion and the frog. He has disabilities, too. He is what he is."

"That doesn't mean he has the right to attack her."

"Regardless, he sees her as a target. Which isn't the case, is it, Elsa?"

"No, it's not," she said. "I'll get him."

Murray watched them gently lift Elsa into bed with a hug and a kiss on the uninjured cheek. Through the girl's bedroom door and out the hallway he could see Dad quietly close the door to the master bedroom with a shake of his head and continued discussion.

Murray reactivated the butterfly and flew out of the little girl's room to search the house. Into the hallway, he turned away from the bedrooms to the family room. He passed the couch, TV, coffee table and found the kitchen table with an open laptop. The butterfly floated easily to the small computer and folded itself into a perfect rectangle and glided into the USB port. The executable file activated instantly and allowed Murray full access tracking to the keystrokes and actions of the device.

The trap set; Murray could now wait patiently.

Dad came out and popped open the laptop, opened his fully encrypted password manager and logged into the company server via the VPN (Virtual Private Network) and rotating public-key cryptosystem. He checked his communications and fiddled with a presentation he'd been preparing before giving up twenty minutes later. He shut the laptop and turned out the lights on his way to bed.

With the lights out, Murray remotely booted the system, copied the cryptosystem key and devices unique MAC address onto the butterfly drive, then spun the laptop down. He flew the butterfly through the open window into the cool California air and into his waiting hand.

Murray plugged the butterfly drive into his tab and downloaded the key, address, password manager and database. He plotted the keystrokes in a moment and opened the passwords right in front of him.

"Got 'em. Thanks, Glen."

Saturday

Substation 19

Fri. Night / Sat. Morning, August 4, 2029 2:03 a.m.

Early morning, 2 a.m., and Glen arrived at electrical Substation 19 in his Wrecan truck. He motored home this afternoon had dinner, put the kid to bed, kissed the wife and fell asleep just in time to wake up and come back down to Santa Monica.

Only a police cruiser and an unmarked vehicle hung around as the last remnants of an all-night get together. Most of the police had come and gone.

Tight, horizontal yellow police tape ran around the chain link enclosure holding the island of transformers that prep the power as it flowed off the grid. Most people drove by without even noticing it. Inside the fence was the substation that distributed the power for stop lights, pocket comps and the frosty six pack at days end.

Glen parked, popped out and threw his hand out for a shake, "Greetings, Detective Kim."

"Cut the crap, Glen. Your boys already came and went."

"I'm follow up. The big boys wanted me to lay eyes on it."

"Boss didn't want to get out of bed?"

He pointed to the sky, "Last quarter, waning crescent moon. Don't get to see many of these."

Detective Kim raised an eyebrow.

"Our linemen are great but they aren't investigators," Glen said.

"A simple power outage seems below your pay grade."

"Not this one." Glen had already viewed the pics and vids.

"The Feds coming out?" Detective Kim said.

"Could be. Depends what I find."

"Knock yourself out. I'm into overtime..."

"C'mon, Molly, lemme borrow just a few more minutes of your time."

She looked him square in the face and hoped for a joke somewhere in there. He didn't flinch. "You don't need me," she said.

"It'll only be a couple. I'll buy you one of those home mortgage coffee things you love."

"Just get on with it."

He followed the perimeter of the chain link fence surrounding the transformers and marked the I.P. enabled security cameras. He checked these feeds when he got the call earlier. The video archives showed only the arcs and sparks of the transformers as they exploded.

"They took out seventeen transformers?"

"Seventeen. I haven't seen a deliberate take down like this since Iraq," Glen said. "The third time. Yemen, maybe."

"Boasting is a bad look, Glen. Besides, you're just proving this is the type of mess Wrecan pays you for."

"Is this why you don't have a partner?"

"Could be. Probably. Clearly."

"These men..."

"Or women - Don't jump to conclusions."

"Our *perpetrators* left clean shell casings?"

"No fingerprints."

"AK-47."

"Pros."

"Pros."

The power failed on this particular stretch in Playa Vista past the wetlands over to Marina del Rey, Venice and even part of Santa Monica. The failure cut vital electricity to homes, businesses, tech companies and studios. Fortunately, most of the power had been re-routed. But a whole chunk wasn't.

"Okay, now look at this," Glen said. He indicated two of the cameras. "I'm serious." He waved Detective Kim over to his spot.

"Those two were taken out," she said.

"No, they weren't, but they do monitor the enclosure in this direction. Watch." As he backed out, Glen walked toward a short pile of gravel. The forensic flag markers for the casings lay within a few feet to the right of the small pile.

"I don't even need to double check," Glen said.

"But you will," Detective Kim said.

He activated his pocket comp and switched between the feeds at the station. He was invisible. The piles of gravel lay exactly outside the view of the multiple overlapping video camera surveillance.

"Someone left that gravel as a marker."

"Either these perps watched a lot of action movies or..."

"Yep. Serious surveillance."

"And access to these feeds. Hey, how are you getting this feed? Your other guys said they cut the phone lines."

"The cameras default to the lines but they fall back to wireless with battery backed satellite cell service. Can you show me where those other cables are?"

Detective Kim and Glen walked a couple hundred yards off-site to where a large metal cover was pulled askew of a subterranean box. A slew of fiber optic cables ran through it. He gave the cover a kick and it didn't budge. "Heavy."

"It'd take more than one perp to move this."

"No doubt. And the fiber optic lines were cut clean through."

"They cut Internet and electricity. Somebody's up to no good."

"And they are using SEAL level shit to do it."

"Twitter and the TV news are claiming it's vandals but nobody goes through this much trouble because they didn't get their owner's share."

"Shunned employees want money."

"Ya, these bastards want power."

"Or the lack there of."

Agent in waiting

Sat Aug 4 - little after 9a

That morning, Murray waited in the anteroom of Willie's shit hole 'talent' agency. The kind of agency that hit up bored, overly proud moms at the mall telling them their little darlings were "just made" for the big screen, small screens or stage. Their talent "just shined through". Asshole.

A third of the agents were chi-mos or pedos and another third were cons. At least, Murray figured, he earned his money the old-fashioned way, he stole it. Well, and spied on people.

He swiped through his pocket comp and looked at Chirper. God, he missed Twitter. But he wasn't going to pay for that crap. Fucking knockoffs. He couldn't figure out why he couldn't stop looking at the damn app. He knew. Boredom and the chance to look into the lives of people he didn't know, one dopamine hit at a time. That and the chance to watch a guy try to eat corn on the cob via electric hand drill. Of course, he was surprised to lose his front teeth. This latest bit on the news pages about privatizing the grid had stirred up a shit storm with the libs, too. Good for business as far as he could tell.

The room was grimy and painted brown with greasy carpets. Old, printed Hollywood Reporters were stacked and falling around the room. Piles of round 35 mm film canisters and rectangular 3/4" video tapes clung to the cobwebbed corners. This stuff was from the stone ages with the dust collection to prove it.

Willie, the unshaved lout, popped his head out the office door and looked at Murray, then looked back inside nervously. He put a finger up to Murray then ducked his head behind the door and said to someone inside, "We'll need to take a break, mam! I just have a very important deal to close with this gentleman."

Willie offered the opened door and out walked a perfect stage mom, looking somewhat familiar, with a paunchy little girl in a lacy, frilly dress and pigtails, to boot.

"Please have a seat. You don't mind waiting. I'll be right

back with you."

The stage mom took in the room and saw Murray with squinted eyes.

"Ya, I'm from RKO," Murray said, crossed to the office and closed the door behind him. He turned back around and addressed Willie, "Do I know her from something? Why do you waste your time with these B-list broads, anyway?"

Murray sat in one of a pair of brown (of course), worn pleather wing-backs.

"Why do you think I brokered these deals? I need the money, asshole. Besides, did you see her and her little Shirley Temple?"

"Who?"

"Shirley Temple."

"Shirley."

"Temple. Ya. Shirley Temple."

"How old are you?"

"For Pete's sake. Taylor Swift. You know who Taylor Swift is."

"That old lady?"

"Give me the goddamn files," said Willie and wiggled his open fingers at Murray.

Murray pulled an old flash drive from his pocket and held it up with a shake, "The money."

"I don't have it, yet."

"The money."

"They won't pay me until I give them the info."

"Pay up."

"You know they haven't paid me yet."

"I know you'll never pay me unless you. Pay. Me. Before I hand it over. Make the transfer."

Willie pulled out his tab, made a flurry of key taps then hit the final button with force. Then he swiped and checked something else. His attention shifted.

Murray's pocket comp pinged with a notification that a lot of digits were deposited in his bank app, "Didn't pay you yet?"

The agent just smirked and shrugged.

"Asshole."

"We can only be who we are," Willie said. "Now get the hell out of my office and send that lady in here with the beautiful child."

The door burst open and the lady and the child shot tasers at Murray and Willie. The lines came out of their wrists like electric Spiderman webs, one line per wrist.

The woman's taser hit Willie straight in the chest. Willie grabbed at it, then his chest.

"What are you doing?" Willie said.

First, she gave him a light shock, "You are double crossing us. I have been alerted through the interception of your communications."

"I would never," Willie said as he rattled from the jolt.

At the same time, Murray was sitting three quarters to the door. One taser line hit the wing back in front of his face and the other hit the arm rest. The tasers came from the kid's wrists and were stuck. The damn kid shook the lines that would not come loose.

Murray jumped up, "What the fuck's wrong with you?"

"No. No, no!" Willie said. "OK. Everything can be negotiated. We will take your deal."

"We?!" Murray said.

The mother fired zolts of bolts through the wire and the bolts flew out of Willie's fingertips. His eyes sizzled and he collapsed dead.

"Unacceptable," the mother said as she looked at her cohort. "Can't you ever get this right? Must I do everything myself?" she said and retracted the taser wire from Willie's chest back to the fold of her open wrist.

"Oh shit, you're a modified Real Doll™ *patent pending*," Murray said even in this moment wondering why people need machines for the most basic of needs.

"I am not," the stage mom said. "I am not rendered for teledildonics. I am rendered for surveillance and acquisition."

Her body made a *zooowooomb* rising sound as the lines recharged. The little one ran to the chair and shook its own lines in a fruitless attempt to release them from the wingback.

In the process, the short girl lost the pigtails to reveal deep short black hair underneath and, in actuality, the head of a man.

As the moment of inaction presented itself, Murray did the only thing he could think to do. Murray ran and, with a flying, yelling kick, he knocked the big one square in the side of the head. The force knocked her over just as the taser shot from her palm into the wall. The wire hit directly into an electrical line hidden in the wall which blew, sparked and zapped. She shorted out into a pile of smoke and sparkles.

The little one had finally pulled the end of the taser lines out of the pleather and flailed its wrists unceremoniously. The lines wouldn't zip back in so the little guy hurled itself at Murray. The little bastard grabbed Murray's ankle with both arms and bit.

Murray stepped down hard on its neck. Then its head and shoulders. Murray stomped and stomped on the little thing until it stopped moving. Once the little robot released, Murray lit the fuck out of the office.

Two steps into the waiting room he turned around and loped over the robots in Willie's office to his desk.

Murray, index finger extended, pushed Willie's head one side to the other. Nothing. He grabbed the flash drive from the desk. This time he stepped on both of the assailant robots' heads on his run out like a kid playing lava in the living room, "And here I left my gun at home."

He passed through the waiting room and ran into the main hallway.

Murray mulled what just happened. Somebody killing Willie was no surprise. He was scum but what the hell does a modified sex doll want with passwords. The good news was he got his money. And, if someone would kill for the info, they'll pay more. Not bad, really.

Murray pressed the elevator button.

He stood and looked at the elevators, thought better of it and headed for the stairs. He tucked the drive back in his back pocket as he ran for the stairwell door. He figured eight flights of stairs were better than the chance of getting trapped into a fight in the elevator car.

The fire door clacked closed behind him. His steps echoed through the cool air of the cement stairway. Not a hint of movement here. Nobody took the stairs. It was quick work to the ground floor. There were two doors at the bottom, one to the lobby and one to the outside. His only thought was to get out.

He bumped the door and burst directly into the clumpy, dilapidated parking lot through the emergency exit. Wait. He jumped back and caught the fire door as it nearly swung closed.

He searched around the stairwell.

Just to the right of the interior door to the lobby was an old latched glass case with a fire extinguisher. He opened it and placed the drive on the thick layer of silty dirty dust between the wall and the extinguisher. He closed the case, wiped the accumulated filth off his hands and ran out.

It looked clear. His glance around offered hot sun, an unattended parking shack and an asphalt crumbled lot with faded, barely-existent white lined parking spaces and a hamburger wrapper carried by the hot Santa Anas like a tumbling tumble weed. Nobody.

Across the street, the roar of a box truck echoed as it pulled out of a studio gate past the guard shack. The truck slowed to a stop at the curb next to the block length series of indifferent plaster sound-stage walls.

Murray took a left down the side street toward the main drag. He walked a block all calm, cool and collected. He looked back to the big white building, all sixteen stories of it. The thing loomed like an art deco headstone at the end of a cemetery plot. His head on a swivel, he took a right to his car parked on the busy street, Santa Monica Blvd.

Murray walked to the front of his car and looked down the boulevard at oncoming traffic. He faced red light traffic without any cars coming towards him. He stepped out, walked to the car door, quickly opened and heard it. He looked back to the road.

The box truck came into view, turned right and punched it straight at him. Murray squeezed against the car to avoid the inevitable smash. The trucks side mirror glanced his face. His car door bent open. Murray fell to the ground.

The truck stopped just past him. A man in a blackish-green suit jumped out of the back of the truck like he was exiting a troop carrier. Strong, agile, trained. He grabbed and flipped Murray by the shoulder, plastic ties ready. The agent grabbed his hands and found only limp wrists. The suit unharnessed a small blackjack, held it at the ready then turned Murray fully onto his back. He checked his neck for a pulse.

Murray opened his eyes, “Hey, buddy.”

The suit smacked him with the blackjack and told him to shut the fuck up.

Murray barely registered the hit itself. His entire existence entailed the sharp tone at the base of his skull and sparkling flashes in front of his eyes. Words didn’t matter. Pain didn’t matter. But the greenish black suit made it through. The Directive. Fuck. Everything spun and then he blacked out.

The Directive agent searched Murray’s pockets and didn’t find what he was looking for.

He dropped Murray’s limp body back to the ground.

The suit touched the comm in his ear as he jumped in the cube, “Negative. It’s not on him.”

Sirens roared in the air toward the scene. They weren’t more than a few blocks away.

The agent pounded the cube trucks side as he slammed the back door closed, top to bottom. The truck took off.

From above, the charred stage mom and loose necked child observed from Willie’s office window in the building above.

Info

Saturday, August 4, 2029 9:20 a.m.

Nobody had turned up anything new on the Substation 19 attack. Not a surprise, Glen figured, this was just the beginning of the investigation.

Glen came in on an off day to gather his thoughts and sequestered himself in his office away from the consoles of the Power Center.

The boys out on the line had done an amazing job making sure that the live-wire they *did* have still worked. No one took credit for the attack. There weren't terrorists, weird environmentalist, anti-government groups or any of the other dozen watch-listers he unexpected. In addition, no single place, other than the substation, was targeted for some sort of elaborate heist to steal diamonds or precious art like in the movies. Most of the public were with power and had barely known anything had happened despite the hundreds of social media accounts that harped on his company and their response.

The initial reports in all the media nailed this as a well-coordinated attack, which was true. Privately, he thought that whoever was doing this was just feeling the system out, checking for vulnerabilities. There was more to come. News commentators grabbed hold and droned on about the infrastructure and business of the United States, blah, blah. Half of the nut jobs linked it to flag burning and the other to gun control. In truth, spies, terrorists, and corporate espionage were all on the table with none more or less likely than the other. The tech companies represent Billion$ to the economy and the Los Angeles area was a major hub of military contracting. Millions of people and intellectual property were all at risk.

Glen knew that Homeland Security was on their way, too, but those fascists did more harm than good. This whole "homeland" thing was a little too on the nose for a former military man. Fascist was unfair because a lot of good men and women worked there. The leadership, however, looked more and more questionable. Glen figured when we heard 'lebensraum' we were really in trouble and not before although that ass-hat appointment at the top traveled in private jets and bought gold bathroom faucets on the government dime. We all paid for those extravagances and the likes of him complain about public employee pensions.

Glen loved to imagine one of those wimps on a cherry picker running electrical lines or chucking up a pole in the middle of a 75mph rain and wind storm - or going IN to a burning building - or had some meth-head idiot try to take his head off because he was screaming about demons that won't leave him alone. Public service is a service to the public. The sacrifice is real but let's be honest, it's a job.

Glen rifled through the files he acquired on site last night. He settled. Rushing wasn't going to help. He just laid the groundwork like he was trained. He organized and archived the files. He organized and archived the video. He grabbed some still image screen caps to drop in the observations report. He had too many thoughts on this one. This was just the beginning, but the notes and details flew. Problem was he couldn't find the theme here.

Prakash popped his head in.

"I need you in the conference room."

"In a couple. Let me finish my thoughts," Glen said.

"Now. And bring the files," Prakash said and left as Glen looked up to the empty space in which Prakash had been standing. He heard Prakash from down the hallway follow up with, "All of them. No copies."

Glen gathered the info and, of course, made copies to his poc-comp. He strolled down the hall to the conference room. Sitting at the head of the table was Prakash. Two men with earpieces dressed in black suits with a deep green blended underneath stood in each corner. Looking out the center of the fully windowed wall, hands behind his back, was a man in jeans and a black turtleneck. He turned around to reveal a dark beard when Glen entered.

"Thank you for getting out to the substation so early the other night," the man said as he took a seat across from Glen, who was standing.

Glen guessed we didn't need introductions. "Last night."

"I understand you have done some outstanding work," the man said.

"Thank you. I'm just getting started," Glen said. "What concerns me is: this looks like a coordinated attack without a solid motive or claim of responsibility."

"Well, we have our theories."

"I am also concerned that this is just the beginning of this type of attack."

The man stood, "We appreciate your effort and commitment. We'll take it from here," he said and held his hand out.

"You'll take it from here?"

"We'll take the whole package: the flash drive with pics and video, your preliminary report."

"That preliminary report is unfinished."

"And your notes."

"Prakash..."

"He has no say in this," the spook said. "Neither do you. We don't need your permission to do this."

Glen caught his breath, allowed the old military mask to hide any reaction.

"Just leave the files and you can enjoy your Saturday with your family."

"Who says I wasn't enjoying my Saturday?" Glen said. No, this was enough. "By the way, who the hell are you? And why are you bringing these Directive guys in here?" With a chin to the two sentinels.

"Glen, I know you've been working hard on this," Prakash said.

"Now, there's no need to get territorial," the man said.

"There's no need to get condescending. Who the fuck are you?" Glen said realizing he hadn't even sat down yet.

"I'm the man taking over this investigation," he said and waved to the door with a swipe. "Thank you for your efforts."

One of the suits opened the door to the conference

room.

"You're fucking kidding me," Glen said.

"Sorry, Glen," Prakash said.

Glen popped to attention and his training took over. He followed orders.

Even if they were fucked.

He pivoted and left.

.tacos_tiendita

Saturday, 2029/08/04 09:40:00

Kwynn awoke pretty late, for her, in Phyllis' living room on the couch. The sun was full in the sky and already radiated the warmth of the day. Heat was relative. Kwynn wasn't *un*-comfortable. This was no Arizona desert bake. She was next to the shining Pacific Ocean and that water did bring humidity. Her lower back gathered the sweat to prove it.

She lay there and listened to the light traffic. Cars rolled by, slowing and revving at the unseen intersections on their way to their own stories and dramas.

She treaded lightly upstairs to the bathroom, the not-broken-window one, it turned out. She peed, splashed some water on her face and looked for a towel when she noticed the morning sun streaked across the window splitting the rectangle into two nearly perfect triangles. One half shaded and clear, in the other half, the sun highlighted the clouded film on the pane. The same glass with a different look in a different state. Further out the view was also split vertically between the buildings of Santa Monica that rolled right up to the empty sand and the beach that flowed into the endless Pacific which itself was split between the blue of the ocean and the infinite azure sky.

"Hmph." She pulled out her poc-comp and took a pic. She engaged the double-blind VPN and placed the pic in a Twitter post, then deleted it. Hiding in plain site is one thing but pics would place her in a specific location. Instead, she wrote: "Miss my peeps out here. Thinking on the dichotomy of life and how the halves of our life can be so different…" Kwynn decided on the next chapter in her own story: food. She deleted the writing and posted, "FOOD. Delicious and tasty morsels for my belly" and traipsed down the stairs.

"What are we gonna eat?" she said to the unmoving piles on the floor wrapped in sleeping bags.

She threw a pillow at James. He took the flying pillow and hugged it under his head in one motion without a word.

Since she slept in her clothes, Kwynn slipped on her slip-ons and bailed.

She skulked through the room, stepping quietly over the guys and slammed the door on the way out. The sidewalk beckoned and she took a right to find some sustenance. Until the first corner she half expected the guys to catch up to her but no one came.

Kwynn found a familiar rhythm as she walked alone in Santa Monica. With more people and crowds in the Promenade, she knew no one would see her. Kwynn had spent most her life alone in shadows and preferred it that way.

Single people in crowds are invisible if they want to be. No one was going to see her. For example, a young family spun in its own orbit. Dad chased a toddler headed for traffic while Mom pushed the stroller and grappled the bags. The bags bumped Kwynn.

A group of boys who would rather be called men never really saw her. Not one of them looked her in the eyes. Wusses. They see the girl but never register anything more.

A group of girls weren't much better. They focused on her hair, her shoes, her clothes. One girl came close to Kwynn's eyes but clearly judged whether her eyebrows were the proper waxed shape and the right color eye shadow (none in this case).

One older guy followed her eyes as she passed. He seemed to look right through her. This man played a beat on a bucket and sang an old blues song. Or was it some old native drum beat. The howling wolf hiding in his voice bared its teeth at her. She jumped on the inside. Kwynn would never allow that reaction to show on the outside. She just kept moving.

Kwynn smelled carne asada. The sizzle of the fat on an open flame gas grill grew louder as she got further from the singer on the street.

She reached an open store front. The window was open with the grill right next to it. These guys were geniuses. How could you walk buy this place, if you liked meat, which Kwynn did, and not grab a taco.

The whole place was open. The place was a small store and restaurant. Canned and jarred food like veg-all and refried beans were on shelves, as well as tortillas and Mexican chocolate. Soaps and cleaning supplies were on the bottom shelves. A bar separated the customers from the kitchen where everyone could see what the cooks were up to. At the moment, one cooked up a massive pile of carne asada while another completed his side work. He chopped onions, cilantro, tomatoes. Sliced some limes, some chiles. Everything would get used on everything else.

Kwynn took a seat in a simple metal chair at a table and ordered three tacos. She had choices; she was going to take advantage. She ordered a carne asada, a carnitas and an adobada. Also, a sidral mundet.

She popped open the bottle on an opener on the wall and took a sip of the sparkling apple soda. It was room temperature. She expected it to be frosty. Maybe they were going authentic.

Within a few minutes the tacos were slid onto her table with the flair and joy that can only be manufactured by pride and repetition. On a paper plate with three lime slices.

Carne Asada was a flank steak seasoned in garlic and spices, cut up and served on a corn tortilla with onions and cilantro, some red-hot sauce. Her carnitas taco was a pork shoulder cooked crispy, but with a green salsa. The adobada was pork in an earthy, spicy concoction of chiles and paprika, vinegar, oregano. The meat sits in the juices long before it's cooked.

Kwynn squeezed on some lime and knocked them back three bites a piece. She'd never had adobada but new can be good. It was.

"It's noon. You're just opening up?" she asked the cashier. She wasn't feeling conversational pre-food.

"For an hour," he said. "We stay open late for the partiers. We don't let 'em in late at night though. That's why the window."

A little girl of about eight walked in the front door. She noticed the empty plate and bottle on Kwynn's table and walked over. "Are you done?"

"Ya? Thank you."

The little girl took the plate and dropped it in the trash.

She stacked the bottle next to three others on top of the receptacle on her way to the back, where things are cleaned. She stopped and turned. She focused her kind but sharp black eyes and admonished her father, "Papi?!"

Kwynn looked at the cashier.

"I know. I forgot," he said. The little girl grabbed a box and lit a match. She held it inside a glass Virgin Mary candle on a small table next to the interior door.

"My daughter."

"Wow," Kwynn said.

"She's a good kid."

Kwynn changed the subject, "So, I got a question: why that huge pile of carne? You cater?"

"You mean that ten pounds of meat? My walk in gave up the ghost. The power surges knocked it, and the front one, out. At least if I cook it, I can serve it for the rest of the day."

"Bummer."

"Claro." He looked over his shoulder, "Chivo, you hear from him?"

The cook said, "Ya, boss has him on overtime today and tomorrow. Booked up all week. He might be able to come by after he gets off and look at the freezer."

This is none of her business.

"Thanks. I'll be back," Kwynn said on her way out.

"That's how we stay open." Then, "Text him, what's he want?!"

Dark Out

Saturday, August 4, 2029, 9:20 p.m.

After that pile of Directive waste had taken his investigation away, Glen had to cool his heels for a minute. Now that he was home, he was glad he had the chance to relax that night. He had been tempted to go out to the shooting range and obliterate some innocent paper targets but more important matters arose.

Glen stood over his daughter, knife in his right hand as he held a stem from the aloe vera plant in his other. He sliced the fleshy leaf of the succulent open to reveal the bright green sticky goo inside and started toward Elsa.

"No," she said and turned her face away.

Glen smiled, turned her check towards him and applied the goo to her bite mark. "You know this works better than anything else."

"It smells."

"It does. It smells like healing victory."

"No, it smells like alien plant matter."

"Like three-day-old caterpillar guts."

"Haunted eyeball jelly mixed with barf."

"Fish guts and applesauce."

"That's gross."

"Let's not let that boy bother you again at school."

"He wouldn't dare," Elsa said. "Dad?"

"Yes."

"How was work today?"

"Oh, it was fine, sport. Thanks for asking," Glen bent down and kissed Elsa on the forehead. "Goodnight, sweetheart."

"Goodnight, Dad."

Glen pulled the covers up to her chin for her, touched her cheek just below the aloe vera smear and mussed her hair. "Getting better already. I think it's the applesauce."

He turned out the light and left the door open a crack, "Jules, is her chair plugged in?"

"Yep."

Glen sat on the couch next to his wife and clicked the stream of a spy flick. They watched the pinwheel load for a moment. An image just appeared when the power went out. The room still glowed from the only light, the flicker of the empty blue TV screen.

"Uh-oh," he said as he switched off the monitor to save the charge. The room was pitch black.

Glen clicked the monitor back on and the blue glow illuminated the room again. As a tech geek as well as electrical company employee Glen had the computer and the TV plugged into the battery back up in case of emergency. He grabbed his laptop from the kitchen table.

"I'll peek in on Elsa," Julia said.

"It's dark in there and it'll still be dark in there with the power out," Glen said.

She did it anyway.

Glen looked through the front window to a sheet of black. The moonless sky was star speckled while the land beneath lay sleeping.

Doubting he would access any network, he spun up his laptop anyway. He moved the modem and router to his battery back up to provide power while he waited. The laptop finished the startup sequence.

Nothing. He couldn't get access to the world, let alone to the office. He picked up his pocket comp and texted his boss, Prakash: We're down here - You?

Yep - All of SoCal without power - Shit storm Come in.

See you in an hour.

He packed his laptop, tab and kissed his wife on the cheek. "I will keep you posted," he said as he rushed out the door. "It's probably nothing."

Glen started up his truck and drove down the winding gravel drive. His house was a company house. It was cheap and on twenty acres, an extreme rarity in LA. He unlocked the gate, pulled out, locked it again and entered the perfectly dark, suburban neighborhood. He drove down the hill to no traffic lights at the four way stop and hopped on the freeway.

"It's probably nothing."

Jacked Up

Saturday, August 4, 2029, 10:03 p.m.

"Did we do that?" Glen said.

"Not a bit," Prakash said.

Glen and Prakash were at the console of the Southern California Wrecan Power Center where they monitored and controlled their very important piece of the grid. It looked like the power was up.

"Anymore thought on the rolling blackouts?"

"Not a bit. Aren't these," Glen motioned to the surroundings, " close enough for you?"

Nothing was out of sorts except for the power, of course, which was now unexpectedly back. All systems were: "go". There weren't any malfunctions alerted nor had even a transformer registered offline.

"You see," Prakash said. "We have plenty of resiliency. All is back and fine."

The re-establishment of power, the full flow of power, was a surprise. Typically, you need to charge the lines and fill the grid. If the lines aren't filled with energy, we get the brown outs. Picture a series of dams in a water channel. Each section must be filled before filling the next section. With electricity, a trickle will only barely feed all of our hungry devices. The refrigerators, TVs and computers; everything gets just a little power in a brown out. Hence, the brown, not quite black, out.

Glen scrolled the logs of the main server which was, amazingly, a legacy Windows machine. He scanned the error log and wondered what failed. He scrolled and scrolled reviewing for anomalies and the list was long. This legacy machine threw thousands of errors a day simply because it couldn't properly communicate with the network.

"This will take some time, P."

"Go home, get some rest. The forensics won't go anywhere," Prakash said. "Besides, I can't keep paying you overtime."

"I'm on salary, boss."

"I will see you in the morning."

Glen dropped a copy of the logs on his tab and packed up. "This doesn't add up," he said as he looked to Prakash sitting at another workstation then past him. "What's that?"

Behind Prakash was another workstation computer that rebooted.

"What?" Prakash said.

"This is jacked up. It looked like someone was clicking through schematics."

"Probably just the reboot closing windows."

"I guess," Glen said. "It's offline anyway." This computer didn't control any power. It was connected to an out of network testing group.

"Pull the router logs. Perhaps we can track this a different way."

Glen popped out his tab, pulled up his Wi-Fi and accessed the local router to grab the information.

"Is this bad? This is bad."

"Ya, I don't know what this is but we better find out how bad this is."

.more_tacos

Saturday, 2029/08/04 21:45:00

"Go down and bring me some tacos back," Phyllis said. "Gimme a carne and a cabeza."

"What are you a zombie?" Harley said.

"Ya, I don't get this smart without some extra brains once in a while."

Kwynn grabbed the boys and set off to do just that. Kwynn had told the story of the taco shop and Phyllis wasn't about to cook without power. Not for a late-night snack. She liked to cook, mind you, she just hated cooking by candle light.

Phyllis had knocked out a great Caesar salad with chicken grilled on a BBQ and lettuce from her garden but that was in the afternoon. They needed midnight snacks. They needed tacos.

When they got to the shop, Kwynn was embarrassed. She had been worried about these guys at the shop. Like they were going to starve.

Ramon's Tiendita had a line at least two dozen long. While they waited, she looked it up and found they were pretty savvy for restaurant guys. The restaurant had solid ratings on Yelp, they updated their social media consistently and, unbeknownst to Kwynn, the Good Grub show on Food Network had featured them in an episode that very afternoon.

How did everyone see the show with the power out, you ask? Pock comps have batteries and the fooderati, literati, cinerati and most of the other high end, well off peeps carried a satellite plan on top of their cellular. They weren't going to go without just because the huddled masses would.

When they finally got to the front of the line the owner gave Kwynn a big smile, "Couldn't stay away?"

"I felt bad. I thought you'd be losing all your profits for the month with the broken fridge."

"We will. Today will help but, between you and me, we're screwed."

"Didn't get the guy out?"

"No. Too many broken walk-ins and we're too small. That power surge fried us all."

"Let's hope not."

"Oh, ya. Trust me, there's a lot of *gonna be* rotting food out there."

He handed their tacos through the wide-open window front. She and the boys stepped to the side.

Kwynn set Phyllis's tacos, in a bag, on the ground between her feet and dug into hers on her paper plate.

The boys had hammered their own by the time she looked up and wiped their hands of the juices, a beautiful medley of grease and salsa, cilantro sticking to a ring finger.

She ate her own, chicken this time, and picked up the bag with a peek into the store.

A purple laced white canvas left shoe broke the light to reveal a presence on a plastic leather seat. The little daughter curled in the corner of a booth, sleeping with her pock comp on her chest. Kwynn lingered on the vision.

"Let's go!" Harley said.

Kwynn stayed down a beat, her thought: to act like she was tying her shoe - the slip-ons. Then stood up, flummoxed.

James caught a sight of the girl as well, "Bummer for her."

"It's what she knows. She's fine," Kwynn said and walked away.

James and Harley shared a look.

"You want to talk about that?" Harley said.

"I don't," she said as she headed back towards Phyllis'.

"You had pretty strong feelings there," James said.

Kwynn did have pretty strong feelings but she wasn't going to talk about it with these two.

It's enough fighting the demons.

It's all in the past.

Sitting in a dark room, Dad's face glowing green from the code on the four screens wearing his worn-out Rutgers sweatshirt. Him not pausing to eat let alone feed her. Once, she complained so much he swiped his card and bought out the entire candy machine. He piled the candy and chips in front her.

Then went back to his screens in a manic panic. Soon enough that was his habit. He'd bring her there and pile all that crap right in front of her.

It lost its luster after a couple times. She would eventually sneak out and roam around the mountain facility. He told her about the future of the place. How it would be world class when he was done. How it would be self-sustaining with wind and sun power, cooled from the mountain air. It would start with spinning drives, even that resistance used to create more power; until the bio-drives were invented. Then they would have a truly free computer farm. They would be able to learn and grow. They would be able to think on their own and contribute to the world. They would be autonomous and add to our world. It would be the beginning of utopia. She also slept a lot.

Then he was gone. Thirteen, a mother that died giving her life and a father who was gone all the time. Then he was really gone. Kwynn had entered a story contest around the pile of candy time at a faraway bookstore. She won. The matron of the place took a liking to her. Since then, she had spent time with Mrs. Bridwell chatting on her pock comp and playing online battle royales.

Nobody noticed.

A few foster families really cared, but she couldn't. Just doin' her time.

Kwynn was moved down to Tempe to some foster care that led to college. Her aptitude and interest were all directed to the books and studying. Let's say she never looked up and the system noticed. It was like there was always someone there to help her out. Teachers, social workers, everybody lined up to help Kwynn and get her in the program. She had something and nobody wanted it wasted.

Including her. She knew there were good people out there. She also knew that little girl would be alright.

A text yanked Kwynn from her revelry.

CALL TIME: 3:30p

"Yo, we've got most of the day off," Harley said.

"What're we going to do?" Kwynn said.

"We should rest," James said. "It'll be a long night."

The other two just laughed.

Maybe she'd have time to crash TheRanch tonight after all.

Sunday

Markets

Sunday, August 5, 2029, 10:15 a.m.

Glen and Julia took advantage of an opportune day off to bring Elsa down to the Farmer's Market. It was a quick jaunt down to Santa Monica, especially on Sunday morning. As always, the Farmer's Market was out on the Promenade, a few blocks from the pier on Third Street. They parked below an office building in some cool, for August, shade. The spot was an underground garage of a small building with a tax accountant, dentist and insurance agent who all clearly had something better to do than work on this summer day. While Julia lowered the wheelchair from the back of the van Glen messed with something for his daughter.

"Would you look at that," Glen said as he turned his back. "Not only do we have sunscreen…"

He produced an aloe vera plant in a 6 oz. Mason jar with a smile.

"…I remembered your medicine!"

"Very funny, Dad."

Julia readied to leave the lot with a packed bag containing waters, snacks and an umbrella. Glen plucked Elsa off the back seat and placed her in her wheelchair. Julia lathered sunscreen lotion on Elsa and just shot the spray sunscreen on Glen to a grimace, who then dutifully rubbed the cool spray in to his skin.

They walked outside the parking garage and the reasons for protection were unmistakable - their skin tinged as they stepped into the sun. Everyone was long past enjoying the blazing yellow ball at this point. It was hot. It was summer.

Elsa said, "You know it's a good day when you feel the sun and smell sunscreen."

Heat notwithstanding, nobody could deny the smell of sunscreen usually meant good times. Ella flopped the umbrella as she opened it and hit her mother in the cheek just as Glen thought the traffic lights were out. Glen cared to Julia's cheek and by the time he looked back the crosswalk indicator was green and he forgot all about it.

The market was a joy. Just as they entered the space a vendor handed them a slice of apple.

"These are from my farm. Generations ago the trees were planted. Their ancestors were grown by my ancestors," he said. "They are Fuji."

The apple was cool, crisp, sweet. Delicious.

Of course, they bought half a dozen from the wife at the apple cart. The vendor started his pitch again to another couple. "These are from my farm..."

At the next booth they were offered peaches that were just as luscious. Glen bought three and they walked around with peach juice running down their arms and around their smiles.

This bedouin place of tilt up tarps and fold up shade makers was full of neighbors and vendors chatting and laughing. Two men had their dog in a pram. A preschool child pulled and ran from his bag-filled, now bag-spilled, father.

There was a local cheese vendor, an olive oil farm, strawberries, cucumbers, and carrots bigger than rabbits. Tomatoes exotic and run of the mill in as many different colors of red, orange and yellow as the sunset, all of them beautiful if not perfect. Beans, radishes, onions and garlic.

No cherries.

Glen asked each vendor. No cherries. The season had passed.

He did have the chance to catch the tail end of the Santa Rosa plum season. A beautiful dark plum with cherry red meat and slightly bitter, tannined skin.

They bought too much of everything.

It would never fit in their kitchen, at least, not neatly. It didn't even fit in the stowaway area on Elsa's chair. Glen stopped to straighten up the mess of bags so Julia took a seat on the nearby bench.

A moment later, Julia held up her poc-comp to Glen,

"Have you heard about this?"

She showed him a tweet that stated: "IT HAS BEGUN. The power is in our hands and it will bring Independence." It had 1,505 re-tweets, 456 comments and 9,935 likes with engagement exploding as he read.

"Did you read the sub-tweets?" Glen said. "Most of the replies are simply arguing and keep rattling off, 'NO MORE POWER GRABS'. A bunch of trolls."

"If you say so, but I know a bot campaign when I see one."

"It's nothing. It'll be fine."

"Did you see both of those sayings are trending?"

"The POWER GRABS / IT HAS BEGUN stuff?"

"They're talking about you."

"Leave it for marketing."

Elsa looked between the two of them looking at the device, "Enough shop talk, can we get this stuff home before it rots?"

"That's the plan," they both said, forgetting it all, as they headed for the parking garage when a huge sound rolled from the beach in the direction of the pier.

They all looked at each other, a little shocked. Car alarms blared throughout the neighborhood.

"That was an explosion," Glen said.

Elsa agreed, "A big one."

.a_trip_to_venice

Sunday, 2029/08/05 10:13:00

Since Kwynn and Harley were ecstatic to learn call time wasn't until the afternoon, they knew fun could be had. Kwynn wanted to go to one of the many places recent college grads visit when in LA for the first time: Venice Beach.

The trip took some cajoling on Kwynn and Harley's part to get James on board. After the late-night delivery of the film and dropping the truck off, then tacos and watching a movie Kwynn had saved on her tab, James was being a wimp and she wasn't going to let him. Kwynn was tired, she didn't even try TheRanch last night but she would figure out a way to see LA while she was here.

"It's Sunday. We have a whole day off," Kwynn said.

"It'll be good for us," Harley said. "Culturally edifying."

Kwynn walked out the door, "Besides, what's with the between places stuff? How do you not have a place to sleep?" she said. Just keep moving and change the subject.

"That's a loaded question," Harley said.

"We just moved off another job in Spain and haven't settled here yet," James said, with a look at Harley, as he followed her momentum.

Truth be told, Kwynn didn't really care that much. If they didn't want to tell her the whole story, she didn't want to hear it. Plus, they followed her lead to sightsee.

Venice Beach, on the other hand, was all she bargained for and more. First there a mass of locals. The eccentric elite lived in Venice. Home to entertainment moguls, actors (big and small), and musicians of all musical shapes. Second, there were tourists of all stripes. To top it off, that particular day was a Hare Krishna free food and mindfulness festival.

Festival of the Chariots. More people than fit in Dodger Stadium streamed through the cluster of tents all striped in bright blue, red and gold. The tents served as a center of families and friends that shared feast and conversation, all set before a long, sandy beach with the blue Pacific Ocean as backdrop; the ocean's blue darker than yesterday's greener blue.

Kwynn caught a glimpse of a young man in a dark leather top hat and large, leather overcoat. He sang and played his acoustic guitar from atop a short wall like a bard in the back of a horse cart. Intrigued, she stopped.

"The fair lady finds interest!?" the musician said addressing her, the passing crowd and his band mates. Kwynn's presence gave him a chance to engage the crowd with his shtick. Seated next to him on the cement brick wall was another young man pounding a beat on a small box contraption. A young woman tittered sing-song behind the two.

Kwynn laughed nervously and they laughed along with her.

"C'mon, maybe you have some mana for our souls," he said.

"Or money for our pockets," said the percussionist sitting on the cajon.

She bowed with a wave of the arm and produced a fiver. Kwynn held it up, "But I'll need a song."

"There's a cost for everything," the girl sang and the leader strummed some palm muted chords on his guitar, singing a variation on the words "there's a cost for everything" with the beat set by the drum box and the song bird fills. "There's a cost for everything."

Kwynn giggled and dropped the cash onto the worn, dark green velvet of their open guitar case.

Twenty steps ahead James realized Kwynn no longer walked with him and Harley. He circled back to find the girl singer flittered around Kwynn like a Greek siren while she tapped her finger cymbals in concert with the drummer. "There's a cost for everything."

"It's costing me my ears," James said as he embraced Kwynn's shoulder and walked her down the boardwalk.

"I was having fun," Kwynn said.

"Those are not the type to mingle with," James said when the rush of skunk smoke almost knocked them over. Kwynn looked over with a single eyebrow raised.

Dr. Green reeked of pot and patchouli oil.

Dr. Green was a store front manned by a beautiful man and a beautiful woman in lab coats with clip boards hocking marijuana as the heal all herb. Clearly, neither was the doctor. "Come inside," they said, "relieve your pain."

As Kwynn contemplated what pain they were looking to relieve, James said, "Someone's following us."

Harley looked at him, then around, "You're being paranoid. Nobody sees anything."

"Maybe. But something is up."

They walked along a busy boardwalk constructed in squares of concrete and asphalt held together in some spots with a mix of sand, gum and cigarettes. The many vendors sold tourist shirts, plastic sunglasses, beach toys, henna tattoos, burgers and corn dogs. The buildings were a mix of one and two story all painted turquoise or yellow, red and bright white. Kites and wind sails fluttered on the subtle ocean breeze. They shuffled over the sand dusted boardwalk until they opened into the central area while dodging a squadron of pigeons to even more surprises.

Kwynn had passed the basketball courts filled with ballers and hustlers who talked trash and shot hoops. The famed outdoor workout area contained iron weights and stretch polyester clothed muscle builders who could flex the muscles in their thumb. She watched skateboarders from five to sixty-five pulling Ollie's and toe flips, manuals and rail grabs. But most amazing was when they came upon a large chariot in the middle of the festivities. Then two more chariots exactly like the first.

In concert with the theme, the three extravagant Indian-styled carts were bright with colors of blue, red and gold. The colors matched the stripes of the myriad tents. The carts were tall, two-story floats covered in wreaths, flowers, balloons and more. All symbols of prosperity.

"What are these?" Kwynn said.

"Don't ask!" Harley said.

James answered, "The chariots carry the Lord Jagannatha, Lord of the Universe, his lord brother Baladeva and his sister Lady Subhadra. In the mythology, they have been cloistered in a temple and ventured to greet the people of this world."

The crowd sang and danced around the chariots in a parade.

"See?" Harley said.

"They say if you are lucky enough to pull the chariot, you pull God close to your heart and drive out all unwanted things."

"It takes more than pulling a cart to solve your problems," Harley said.

The thousands of people moved like water around rocks. If they even touched it was momentary. Many dressed in celebration of hare Krishna with orange robes and shaved heads but were otherwise people in a crowd. Exotic only to Kwynn.

A half dozen of those in orange passed, danced and chanted through the crowd. The circle of tents sat on small knolls that opened to a park amphitheater. The group within faced a stage and danced to a mix of Eastern sounds and Western DJ beats driven by sitars and flutes, African dance beats. People of all colors, shapes and sizes danced like damsels and dragonflies to the song.

"I can't believe how many people have their kids on their shoulders," Kwynn said to no answer from the boys.

"How about a snow cone?" James said and pointed out a booth on the other side of the nearest group of tents.

"I figure a hot summer day is better with a snow cone, Jimbo," Kwynn said.

James looked back stone faced.

Harley laughed and said, "He's not the Jimbo type."

Kwynn was drawn to one of the gathering of tents where small groups sat in the shade listening intently to gurus discussing aspects of meditation and religion. This one that attracted her overflowed with people sitting inside and others standing around the tent poles on the outside.

An old Indian man, legs crossed, sat on a dais. He spoke intently to the rapt audience. "This is the call and the threshold," he said. "Here we see and feel and are taken over to the parallel space - a dimension of the simulacrum. A place where your past place is crammed into the same space as your present. Where you find your hidden talents only exist once you have pushed through the boundary. Talents, all. Spiritual, physical, mental. This is a wall unseen and only really felt once you have pushed through it. Passing into that state of mindfulness, you may see the daemon of a few of these people.

Look around. Use your third eye. It is extraordinary and surprising. Many of the daemon are like a well-trained dog - controlled and pleased, if not happy. In comparison, many who are less skilled and overwhelmed by these sprytes, you will see them jumping and circling around them like a puppy off a leash. They seek attention. They lack discipline."

James looked to Kwynn and Harley, "He speaks sense."

Kwynn looked at James. Whatever. She then turned her head next door to the snow cones and was surprised to see a kindly old Indian woman, head wrapped with a scarf, looking intently at them waiting for their order.

"Would you like some?" the old woman said.

"I don't see the price," Kwynn said.

"These are free. We are simply sharing mana for our souls."

Kwynn took three raspberry blue snow cones with a thank you. They took to the boardwalk and Kwynn turned to face the beach to take a pic. A four-wheeled cycle bared down the boardwalk right toward them. The three split with a leap as a toe-headed tourist family raced past. The boy and girl fought to steer the four-wheeled cycle down the boardwalk as the parents apologized from the back.

"I want to try one of those!" Kwynn said.

James shook his head, "No."

"I'll pay," Harley said and ran over to the vendor booth.

"Besides," she said, "it'll be faster to ride down to the pier than walk."

"To the pier? That's two miles away," James said.

"Then we better get moving," Harley said as he gave the vendor a twenty and hopped in the driver's seat.

A little bit of pedaling later, they pulled near a swing set with a perfect view of the pier running out into the Pacific and covered with booths, a roller coaster and a Ferris wheel.

"One more shot," Kwynn said and hopped out to click a pic. She clicked and then a huge explosion flashed and boomed down the beach. A plume of smoke and fire rose above the pier and the Ferris wheel toppled.

James pulled his phone out to record what was happening in video.

"What is going on?" James said and looked away from his phone to see Kwynn and Harley running upstream. As the crowds ran away from the explosion, Kwynn and Harley ran towards it.

"Call time is in two hours, you guys!" James said and followed.

The Unlikely Meeting
Sunday, 2029.08.05 10:55:00

Bob caught his strap sandal on a tree root-raised piece of sidewalk and nearly fell on his face.

"Watch where you're going, Bob," he said to himself as he walked down Ocean Avenue just by the Santa Monica Civic Center reminiscing about Tongva Park. What was once Tongva Park. The whole area was once the Tongva nation, so to speak. The Tongva were the original inhabitants of the entire region including the Channel Islands before the Spaniards and the 49ers after them. In any case, this latest rendition of land appropriation had rolled the park over to make a bank of electrical substations. It looked to Bob's eyes to be some sort of boondoggle blending of private land, public land and the needs of the Power Company. According to them, it often seemed the needs of a legacy land owner and a large company aligned perfectly with the needs of the people. Quite poetic.

Bob got a notification on his poc-comp. "Old school Hollywood agent, Willie Smith, known for turning children into stars was attacked and killed today in his offices."

"Asshole finally got what he deserved," Bob said to himself. "Show your junk to enough people someone is finally going to offend you back."

Bob looked past his revelry and saw a pair of technicians, one tall and one short, really short, worked behind the fence of the power sub-station.

Curious, as always, Bob looked them over through the fence and realized what they were doing in the enclosure. Realized wasn't the word. He just knew these guys were up to no good. He could feel it in his bones. Well, that and they wore Wrecan jumpsuits and this was an Edison substation according to the signs.

"What are you doing in there?" he said to the two workers inside the electrical pen all neighborly and unobtrusive.

"None of your business," one of them said as she turned and walked his way. The tall one. "We're with Wrecan," and showed her badge.

Bob tilted his chin to her in acknowledgment as he watched her partner plug a lap top into the control board. "I'm a bit of a grid nerd. Why the 'puter?"

"Just updating the firmware."

"On a forty-year-old box of wires?"

"Yes, we both know this station is pretty old. Would you like to see?"

The worker opened the gate to allow Bob to enter.

Bob looked her over, "That'd be cool." A closer look is better than nothing, he figured.

He entered the enclosure and she motioned him to the other worker at the control panel. As Bob walked past and with his back to her, he got a massive jolt and fell right on that back.

That was the last thing Bob remembered until he woke up with clear blue sky in front of him. Still inside the 12-foot fenced electrical pen, a black backpack weighed on his chest.

Jesus, this can't be good.

He looked inside.

"I fucking knew it."

A bomb ticked with a timer at 01:58 from zero.

He looked around, there was no one. He could leave it and run like hell. No, this could be bad. Spinning around in his mind for an answer he alighted on one. The pier. He figured he'd throw it off the end. Why not?

Bob slipped the pack on and tried the gate. Locked. He put his fingers in the fence followed by his toes and stayed there 18 inches off the ground like a koala in a tree. Bob stepped off.

1:45 Gate was locked so he ran the perimeter. Behind the transformer and an oleander bush he found some graffiti, blackberry brandy bottles and a small hole dug under the fence. He shoved the backpack through and shuffled underneath.

He broke into a full sprint, which, considering his age, wasn't what it used to be. After avoiding three trucks and a Prius, he ran under the arched Santa Monica pier sign. He passed the plinking and galumphing of the carousel out on the long trek to get above the water. The carnival bells crashed; children squealed while he ran into the cloud of fried food in the fun zone looking for a place.

Directly in his path was 5-0.

The bigger of the two policemen said, "Slow down, bub. What's the hurry?"

"This!" and slipped off the backpack, and held it to them.

1:00 They stepped back and pulled their guns. "Easy, buddy. We don't want that."

"It's a bomb," Bob said.

"Okay, okay. Take it easy."

"I have to get this off the pier," and Bob darted in the direction of the end.

They both tackled Bob and the smaller cop opened the bag to the bomb. "It's a bomb!"

"That's what I said!"

:45 Bob rolled away from the policeman.

"Get off the pier!" Bob yelled at the surrounding crowd. "It's a bomb get out of here!" to the bemused looks of the jaded Los Angelenos who have heard this thirty times too many.

He spied a fire hose rolled next to the milk bottle stand. A twelve-year-old threw a baseball at the stacked bottles while Bob pushed past to the hose. He grabbed hold and spun out the two-inch hose while he turned the blue handle of the water valve. A firm stream flew from the hose.

Bob pelted the crowd with hundreds of pounds of water pressure.

That'll disburse them, he thought. Somebody will help.

When the bomb exploded off the side of the pier, a massive wave of water broke over the pier propelled with a boom that knocked the crowd dizzy and flat on their asses. The flash ignited the dozen umbrellas of a waffle cone shop and the Ferris wheel was knocked off its axle. It rolled a quarter turn through the roller coaster and tumbled into the ocean.

One policeman gathered Bob, while the other called into precinct. The sirens of the approaching fire trucks roared quickly to the scene.

.from_the_other_side

Sunday, 2029/08/05 11:02:00

Kwynn, James and Harley watched from behind a quickly erected barrier. The pier itself and the carnival booths were engulfed in flames as the fire trucks pulled up and sprayed water beyond the erected barriers and worked to restore order from the chaos.

Amazingly, no one seemed to be hurt.

James turned to a young skateboarder who stood watching with them as the flames were doused, "Did you see what happened?"

"Ya," the kid said. "Listen. An old guy starts screaming: It's a bomb, it's a bomb! GET OUT, GET OUT. Everyone just ignored him but he kept at it and started pushing people around screaming about the bomb."

"No one believed him?" Harley said.

"Nope." He looked up at the crowd, "Ok, nothing's going on here. Check it out," and the kid brought up the video on his phone.

They all crowded over his shoulder to see the middle-aged man screaming and pushing people.

"It's a bomb! Get off the pier!"

No one went anywhere until he broke a glass case and grabbed a fire hose. He turned the fire hose full throttle on the crowd and he knocked people over with the stream. So, of course, they disbursed.

"Get off the pier, it's going to explode!"

He doused the crowd with his hose when behind him an explosion rocked the Ferris wheel and the booth burst in flame.

"Why would he do that?" said the kid.

"Can I have this?" said Kwynn as she looked on Chitter. It was already nested in hundreds of posts with a #ItHasBEGUN and #ShutItDown. People were already using this weird thing for their own purposes. She found the original. It was viral. The likes and shares rolled over like a slot machine. She followed and liked the video instantly so she could find it easier later.

She loaded the video. There was something they were missing.

"I already put it on Chitter," the kid said. "Check it: KewTeeBae even liked it!"

"No way," Harley wagged to take a look.

The kids comp rang.

"You can use it but I want cash," he said into the phone as he walked away. He put his hand over the phone to them, "It's the news," and he went back to the phone, "... and full credit. Verbal and visual." He gave a silent wave goodbye.

.Phyllis'_house

Sunday, 2029/08/05 01:17:00

Kwynn, James and Harley returned to Phyllis' house.

"You're late," Phyllis yelled from the back porch when she heard them rustling around. She walked through the kitchen, "Where are your heads? It can take you two hours to go twelve miles around here."

"We know we aren't in the sticks, Phyllis," said James. "Didn't you see the explosion down by the pier?"

"I heard it and watched the smoke rise," Phyllis said, straightened a "My house is dirty enough to be happy" crochet on her wall and shook her head. "So?"

"So?" said Harley.

"So, the show must go on," Phyllis said. "The permit is for today. They shoot today. So, get."

"The most amazing thing about the explosion was the guy there. He took a fire hose to everyone to clear the pier before the explosion," Harley said.

"Ya, it's a strange way for a terrorist to act. Besides, I don't imagine many terrorists are of the graying set."

"Bob," Phyllis said.

"Bob?" Kwynn said.

"Bob," Phyllis said. "Bob is the guy at the pier."

"Bob is the guy at the pier?" Kwynn said. "How do you know that?"

"Because that's what Bob does," Phyllis said.

"Bob blows up piers?" Kwynn said.

"No, Bob is in the middle of whatever happens. He knows and he's there," Phyllis said. "Now, go get your stuff together before you make yourselves late."

The three gathered and grabbed their gear. Laptops, tabs, chargers, comfortable shoes and warm jackets. You never know on a shoot. It's like camping but with pay and smoothies.

"Bob," Phyllis said and changed the subject. "Do you know where you're going?"

All three looked up from their bags that were lumped

around her couches. They pulled out their pocket comps where they stood and began searching their map programs.

"Looks like we can take the 10 and work our way up Sepulveda," Kwynn said.

"No way, we should take Santa Monica all the way up," James said.

"I think we should take the 10, loop around the 110 and back to the 101," Harley said. "We'll be moving faster."

Each used a different map application and they compared commute times when there was a commotion out on the street out front. Phyllis looked up but the other three kept on their devices.

Kwynn found another #hashtag marking resistance and anarchy and climbed down the well and watched a video by AuntiFa. James checked his emails and furiously typed a reply to something. Harley found the video the kid had posted of the explosion. He watched without a word to anyone.

"Kids," Phyllis said. "I think you may want to see this."

No answer.

"No really," Phyllis said. They continued on their devices and typed. No acknowledgment.

"They're nekked you guys."

It was an offshoot of the National Ride Your Bicycle Naked Day, Santa Monica chapter, which meant, this week, they'd have a ride. It was summer and a couple dozen young men and women were out enjoying a bike ride with their various bits and pieces bouncing and dangling in the shining California sun. The group quickly passed and turned down a side street.

Nobody looked.

"They even had a sign and dogs," Phyllis said. Nothing. "Ok, you gotta go." Nothing.

"Really, you gotta go."

"KIDS! You GOTTA GO!"

"You don't hafta yell about it," James said. "Jeez."

.the_hollyhock_house

Sunday, 2029/08/05 19:49:00

"What're these designs this house is covered with?" Kwynn said.

"Well, designed by Frank Lloyd Wright," said James, "the Hollyhock house was groundbreaking, and bank breaking, for its time. A beautiful open home with the hollyhock flower as its talisman, some say it changed architectural history."

"Why would you ask him?" Harley said.

"Originally built on 36 acres for an oil heiress single mother in the early 1920's..."

"Just making conversation," Kwynn interrupted.

Said Hollyhock house is the location of the music video shoot they worked just east of Hollywood. Set on a hill and made of textile bricks with a graphically modular shape and design, the house struck a modernist, classic and nostalgic chord simultaneously.

The shoot was for an act that was blowing up. They sourced from only twenty miles away, and a world apart. This act funded a high budget video because that's what became the gold chain of Hip Hop acts in these days. Vids for social media. Was a day when you had to shoot a video for MTV, before that they shot them to be on Soul Train or Merv Griffin. Now most acts shoot and edit 'em with their own pocket comp. Major talent and real opinions too big for the small screens but made just for them.

Added to the excitement, the director exploded in one of his meltdowns. The salty crew knew the drill and busily kept at their work: set lights, adjusted props and loaded the film, yes, film, into the camera as the dolly tracks received a last leveling to ensure a smooth roll.

At times like these, PA's like Kwynn, James and Harley do one of two things: stay completely out of the way or scurry around trying to look busy by walking fast with something in their hands.

"When I arrive on set, I expect the set to be ready,"

Herr director, Dieter van Eisenstein said. "Vhen I arrive on set. I expect talent to be ready. I could be in the editing bay finishing my Fidelity spot."

The sun dropped near the horizon under a horror movie red. Dark clouds surrounded the amber orb, and provided the end of day drama earlier than normal.

"Wow, look at the sunset," Kwynn said.

"It's the brush fire," Harley said. "They're bad but they make for a helluva sunset. Give a whiff."

Kwynn hadn't noticed that smell of smoke and felt a slight irritation in her throat like the very inception of a cold.

"We better look busy," James said and threw his chin towards the producer with her eyes straight on them.

The first camera set up was an exterior on a hill overlooking the uneven grid of city lights and buildings. Cars and trucks snaked the 101 and cars and trucks rolled and stopped on Sunset Boulevard. Large 10k lights were set high above the space as fill, lightening the deep shadow. An animal trainer had a white tiger on a leash while beautiful men and beautiful women dressed as Egyptian slaves were placed around the veranda when the stars arrived to film.

The Assistant Director announced, "Start the sync track. Camera roll."

"Speed." The digital clapper-board smacked. "Action!"

The camera started tight on the artists in a face shot. Their three faces in profile to the chromatic, setting Los Angeles sun. The camera slowly dollied to a wide shot.

They lip synced their treatise on America and race and wine and whiskey when all the entire crews pocket comps buzzed and let out a huge five second tone. The lights in the city blinked out. The artists stopped and turned around to see the outline of the urban skyline. Red and orange sky, dark land. The silhouetted Century City skyscrapers in the distance broke the even line of the horizon.

"Keep going," said Director van Eisenstein. "We have generators. This doesn't affect us. Besides, it makes my CG much easier."

But he had lost his crew and the A.D. stepped in, "Start

from the top."

All of the poc-comps toned again and the entirety of the people on set, minus Herr Director and the A.D., had their hand on their devices. A message scrolled across all of their screens: AND IT BEGINS. THE END IS NEAR. AND IT BEGINS. THE END IS NEAR. AND IT BEGINS. THE END IS NEAR...

James looked over to Kwynn, "I can't access anything on my phone, just the scroll."

"Me, too," said Kwynn and Harley in unison.

"I'm going to try a reboot," said James.

"Won't help," said Kwynn. "I'm going in airplane mode. At least the texts will stop."

"Let's see if the phone works," said Harley as he dialed Kwynn. He got nothing but a busy signal. "They've clogged the network. We're practically bricked."

"Ya, no network, no comp or phone," said James. "Do you think it's BOT's?"

"Bots?"

"Ya, Bots - Robots - taking over our systems?" James said.

"James, Bots are people," Kwynn said.

"I thought bots were algorithms," Harley said.

"Ya, algorithms are only directives written by people," Kwynn said. "Even with machine learning, they only do what we tell them. Just stupid machines."

"Put the phones away," the AD said over the ruckus on his megaphone. "We've got work to do! Back to the top," he said as the crew got back to doing what they do: create alternate realities in ordinary settings. The show must go on.

Then every phone on set rang, and different devices all rolled in sequence as it popped around the crew like a whack-a-mole.

Jail

Sunday, 2029.08.05 20:42:00

Bob sat in the holding cell at the Santa Monica Police Department with a hundred other men, each there for reasons malign and benign. Really, all malignant.

The prisoners congregated in a 100x100 foot space with benches spread throughout. Benches that were bolted to the ground so they couldn't be moved or used as weapons. It was a central room, where a couple dozen cell pods made up the outside walls. Each cell had enough stacked bunks for four to sleep.

Bob kept to himself but soon enough was befriended by a couple of good-natured small timers. Humans are social creatures and no matter how hard the people or the times, eventually people talk. These two were caught as part of a racket that broke into containers coming off the transport ships out at the Port of LA.

"You ever been in one of those containers?" one of them asked.

"Can't say that I have," said Bob.

"Bro, they carry a lot of crap," he said.

"Most of that crap comes from Asia. You'd think most of its from China, wouldn't you?" the other said.

"I guess," Bob said.

"You'd be right," he smiled. "Busiest port in the world."

"By volume," the first said.

"That's why we hit it. Too much stuff for them to keep track."

Somehow, they didn't get caught at the port despite the amount of security. They were busted on the transfer.

"Ya, possession of stolen goods."

"Better than B&E."

A thin, smoky smell drifted over to them.

"Ya smell that? Stay away from those guys," said the first one.

"Smells like burning toilet paper," said Bob.

"Crack - one those dudes is smoking over there and nothing good will come of it," said the other.

Bob nodded, bottom lip out. Good to know.

Pop. Click. The lights went out.

"Yo! Guards, the lights are out!"

Bob looked into pitch black. The entire floor was dark. This could get interesting in the completely wrong way. He settled himself and closed his eyes.

Bob relaxed and listened around the room. After the initial cussing and yelling about the lights, the room vibrated with a sense of menace. It shook the air. Bob felt it in his bones, thumped behind his sternum, something was getting ready to happen.

Whoosh - the lights came back up. Bob opened an eye, cocked his head. Listened and mentally checked the cell. He wondered if it was emergency power or power was restored.

He walked to the entrance and peaked out the cell to the booking room. All of the officers were looking at their phones. A big sergeant walked straight at the door. He didn't look at or acknowledge Bob right there.

"Bob. You got bail," he called into the big cell.

More surprised than anyone there, Bob told him that he was him.

"Then let's go," the sergeant said as the door buzzed and he pulled it open.

Bob walked out of the holding cell. Not a single soul noticed he left.

The sergeant escorted Bob to a window. A uniformed desk officer sat in a small room with a Plexiglas window before him and a slot below it.

He looked at Bob.

Bob looked at him.

He looked at Bob, raised his eyebrows.

"Oh. Bob."

"Sign here for your personal items. Bob."

As Bob did so, an envelope was pushed through the slot.

Every pocket comp on the floor and telephone on a desk

began rolling through their rings in unison.

Bob turned his on and, now, his began ringing while a full ream of texts flooded the device.

The first call came up (000) 000-0000, declined it, but he knew the second. Bob answered.

"You didn't have to do that."

"You asshole. Of course, I did," said Phyllis on the other end. "What's all this about?"

"I have some ideas. Let's talk. I'll be over."

The Dark City

Sunday, 2029.08.05 22:55:00

Bob walked out of the police station to a bustling city. A wall of glow-faced strangers swiping at their poc-comps as they walked down the street didn't surprise him. The car headlights rotating past him and the noise of clicking, clanking and laughing from the restaurants and bars didn't surprise him.

Bob took a right and headed toward Phyllis' house. The Ferris wheel and fun zone and the beach front shops packed with summer crowds didn't surprise him.

What surprised him was the gathering of six men as they broke quickly to encircled him as they walked down 3rd street.

Bob stopped suddenly. Trying to surprise them.

Unfortunately, he was surprised by a burlap sack over his head and a man on each limb. He tried to hit one of them but he was now horizontal and being carried away. He screamed and gyrated trying to break free when he got a boot between his splayed legs. This stopped the wriggling but intensified the screaming until he felt a cool alcohol-like substance come through the burlap. Chloroform. Did that surprise you? Me, too. But Chloroform is a trick. We all fall for it. It doesn't work that well or that fast.

They hit him in the back of the head.

Hard.

.midnight

Sunday, 2029/08/05 23:52:00

With the clock nearly midnight Kwynn had grown a very large aversion to this song. Who knew working a music video shoot meant you would here the same song on repeat for most of the entire shift she'd worked?

It had started out great. What an awesome song. Then, she learned the words. After that she really got into the structure. How they blended the samples and the beats. The hook and chorus. Then she flat out got sick of it. That's where she was at now.

"Kwynn, come here."

It was the production manager. At least she knew her name.

And it was time for an errand.

Kwynn hopped in James', or was it Harley's, crap car and headed to Queeqwegs. Frappa-Dappa-Dippi-Do's for the crew. One hundred and twenty blended coffee-shake caffeine-riddled, twelve-hundred calorie, sugar-infused cups of energy and joy.

Don't worry, the attendants weren't unhappy to see her. She expected to get dirty looks and remorse. Nope. They've been on this ride. Just another day in Hollywood.

Thirty each of four different flavors while she waited. Chocolate, Vanilla, Carmel and Coffee. How do you not make coffee flavored coffee?

Kwynn could get into this though. She sat and swiped and waited. And, was getting paid.

The power outage was all anyone was talking about. Really, they all talked about the IT HAS BEGUN texts. A dozen, or more, of the peeps that made their living on these things, stars of media, the hype beasts, had made vids and memes, jokes and references back to older memes based on IT HAS BEGUN. Kwynn laughed and gawked, swiped and waited to the grind and hum of the blenders, time after time.

One of the attendants walked up, "We're out of ice."

"Oh," Kwynn said. "What's that mean?"

"We've used what we had but the outages knocked out the freezers at the grocery store and the liquor store next door sold out. We're three quarters through the order. Can we give you hot drinks instead?"

"Ya. I guess it'll have to do."

The attendant smiled and let his cohorts know.

She pulled out her tab. She felt an urge, even felt some sort of push from outside her but she hadn't quite figured out the language. It tickled outside her imagination trying to get in. These ideas were always bringing her snippets and feelings like morsels of a wonderful chocolate chip cookie but she didn't know how to handle them. Didn't know what they were. There was something about these outages that made too much sense. There was something familiar about the whole thing.

Pong. She got a dozen new follower on 'gram and more on Twitter.

The rest of the drinks were done. Knocked out in record time. Kwynn didn't know how long it should take but they were ready now and that was the fastest record for her.

Now came what she didn't think about. Where do you stack one hundred and twenty drinks in groups of four, by yourself in a crappy commuter car. The answer is on the seats, on the floor, in the trunk. (She's not drinking anything that has been in that trunk, or on the floor for that matter.) What they don't know won't hurt them.

Kwynn drove at a whopping 15 mph over the three blocks down Hollywood Boulevard back to the Hollyhock house. She yipped when she crossed the driveway, and squeezed her toes up the pockmarked, potholed hill as she waited for some sort of flood of coffee beverage apocalypse. But she made it safe. The drinks made it safe. She even got the coffees to the production motor home without losing any drinks or her job. Not even a complaint about the hot drinks. Not that she mentioned it. A win for Kwynn on this night.

Until she heard that song again.

Monday

Sun Rising

Monday, early morning

Bob awoke tied to an office chair in a big construction space. Clearly, tenant improvements were under way in a tall office building. Exposed metal studs and dangled electrical wires webbed through the space like veins through an appendage. The windows faced west over the Pacific and he was a dozen stories up. It was predawn and the sky glowed at the top while the light chased the dark into the horizon. A brown haze of fire smoke lingered in the foreground adding another line in the layer of colors in the sky.

He looked for options around his immediate construction area. There were piles of CAT9 ethernet cables, electrical wire and more studs. Six-foot-high stacks of drywall, a saw horse and a chop saw. Perfect.

Bob pushed off with his feet to roll his chair over and he didn't move. Great, no wheels. He tilted over, banged his shoulder much harder than he thought he would, and inched himself, on his side across the floor, to the foot of the sawhorse and kicked the legs out. He quickly scooted to the side and hoped to avoid the chop saw falling on top of him. It fell clear of him with a bang.

Bob rotated the chair behind him and shuffled on his side to the saw. He flipped the switch a few times with his chin. Nothing. Power still out. He maneuvered himself and flipped the chair again putting the saw behind him. He scraped the rope on the saw blade.

Thrummmm-ZWINNGgggg!!

All the lights turned on and the blade spun in motion.

"Bob!"

Yes, Bob peed just a little bit.

"I'd keep my hands away from that blade," Bob heard behind him.

"That wasn't very nice. Were those your guys at the beach today?" said Bob.

"No, not ours. They must be part of some terrorist group. Thanks for that," said the middle aged, slightly balding man, fit and trim beard. Black turtleneck, blue jeans.

"You're welcome, Arno. Don't be so smug."

"I'm not so sure this time," said Arno as he turned off the saw and pulled it away from Bob, whom he left on the floor. Arno walked to the elevator banks, pushed the button.

"Why all the dramatics with the rope and the office building?" said Bob.

"I couldn't be sure how long you'd be out. You had to be indisposed until they got the power back. Besides..."

Ding! The elevator arrived. "I never miss a chance to fuck with you," Arno said. "Gotta go check on someone."

Arno walked in to elevator and gave Bob a four-finger wave as the doors closed.

The next elevator opened and out walked a crew of construction workers.

"Woh, what's this?" as the group rushed to see what was the matter. They untied Bob and stood him up. "We should call the cops."

Bob begged off the bids to call the police by the construction workers and within minutes ducked down the same elevator bank Arno had taken.

Man, he had a headache. Even the smooth movement of the high-class elevators rocked his splitting head. The elevators doors opened at the bottom and he crossed the surprisingly small foyer. Nothing but a little space and a security desk.

He pulled out his pocket comp to check the time. It was shut down. He booted and walked into the coolish shade of the building outside. What existed of the morning coolness was already cooking off.

His phone was up and pinging like a nickel arcade. Some garbage about the end coming and the beginning. He also had fifty alerts from his monitoring application that clients' websites and applications had failed. And recovered. And some had failed again. He had four times that many texts from his clients telling him they were down or up or down in more colorful language.

Typical Monday.

The Fire, The Grid

Monday, August 06, 2029 5:52 a.m.

On the other side of town, the morning came fast. Well, predawn. It was that liminal time of day when change comes. Dark slowly gives way to light, purple to yellow, and we start at the beginning again. Sunrise, new day, new chances. Glen looked out the back window to the dayspring with a fresh cuppa and itched the back of his head.

Glen spent the night rolling through the error logs searching for a clue. He would find something interesting then tracked it down, found a dead end and kept looking. It was tedious, boring work but a list of errors will give you answers if you take the time.

"Worrying about the power outages?" Elsa rolled in itching the back of her head.

"Yep. Well, no. Nothing to worry about, kiddo."

"This seems really intense, Dad."

"How so?"

"I don't know. I'm scared and I'm usually not."

"Don't be scared."

"I'm just scared it'll get worse."

Glen heard a rustle and pop in the driveway. He opened his door and his cat ran around the corner and past him out into the field. Wallie, the cat, wasn't afraid of much. Living in the hills as an outdoor cat meant he was tough and smart. Coyotes eat you otherwise.

He heard a noise inside the house. He half closed the door and Julia came out with a stretch and a yawn.

"That damn cat just ran out," Glen said to her and put his attention back to the door. A fireman in his turn-outs stood there.

That's when Glen registered the smell. The Fire. During certain parts of the year, Californians get used to the smell of fire and ash falling on their cars. Dry grass burns mighty easily. He followed the direction Wallie went with his eyes and there up the valley was heavy black smoke with some white mingled in. Damn cat.

"Go get dressed, Elsa." She was already on her way. He turned his attention to the fireman. "Is it what I think it is?"

Julia pushed her way through the two men, "Excuse me. I better get that cat."

The fireman nodded and to Glen, "With the winds coming in, this fire up the way is threatening your place. You're going to have to evacuate for a while."

Glen understood. The few dozen acre property Glen lived on was where a small group of transformers congregated. He noticed the uptick in the wind but also the addition of the white 'smoke', which was actually steam, from the water the firefighters were throwing on the blaze.

"Looks like you're making progress, at least?" Glen said.

"Yep, but these winds pick up as the day grows. This valley is a chute. If it lights this way, it'll rip right through here."

"Okay, we'll pack up and get out."

The roar of a helicopter suddenly flapped upon them then a WHOOOOSH of bright pink retardant fell on them, the cars, the house.

Then a fire engine siren and persistent honking horn came from the dirt track up the property. They heard it before they saw it but the engine took the curve a little more red Ferrari than red fire truck. They blew past Julia looking by a culvert for the cat. The engineer stomped a stop next to the house.

"It's coming!"

With that pick up of the wind, the chimney took hold. The fire was sprinting toward the house.

Glen grabbed Elsa, the laptop and the keys. He thew her in the car. "My wheelchair!"

"I've got the sport."

He hammered the minivan to Julia up the way. He tried a power slide but on a front wheel drive: not so much. With the hard turn, he stopped. Julia got in and he punched it. Then stopped. "The meds."

Elsa's immunotherapy medication. He pulled directly up to the front door and ran in. He grabbed the bottles, grabbed a laundry basket sitting on the couch and hustled out. Glen hopped as he threw the basket and meds to Julia.

Glen pulled around the house and could see the fire coming down the canyon right towards them. He got to the gate and the fire truck and battalion chief suburban were parked, waiting.

"Get out of here," the chief, it turns out, told them. "We'll do our best for your place and the neighborhood."

"Stay safe, gents."

Glen's set of problems just increased. There was the power and work stuff but, obviously, he needed to get Julia and Elsa out of here right away. There was a queue of cars as he approached the freeway.

"How much of Elsa's meds do we have?" Glen said.

"You just refilled this week but there isn't much," Julia said.

"They were making me go back to the pharmacy later this week. We'll be fine."

"Oh, baby. I don't know."

"You need to get in to work. This one's not so different."

"We've weathered a fire a year here ever since we've moved in. This one's different."

"It's just the short meds plus weird outages - and a fire," Julia said.

"Nah, you're just worrying. You like to imagine the worst."

"I'm a mother, I have to prepare for the worst. If a fallen tree can take out the whole Northeastern power grid, I hate to see what you and Prakash can do to us."

"I always appreciate your belief in me, babe."

"That's what I'm here for: unconditional love and support."

"Grab a hotel room and wait it out. Besides..."

"Besides, it's on the company dime," she echoed.

Small Spot

Monday, August 06, 2029, 6:42 a.m.

After getting Julia and Elsa situated at the hotel Glen decided on a field trip before hitting the office. Throughout the grid there are substations that work to relay and step down power to the general public. The transmission lines carry hundreds of thousands of volts. After leaving the substation and traveling through transformers the voltage steps down to tens of thousands of volts. These are the army sergeants of the grid. They may not create the power but they do a lot of the work.

There was a substation up in the hills that didn't get much attention but Glen was thinking could be the fulcrum. He had been studying the path through which the electricity was routed and with the station by his house debilitated, this one was carrying more than its share of the load.

The housing had infringed on what was once a remote outpost half a century ago. Shoot, these houses were built more than twenty-five years ago. He parked on the street outside a condo complex and grabbed his backpack from behind his seat. The brown-on-brown complex was indistinct next to a perfectly laid sidewalk that was wet from the sprinklers that watered the hellstrip of grass splitting the road and his walk. He stepped off the curb at the corner of the useful road into a bit of seemingly discarded space.

Glen readjusted his backpack as he swung his legs over the metal barrier guardrail that blocked that dilapidated road he started down. He walked on the half-dirt track, half-chunk asphalt road toward the chain link gate that led to the intermediate power station. Originally, the road was meant to be a main artery and pass this way but the road had been abandoned and allowed to rot. The double-sized charcoal chunks of asphalt broke away as the trail meandered between dirt and the old road. The dry grass scraped at his knees while the sun broke through the dusty, silty dirt cloud he created beneath his shuffled feet.

The barely man-height fence and gate awaited him two

hundred yards in. He scoffed at the chain on the gate. Seven locks linked each other to the two drooped sides of the gate; all held together with the chain. Seven locks. Nobody could share a key. They had to have their own access with their own lock.

He pulled the gate wide against the chain, and slipped through the opening. He turned left and, fifty feet on, the fence had fallen and grass grew through it. Security.

The fence ended into a small murky pond fed by a trickling creek surrounded by eucalyptus trees, pines and a stand of palm trees. None of the trees were indigenous to the area but obviously seeded by birds. He entered the area and felt sequestered. As the bright sunlight transformed into the shade of the trees, a wisp of coolness wafted his way. He shivered as three bright blue damselflies stopped and each peered at him in succession. Just as quickly their four wings carried them away.

The water must've been only a foot or so deep but he couldn't see the bottom. A breeze came up and he heard a rustle under a palm just a few feet taller than him. It carried fronds from ground to tip. Must be a squirrel. He walked past the palm to the tinkle of the creek and looked for a way to cross without getting his boots wet.

Another minor gust blew, shuffling the fronds. He looked to it and around. It was a high noon, summer day and he got another chill. If he didn't know better, there were ghosts in here. That was no squirrel.

He hoofed the trail a bit more, skirted the pond and eventually came around the other side. His spirits seemed to follow him until he came back out into the light. Something watched him and he couldn't see them but they sure could see him. He just knew it. Somethings you just know.

Maybe it was just not sleeping the night before.

He walked on up the rise with the dust in his nose and rocks crackling under his boots. He entered the fire area. Somehow the fire had turned and avoided the riparian stand he had just passed but here the ground was deep, dark black. The trail was the same as ever, simply dirt and rock but the land around it was charred. No dry grass remained. The few small pieces of shrubbery were transformed into waist high skeletons above the charcoal terrain.

Glen heard it before the shack came into view. Around the bend in the valley, he was not pleased to hear, then see, man-made lightning. The transformers were arcing, sending bolts twenty-five feet in the air. It looked like Dr. Frankenstein's lab or those Tesla machines, lightning without the orb. The power arced and lit off like a whip, snapped then buzzed, held and snapped again. If you ever wondered why they called it a live wire, you could see the energy and life now.

"We gotta bypass this," he said as he pulled out his phone, his dead phone. Glen shook his head and trekked back up the track. He bypassed the pond on principle and eventually got to his truck.

Glen plugged his phone in for a charge as he drove down the road. When he looked up, he had to swerve to miss a mess of cars lined up on the side. "Keep your eyes on the road," he said and shook his head.

The line of cars ran for nearly a mile and into the gas station sidling the onramp. There's gonna be a run on gas. And his phone lit up. When it finished its boot up, he grabbed the poc-comp and called Prakash.

"P, we gotta bypass this transformer," he said. "Now."

"We can't. The other relays were destroyed."

"Don't matter, this is going to get worse. And it will work its way back up the line. We gotta protect the rest. Trust me on this one."

"I will see what we can do."

"I will be there in a jiffy."

Down the Street

Monday, 2029.08.06 06:52:00

Murray walked down Electric Avenue with an overall ache and a limp as the early morning rays just peaked through the deep canopy of bright green Ficus trees. The heat charged light dappled through the leaves as he crushed another type of leaf underfoot. He passed through the sweet musk of eucalyptus and he stumbled on the lifted sidewalk caused by the tree roots underneath. He shook his head for not paying closer attention.

For most people, the pain and confusion would mark an extraordinary day. As Murray, and as a victim of hit and run, let's just say this isn't atypical.

He passed the parking lot and crossed onto Abbot Kinney. The little road carried a Venice vibe of stucco and brick buildings filled with mystic book stores, trendy dress shops and a Queequeg's. Always a Queequeg's.

Murray considered some caffeine, thought better of it when he stepped around the line of head tilted thumb monsters coming out the door and approached the exterior stairway to his office. The coffee would be there but the people will be gone in an hour. He'll come back.

Before mounting the stairs, he grimaced. Then he took it one stair after the other. Twelve steps up, a right turn and one more step into the second flight his pocket comp rang. The ID wasn't necessarily who he was hoping for. He clicked 'Accept' and put it to his ear.

"You look like shit."

"Thanks, Arno. I feel like I was hit by a truck," Murray said.

"That would make sense," Arno said.

"What do you want?"

"I'm sitting across the street eating a breakfast burrito at the tiendita and wondering when you were going to show up, and here you are."

"Here I am," Murray said.

"It hurts to watch you. You know that?"

"What do you want?"

"Well, I'm finishing my chorizo, egg and potato. By the time I finish, you should be up the stairs and we can talk all proper and polite, face to face." End.

Great. Arno. This is all a little too real. On the plus side, maybe this means a cash deal. Murray slowly gained each painful step until he reached the second floor, walked down the hallway and opened the door to his one room office.

He peeked through the glass door to some mail on his floor. He checked a tiny slip of paper stuck between the door and the jamb shin high and unlocked the door. He picked up the catalogs absolutely no one would touch but to throw away and threw them away.

Arno entered behind him and shut the door.

"Where's the intel?"

"What is it with all this cold war shit? I'm a P.I. for chrissake. I don't have it. Your suits made sure of that, didn't they?"

"Well, time was of the essence, as they say."

"But not anymore."

"No, it is," Arno said. "But I never marked you as a killer. What happened to Willie?"

"Some 'droids came in and tried to take me out."

"And they got Willie."

"And they got Willie. I haven't figured out the rest."

"Don't fret your little mind. Give me the drive and you won't need to worry. That's all they want from you."

"I told you, I don't have it. But if I did, what would you offer for it?"

"Your life."

"That won't work. You and I both know I'm used to threats."

"Who says it's an empty threat?"

"You won't find it without me unless you go through the trouble of stealing it again. I'm easier. And cheaper."

"Cheaper."

"Cheaper than a whole mission. Make me an offer."

"Who's to say we haven't already paid for the mission,

Murray?"

"Too late for that play. Might've worked though."

"It's not a play. However, and unfortunately, I don't have authorization for your termination. Or a cash payment."

"I take credit cards. Transfers, too."

"I will run it by management."

"This all became real bureaucratic real quick. This is a side I've never seen before, Arno."

"The pendulum swings, Murray. And against my better judgment, I have a soft spot for ignorant flatfoots," Arno said, walked out.

Murray finally took a seat. This was going to be lucrative or the end of him.

Same as it ever was.

And Back Again

Monday, 2029.08.06 07:05:00

Same as it ever was…

Murray looked at his pocket comp and checked his map app for the traffic. He considered the time it would take him to get back to Hollywood, and the flash drive, from where he was in Venice. Murray knew the answer but checking meant he didn't have to face the real issue: What would he do if Arno didn't pony up. With Willie, and his bag of questionable tricks, dead, his income stream would slow considerably until he found a replacement. This flash drive needed to pay off.

Murray clicked on his desktop computer to double check the money he knew was supposed to be here. The computer was in back up mode. Might as well be dead. The damn system was locked up caching and uploading the backups to the off-site drives. Useless.

Well, luck favors the brave, he figured as he scrolled his contacts on his poc-comp again for inspiration. He imagined each client's bank account as he leered at their information. In his revelry, he looked out the window to the sidewalk below. Standing across the street was the stage mom, all blonde and buxom. At least he must have finished off the little one.

Murray skedaddled out of his office and turned the opposite direction from which he entered the building. He headed down the hallway, chin to his chest and came to the back exit to his suite of offices. He opened the door and there stood the kid. Sort of. Now it was the kid that wasn't a kid anymore. The face was the same but it had a thin mustache, black hair and a pint-sized trench coat. These two looked like Boris and Natasha. What's next, Moose and Squirrel?? They both stood frozen, eye to belt buckle.

Murray closed and locked the door and headed the other way. The door flew inward behind him and the door on the opposite side of the hallway flew open to reveal Natasha. Murray was dead in the middle of a gunslinger's standoff. The little one even wiggled his fingers like he had a gun on his hip.

Murray considered his options.

"Where is the drive?" Natasha said as she sauntered closer to Murray.

"I don't have it."

"You are lying," Boris said as he did the same.

Why is this little thing sauntering?

"Give us the drive."

"I don't have it," Murray said and had an idea. "Shoot me if you have to, but I'm not handing it over."

"That's a wonderful idea," Boris said and before Natasha could stop him, he sprung the tasers from his wrists. Murray dropped flat on the ground. Boris' taser flew over Murray. The lines locked into Natasha and the charge knocked her over.

Murray popped up while Boris couldn't get his taser lines out of Natasha. Murray kicked Boris in the head. Again. He stepped over him and lit out the back door.

"You are an idiot," Natasha said.

"I can't get my taser lines back," Boris said as Natasha removed them from her chest.

"Oh, thank you," he said.

"We will follow him."

They ran out the back door only to see Murray hop in a taxi and drive off.

"Who takes taxi's anymore?" Boris said.

Dark Govt Meeting

Monday, 2029.08.06 08:00:00

Arno walked through the hall of a new age office building flanked by guards in their dark deep seaweed colored uniform of polyester, stiff and loud as the pant legs rubbed. Their footfall clacked off the perfectly smooth and square walls that ran on and on in the corridor. He came to a young short-haired female receptionist in front of a metal government issue desk. She stood still, hands behind her back, with a nod, "Through the doors and to the right."

Never breaking stride, Arno, he and the bodyguards, they crossed the threshold into a conference room.

A holo projected mid-table. The guards backed out of the room and closed the door.

In the holo, standing before a large window overlooking the Potomac, Lincoln Monument in the background, small forest in the foreground, was a middle age woman, hands clasped behind her back.

"Glad you could make it," she said back still turned.

"As if I had a choice," Arno said, sitting. "This isn't all us. These outages."

"No," she said. "No, we have no reason to do it."

"Did you review the materials?"

"Of course. That little operation at the pier? They did it by the book. If I was doing it that would be how I would do it."

"That's what I thought. I've seen similar from other silos."

"We test the system occasionally but this is something, someone, else. Besides it's the west coast. Nobody here pays attention past their bedtime."

"Bob thwarted something, Frankie," Arno said.

"I heard," she said, turning. "Don't clue him in to our involvement."

"What involvement? In any case, a curious Bob is a dangerous Bob."

"Leave him alone. Where is he now?"

"In Santa Monica lock up, I think. Or home. I'm not tracking him."

"No more sloppy, ill-advised kidnappings."

"I would never."

"Enough. No more. Stop fucking with him."

"It's better he's confused than curious."

She ignored this. "And, Arno, I expect you have some sort of a solution to this predicament with the PI..."

"Perhaps I do. Has anyone taken credit for the outage?"

"No. That worries me. That's why you're here. Hold it - Perhaps?"

"The P.I. is hiding the intel and he doesn't know what it is. At least what it's for. He tells me 'droids did the killing."

"Androids acting autonomously. Great."

"Could be QWOUNZEL is the other actor. Are they in the wild?"

"In the wild. Sure," she said. "They are trying but, listen, QWOUNZEL is not in the wild. That's under control. What else?"

"The P.I. wants a buyout for the info, too."

"So. Take care of it."

"The buyout?"

"However," Frankie said and turned back to her view. "I don't want to know."

"Very well."

She held up her hand and Arno waited.

Patiently.

"I don't want him knowing we instigated this information gathering."

"Yes. I have been working under that guise."

"He has only been used to protect our liability, not become a liability."

"Correct. I considered him as insulation all along. As the fall guy."

"I've changed my mind. This cannot go on any longer. Take the info back, finish him and then proceed as planned." End.

Arno stayed at the table and contemplated his next

steps. He had carefully laid out his chess pieces. Now they knocked them over like a toddler on a spree. So be it. All of this for a little corporate espionage. There are times Arno was sure they simply made things up to keep him busy. And why the 'droids anyway?

Troubling, too, that Bob got involved in this.

Fucking Bob.

Where did that lazy ass P.I. hide that drive? Arno pulled out his pocket comp - no service, "This fucking place."

He left the room and walked past the receptionist. Without slowing his gate, "Always a pleasure," to the receptionist. The guards each took a shoulder and matched his stride down the corridor and peeled off when he reached the exit to the street.

Arno dialed Brett, "Meet me at Willies office in 15."

"Why there?"

"You know why." End.

A Dead End Meeting

Monday, 2029.08.06 08:05:00

Murray ended the connection. He sat in the waiting room of Willie's office. "Good thing I'm already here."

A meeting with Arno here meant one of two things: Murray was getting paid or he was in for it. He wasn't going to think about the *in for it* option.

Upon arrival at the building earlier, Murray avoided double checking the flash drive hiding place. He couldn't risk giving away that spot if he was followed. Every lazy desire to be satisfied pushed him toward the drive but Murray walked past the fire exit door on his way up without even a glance. This was going to take discipline.

Now, he sat on the brown couch reviewing ChitterChatter. He waited. God, he missed Twitter. He spun through a few posts about the explosion down at the pier.

Swipe.

Something about some power outage the other night.

Swipe.

The Fire.

Swipe.

Something about Wrecan taking over the grid.

Swipe.

Something about the unions protesting the takeover by Wrecan.

Swipe.

What if it's gone? The drive's there. Who would look for the drive there? He looked back to the comp. Another fire by the Getty. This was cool, they designed the buildings to withstand the smoke and brush fires with reverse air flow. Smoke and heat were bigger threats to the artwork than the fire itself.

Swipe.

Some Cyber Warfare book is on the digital shelf stirring the pot.

He better get that drive.

No, it's safer away from me. A chip to be played. Arno don't abide by chips.

Murray got up and went to the elevator. He pushed the button for the lobby and rode down. He pictured ways that the drive was actually gone; cleaning crews, efficient fire inspectors. His only bargaining chip and it was probably gone. He exited the elevator to an empty lobby. A slice of light arced across the checkered tile and illuminated the latent dust motes of the old building. He peaked around the corner of the elevator banks and stepped out the fire door into the stairwell. Adjacent was the fire extinguisher. He reached in and the flash drive was there behind that fire extinguisher where he left it. Nice. He pocketed it and turned around.

In his eye was a silencer. Behind it was a pistol.

"You don't need to do that," Murray said.

"Oh, but I do," Natasha said and unloaded a bullet into Murray's left eye. He collapsed and Boris pulled the flash drive out of Murray's jacket pocket before the blood ran on his shoes. He didn't want to leave tracks. Something about human fluids always seemed chaotic to him. They left through the checker floored lobby.

A bearded middle-aged man entered through the adjacent door. Arno. Natasha lingered a moment but did not register a difference in heart rate from him. No recognition.

Boris had left the building and paused on the entry steps, accessed his communications protocol and informed QWUOUNZEL: Acquired. Data to follow. He opened his port on his wrist and stopped.

"What?" Natasha said as she caught up. "They are waiting."

"This drive is USB. It is too old. We don't have the proper port."

"Give it to me." She placed the drive on her tongue as they descended the rest of the entry stairs to the building. The plastic flesh folded back and adjusted to make a metal-on-metal connection. The data transferred to her local memory set and she transferred it to the predetermined address as they walked through the empty, crumbling parking lot under the glaring bone yellow sun.

.a_late_night_jaunt
Monday, 2029/08/05 15:42:00

After staying up most of the night and morning on the shoot, the boys were still asleep on the floor beside Kwynn as she booted her tab. It'd been a minute since she was able to attack TheRanch and she felt a disconnect. She would never beat the thing if she didn't work on it. She hit the bookmark and a hundred tabs spun around her like a deck of cards splayed on a casino table.

Kwynn approached the gates of the firewall and inserted a script just to warm up her fingers. There was a pause then a ping of failure. With a crunch of her lips to one side, she hit a script that searched all of the communication ports to see if something had been left open for some reason. There weren't any openings but she found something new: there was a fire-hose worth of information leaving the place.

In all her time hitting this program she had never seen anything go in or out. As far as she knew, Kwynn was the only one who ever did anything remotely close to this place and all of a sudden, the Info-out door was wide open and that information was flowing. Fact was: she couldn't even access any of it. As she attempted to steal packets flowing out, she was knocked away like a mother slapping her child's hand away from the cookies before dinner, not unkind but definitive.

Kwynn never knew her own mother. What little she did know was that her mother grew up here in California. She had heard a story from her father once that Kwynn couldn't quite believe. He had a habit of telling tall tales when he actually turned his attention Kwynn's way. Really, they were more myths to Kwynn's ears.

But this one was true.

Her great-grandfather's grandfather had come to California back in the days of the mighty 49ers and found a place for himself in burgeoning San Francisco. By the time this great-grandfather, Martin, had grown and moved to Southern California to earn his own fortune a war broke out and there was a lot of anger aimed at Japan. There was talk of shipping people off to camps to ensure the safety of America. Martin didn't think that was such a good idea but what he'd also heard rumored was that they were planning to seize property. Not only did he hear this mentioned in the newspaper, his neighbor had told him of the possibility. This man who had been his neighbor, with whom he had shared beers, whom he trusted, offered a solution when it became apparent that Martin's family would be shipped to the camps. To avoid having Martin's home seized, Martin should transfer title to this man and while the war was fought, the man would keep Martin's home safe. After Martin Kurosawa and his family were released from Manzanar following the Surrender of Japan, they returned to find his home had been sold and the neighbor nowhere to be found. Unfortunately, because the title was a legal transfer there was nothing to be done but shed tears once more then rebuild. Martin felt no true connection to the horrific suffering of his ancestral home for picking that fight but he did know that his fortune had been ruined in his father's father's homeland and that homeland was the United States of America.

Her father had made sure she knew this story. She and her father had lost any contact with that side of her family, most of whom had passed, but she heard this story when Dad was frustrated with any other injustice. He had always told her to stand up and protect those who couldn't protect themselves. Those types of things time should not forget. Do the right thing, no matter the cost.

"What are you working on?" It was Harley.

Kwynn shut her tabs, "Nothing."

"I'm not spying, you looked like you were remembering more than typing is all."

"I was," she said. "I'm hungry."

"Me, too," Harley said and hit James in the butt with a pillow. "Wake up, let's eat."

James grumbled, "What do you want to eat?"

"Ramen!" Kwynn said. "I'll find a good place," and she pulled up her Yelp for a good place close by when social media blew up. The video she shared about the pier explosion had taken on a life of its own. It had been taken, edited into memes, dissected and shared with the tags #ITHASBEGUN and #SHUTITDOWN. Two sides fought it out about whether Wrecan was creating a private army in order to take over the west and some other group that wanted systemic change and the power outages were the first step to that change. Nobody had taken credit for the event but everyone had a theory about who did it and where it would take us. Kwynn could only see that all these people were manipulating the event to serve their own purposes.

"Where's the place?" James said, awake now.

Kwynn popped back and found one, "I got it."

"Let's go!" Harley said as he scrambled up and strutted out the door while he put on his cap.

Tuesday

Silence

Tuesday the 7th, just after 3:00

Silence dropped in. Darkness immediately followed.

Bob hated this part.

He couldn't see his hand on the keyboard. He just felt his fingertips. No lights blinking, hummmm of the servers or thrummmm of air conditioning forcing coolness on his face. Waited. He just waited.

Bob was sweating now. Then, the workstation before him glowed to life and pulsed. Click and the lights returned. The back-up generator kicked in. The comp instigated boot sequences on all the server stacks piled in the room.

Fucking thing worked. Bob knew it worked but you never really knew something would work until it did. Too many of the variables we humans take for granted can get skipped when giving instructions to a stupid machine. These are multi-million-dollar stupid machines but they only do what we tell them. A stray semi-colon or a missed directive can screw the whole thing. Rock-n-roll. He won. The emergency system installed and operated. He could finally invoice; not that he'd see the cash for ninety days.

Bob cleaned up. Grabbed his tab and bag, swiped the security card and left the server room for an empty hallway. 3am usually meant empty hallways. He lumbered past an array of cubicles, took a left and two rights, key carded through two more interior doors, gave a wave to the security desk, got a tired wave back and he went outside to the sodium lit parking lot.

As quiet as the building was, there were quite a few cars reflecting the orange glow back at him.

That's when the lights really went out, all across town.

"Oh, boy."

Making Connections

Tuesday, August 7, 2029 7:09 a.m.

The sun and heat tinged Glen's skin. It was seven in the morning, the gauge already said 95 and we wonder where the water is. Glen stood before the property and the view. His house gone. His truck gone. Well, the company house and the company truck. They lost some of their possessions but he was a short timer in this house. Company housing is never truly your home. The family was safe in a hotel, that's all that mattered. Except for his cat. And the power.

Below him everything was devastated. The entire adjoining neighborhood was leveled. Homes, cars, trees, the perfectly manicured, lush green lawns: all ash. Here and there was a standing bush, a monolith brick chimney and the shell of a washing machine. All Glen saw were the lives of hundreds of families permanently altered. The fire service couldn't truly fight it. Once the homes caught, they continued to throw water on the roofs but the units were pushed back by swirling wind and fire. No home is worth a life.

Firestorms are called so because they create their own weather. The flames and air movement have a pattern all their own. Brush fires are known to create fire tornadoes that will yank the fire hose out of a firefighter's hands and whip the hose in circles while they helplessly stand by.

"Did you see Wallie?" Glen said to Julia as she picked through the ashes of their former home.

"No," Julia said and walked over to his perch over the valley.

"I've got a bad feeling about this."

"What's it say?" Julia said.

"That this neighborhood is fucked. I don't know. It just doesn't seem right. Nothing more. Now's not the time, babe."

"I'm just saying: when you have a feeling, follow it. Someone is speaking to you."

"Not now. Nothing is speaking to me."

"Something is - why couldn't it be God?"

"Why not intuition?"

"Could be."

"Like 'trust your intuition'," Glen said as he shuffled and kicked some chimney bricks to the side. "Better not do this - I just have a feeling..."

"Why couldn't that be God talking to you?" Julia was straight as that chimney once was.

"The voice in the back of my head?"

"Precisely."

"That voice is God?"

She wandered the footprint of the house, headed down the hallway. "Why not?"

"Because he doesn't have time for me. With all the earthquakes and floods. The fires. The power. The helpless."

She rummaged the pile of ash that would've been their bedroom, found a piece of melted alarm clock that they hadn't touched in years but to move it, "He does, Glen. That's the point."

"Nah, he doesn't. But I like the thought."

She picked up a few unidentifiable ash-burnt papers that disintegrated like spent jasmine petals then looked over, "He does."

"It's just a function of our need to name things."

"A rose by any other name..."

"...would smell as sweet. Ya."

"You have to be open to a higher power," Julia came back to Glen, sun on his back, and stood next to him looking down the valley with a shadow stretched thin and long as a giant before him.

He stood still, immobile, "No, but I am open to the idea that we don't understand everything."

"I don't think - no - I got a feeling we don't know the half of it."

"You bet."

"You bet."

"Get to work," she grabbed his hand. "And do me a favor?"

"What."

"Trust those feelings, inklings, whatever - cuz, I do know something's rotten," she gave a squeeze.

"Something is weird. That's why I'm going."

"Go save the world, Glen."

"No, just our slice of it," he said without moving, eyes on the devastation below.

"Alright, cupcake," Julia said and headed for the minivan. "I need to get back to Elsa and you can get a new truck at the shop."

"You sure you have everything? I don't like leaving the two of you alone." He went to the passenger side. "We can go to the store."

"We are fine. Do what you have to do," she said over the hood and pointed to the burnt-out neighborhood. "They need you, too."

They climbed in their van and she dropped him at work. Within twenty minutes of the conversation, he sat at the console and Glen, who prided himself on staying calm, wasn't. He didn't know where to start. The whole Southwest had been knocked out. California, Oregon, Arizona, New Mexico, parts of Colorado and Utah. Holy cow, what happened?

Prakash, the plant engineer, ran in, "What happened?"

"Exactly. What happened?" said Glen. "I'm working on isolating the issue. I'm running through that new monitoring tool and an error log."

"And?"

"And as I scroll through, I'm thinking it rolled through district 43... No, or it started here," he pointed on the map on his screen. "That brush fire by my house knocked the transformer and pushed power down the line."

"Ok, isolate the area and let's see if you can normalize the surges," Prakash said. "Then we can establish a crank path."

"You know it's not that easy," said Glen.

"It is something. Check for other unusual behavior there like unexpected devices or deviating voltages."

"Like these outages? That's unexpected. The blackouts are rolling through every neighborhood."

"Baby steps. Keep good notes. That program learns more every time something happens. Even from this fire that got out of control," said Prakash.

"Hell, yes, it's out of control. This whole damn thing turned me into a country music song, Prakash," said Glen.

"Didn't find your cat?" Prakash said.

"His name is Wallie."

"He had cancer."

"He was on the mend," Glen said. "And, I lost my damn truck."

"I understand but I'm concerned about our grid. 10 million people just in LA without power. A day is bad but this could go a week, more... This could mean a lot of problems."

"The power is there," Glen said.

"The power is there. Set your crank path. No plan to roll out power, no power."

"With the substations down, how will we seed the power?"

"With your plan, Glen. We'll re-energize the lines section by section. Does Elsa have her meds?"

"Ya, we just refilled this week. For the week."

"Good because this will make meds hard to come by."

"I'm aware, P."

"And hospitals, water and the entire food supply. All at risk," Prakash said.

"I'm aware, P."

"Right. Then get on with it. Plan it. Fix it."

"I'm fixing. I'm fixing. Did Tehachapi come around?"

"The wind farm and the Mojave solar plants both pulled off the grid. They don't want to get blown out by the surge."

"And that's our junction to pass through the power."

"It is."

"I will talk to Tehachapi again - you lay the ground work. Sorry about Wallie."

"I didn't find his body. Maybe he found a cave or a culvert up there. He's wily," Glen said. "Like his owner."

Interlude

Tuesday, morning

Bob sat in his chair with his hot, sweet and spicy tea and played his guitar, like he did every morning, because he couldn't get the little bastard to slow down. He was always so excited to start the day. Dawn was his jam. The little guy. Bob, not so much. Moonlight was pretty good for him but like most of life, nothing was easy and rarely how you ordered it. Even supernatural aid.

Bob made his living fixing computers, networks, corporate displays. The cyber type stuff. Cyberspace. Cybernetic. Cyberpunk. Cybercrime. Cybersecurity. Of course, security. Always security. He liked to focus on the space between. Not the internet of wires, waves, servers and switches but that place between that could be run by gremlins for all we really know. The ghost in the machine. Daemon.

But his guy and him, they jam and they work on music and stories and problems. The big ones and the small ones.

It wasn't really by choice, the daemon usually handled that mystic part and Bob's grew attached. Oftentimes, the daemon would swap person to person but these two. They were a pair. TBH, the stories got in the way. Bob couldn't even keep focused on the tech work, the cash machine, because daemon was always jumping on his back with more tidbits. Pieces. Slices. Leaves in the wind.

Bob knew it wasn't the little guy's fault. It was how he communicated but if only he would come out and say it outright once in a while. So, music tames the wild beast and for one to translate his musings Bob had to tune himself to the channel and the little fucker needed to stop jumping up and down on his back. In his head.

Paolo and his wife were the first to help Bob begin to understand. With their help, it was up to Bob to help the next batch coming up. The Council required it. But he wasn't doing anything with Kwynn. Not before she gets some introductions. None of this training-wheels shit.

Besides, Bob didn't really like people. It's not people, per se. They, (snaps his fingers three times), they don't really do as he says. The cybers only do what he says, no more, no less. Much easier, give a directive and let it work. Daemon gives him enough to figure out. But people will die without more help. These power outages don't seem to have a purpose other than making melted ice cream on a summer day. These first little outages are test forays. They portend much worse and Bob can't do this alone. Not this time. Not for long. This is bad.

Bob buckled down and studied the code in front of him. The consultant contract with Global Media Corp kicked up a notch over the last week. The entertainment conglomerate pulled him back in to help suss out the attack Friday night after the power outage. There had been a subtle change to the security patch he had written for them in the event of a full force cyber-attack. When the power went out the attackers hadn't done much, which may or may not be a surprise but they timed the attack exactly with the resumption of power. Exactly. What did that mean and how did they do that?

That type of timing would take... pocket comp phone interrupted him. Multiple rings and attempts stole his river of consciousness. He looked at the device, accepted the call on speaker and was inundated with a pitch in a language he didn't understand. End.

What was he thinking?

Dammit.

Something with the security patch.

He dug back into the security patch and found the subtle change. What could that be?

He followed the includes and found some changes to his protections. The patch would seem to be still working but they had installed deprecated calls. They wouldn't work on the software version of the server his client was on. Bob wouldn't make that mistake. Why would they have done that? Who did it?

He shook it off and ran a script to search for database injections while he checked the log files for access. This was a mess.

Poor Murray

TUESDAY 2029.08.07 08:21:00

Murray awoke in a bed. If the crinkle of the plastic covering on the mattress didn't stop him, the catheter did. His head hurt like bloody hell. He reached to rub his forehead to find his hands were strapped. He looked around the room. A hospital room. Oh, that fucking android shot him.

He blinked and in his left eye he recognized an overlay with a flashing message that he consciously activated, "Good afternoon. Welcome to the land of the living. You have been assimilated and are now part of the collective."

Murray stopped the message. Oh, fuck. He wanted no part of any assimilation. He figured if he kept the message going, they may need his acquiescence to complete the install. Just like idiots who clicked on attachments in emails from people they didn't know back in the day.

He looked around the room again and saw the overlay assessing each electronic device in the room. By focusing on the heart and respiration monitor, he was fed his own vital signs.

Heart rate: 68 bpm. Oxygen: 99%. Body Temperature: 98.7 Damn, I'm doing fine!

If they were going to put all these electronics in him, they must have weaponized him, right? He focused on the plastic water pitcher across the room and didn't quite imagine. He just did it. He shot a laser at the pitcher and the thing exploded! This is going to be fun. He burned through the restraints on his arms and got up.

And fell right back on his ass.

How long have I been out? Oh, Murray focused on his display, 8:20 am. Just about a day.

The door to his room swung open and smiling at him was Arno, "Good thing we had a meeting. I saved your ass."

Murray closed his eyes. Shit. "Hi, Arno."

"Hi, yourself. Sit tight. We have much to discuss. But first you'll need to heal."

"I'm not working for you guys."

"You are now," Arno said as he came around the foot of the bed. "Don't worry. You've been working for us for a long time anyway."

"Great."

"I've ordered you some oatmeal."

An announcement flashed in Murray's display. PLEASE CLICK TO INSTALL UPDATES - YOUR O.S. IS OUT OF DATE!

"Sit back and relax, Murray. Then, when you finish, we can discuss a job for you."

"What about all this?" Murray indicated the intricate healing of flesh and machine that amounted to a total rebuild of his skull, face and, probably, brain.

"Good thing I found you on my way in."

"You know I don't like elevators."

"True. However, you're quite lucky I had one of those new emergency wound kits. Quite impressive."

"Did you use that new synthetic balloon?"

"That fills and supports the wound?"

"Yep, plus once you arrived at the hospital, the doctors used nanobots armed with some impressive steroids. The studies show it will increase that healing at a rapid rate." Arno waved his hand around at Murray's face as he inspected a surprisingly well-healed wound.

"Well," Murray said with a long blink. "Thanks for nothin'."

"We'll have a wonderful time together, Murray."

"I'm not going to be a fucking fleshbot."

"Don't be denigrating. They simply call it bionics."

"It's bullshit."

A hospital worker walked in with a tray and some oatmeal, "It's good you have an appetite!"

"Ya," Murray said and realized he was famished. She set up next to him and prepped to feed him. Murray waved her off and shoveled a bite into his mouth.

"I will leave you to your food," Arno said as he walked out the door. "I'll be back!"

"I know you will!" Murray said, his mouth full of

oatmeal.

.substation_hack

Tuesday, 2029/08/07 08:42:00

"I still don't like it. Why are we here?" James said as he swung his leg over the fence and jumped to the ground of substation 19. The substation our 'friends' tried to blow up yesterday. The techs who broke in had been labeled rogue terrorists but Bob had saved the day by running the bomb out of here.

Kwynn sat in the dirt and leaned against the large metal box that took up a good portion of the enclosure. She pulled out her tablet and placed it on the ground, her display illuminated before her. She traced her pass code in the three-dimensional holo and looked at a displeased Harley.

"Doesn't all the chatter make you want to find out what's really going on?" Kwynn said.

"Ya," said Harley. "No." He kicked a blackberry brandy bottle into a hole under the fence.

"Doesn't it just seem fishy that someone tried to blow this up? Plus, all the power outages?"

"That's what the police are for," James said.

"They can't do what I can do," Kwynn said. "There's something about all this that I can't just let sit. I have to find out. Besides, I have the power to help."

"You don't know anything about this, Kwynn," James said as he fiddled with a locking mechanism on one of the doors to the box.

"I'm just curious," said Kwynn as she fiddled in her holos. "Anyway, nobody will know. I'm good at this stuff, I promise."

"Just don't get us caught," James said looking pointedly at her.

"Relax. I've triple masked the IP through a VPN to an island in Fiji via Yugoslavia and Russia and my MAC address was copied from a shitty pocket comp I traced from a Swedish tourist at the bookstore."

"Just don't screw with anything," said James.

Kwynn manipulated the files in front of her, "I'm site seeing."

Harley gathered a half-dozen of the brandy bottle, a couple beer bottles and a can and lined them up on the far side of the enclosure.

Thirty different routers and hot spots flashed on Kwynn's Wi-Fi interface. She pulled up her kernel prompt and typed in 'view: hidden'. Now added to the list were three additional routers: the city hall encrypted, the police encrypted and the substation comm-link. She copy-and-pasted the address in her browser /config.txt and all of the router information appeared in her window. She copied the MAC address, mimicked the IP and used the passwords to connect to the router and was on the Wrecan Gas and Electric Network.

"Too easy," Kwynn said with a self hi-five.

"Way too easy," said Harley as he chucked a rock at his lineup of waste, looked at James then back to what he could see of the holo then back to James. "Who is she? Who are you?" Harley walked towards her.

"What do you mean? I'm Kwynn."

"No, no. All of the guarding and tracking, we have a right to know."

"We don't," James said. "It's better we don't."

"Ignorance is bliss from the walking encyclopedia," Harley said. "Solid."

"Don't worry."

"She just hacked this place like a warm knife through butter. We're hiding her at Phyllis'. And The Directive treats us with respect. Respect." He got in James face. "You realize they haven't knocked us out and kidnapped us once? Not once." He turned toward Kwynn. "Enough dancing around. Who are you?"

"Don't," James said. "I don't want to know."

Best to pull off the band-aid quick. "Trēowen. I'm Trēowen."

"Wait, what!?" Harley said. "You're Treowen? QTB? Kwynn Treowen Baldesarri. KewTeeBae."

"Knock it off," James said.

"You're sneaky. We're guarding KewTeeBae. I should have seen it. That explains a lot. I mean The Directive steering clear and all, but this: This is big."

That's why Kwynn kept quiet about it. James didn't want to know but she didn't like keeping the secret. It made her a liar. This stupid cult idea that she was so amazing or knew more and could do more was bunk. At least some of the memes had pushed the idea of her more towards Sasquatch than savior but her family was a curse. The sins of the father are visited upon the children. That's the truth of it. But fuck that.

"Can I get back to work?"

"Oh, ya," Harley said. "Don't let me get in KewTeeBae's way."

Kwynn reacquainted herself with where she was. Stupid fanboys. She looked over at Harley and laughed a little.

Where was she? After fumbling through a bunch of directories, Kwynn pulled up the error logs, the same logs Glen reviewed, and traced the beginning of the outages. She switched to the reports log and read to the guys. There was a written report, detailed notes at least, commented into the directory in a text file.

"It looks like it started from a fire up by Tejon ranch," Kwynn said.

"That's what all the sites said," James said.

"Ya, but what they didn't tell us was this was a control burn. They planned it and it got out of control," Kwynn said.

"Out of control," said Harley. "Mistakes happen, I guess."

"Mistakes do happen. What makes me wonder is: the local engineer, project manager, I can't tell. Anyway, lost his house and it's the guy who wrote the report."

"So," James said.

"So, they didn't know about the 'control' burn and he's pissed. This guy, Glen, his family is in a hotel and he lost his cat and his truck."

Bob and Phyllis

Tuesday, later in the morning

Bob stood with one foot on a stair of the back porch talking to Phyllis as she rocked in her chair and broke the ends off of string beans she picked from her garden. The ends stayed in the bowl with the beans and bounced side to side to land at the bottom like in a pachinko machine.

"I don't like getting locked up and I don't see what Arno gets for cutting the power," Bob said with a grind of his teeth.

Phyllis nodded and snapped. Snapped and nodded.

"Okay," Bob stared at her and she kept on with her chore. "This is going nowhere, have you heard anything?"

She grinned, "No, I haven't heard anything. I'm just working on your same question: Why the grid?"

"Why the grid. He says it wasn't him, by the way."

"MmHmmm. And why involve you outright."

"Exactly. Why?"

"I think we're lucky you got in his way. No one had heard anything about something like this. That's the strangest part."

"The strangest part?"

"Yep. The silence is the biggest thing. It's weird. Mostly they, the weirdos, just bang the proverbial pots to get attention. At least most terrorists do. Silence is..."

"Extreme."

"Yep, in a way. To me, its gotta mean things are real good or real bad. The tickle in the back of my mind is feeling more storm than anything."

"Who's the kid, by the way?" Bob asked.

The front door slammed.

"Phyllis," Kwynn yelled from the front.

"You should go. This girl isn't - I don't even know what she's got yet," Phyllis said to Bob.

"If she's anything at all?"

"Yep."

"I'm not sneaking out like a rat."

"Just get out. There's things we gotta figure out first. I'm not dealing with a noob all the way through one of these unless I have to," Phyllis looked to the entry and back to him. "Get."

"Good point." Bob sneaked out through the small space at the side between the shared wall and unattached garage. The opening was hidden and overgrown by purple flowered morning glory vines. The magenta center stars followed his passing through the opening into the neighbor's plush backyard. He headed out to the sidewalk unnoticed but felt something behind him.

Bob continued away from the house and down the street. He looked back to see no one watching him, hit something hard and tripped to the ground. He rolled, ready to fight off… the light pole he clipped. He looked back and forth, shook his head, "Keep your eyes on where you're going, Bob."

.and_it_begins

Tuesday, 2029/08/07 09:08:00

Kwynn, James and Harley rambled back to the porch of Phyllis' house like puppies on parade and came to a stop around Phyllis and her beans.

"Something shitty is going on," Kwynn said with a puff and pink cheeks.

"Enlighten me," Phyllis said.

"With the grid," said Harley.

"And the Company," said James.

"With the grid and the company," Kwynn said. "Don't you look at Instagram and Twitter? This fire was a set up to screw the grid. Anyway, that's what the engineer thinks."

"Which engineer?"

"We sort of took a peek and found stuff we weren't supposed to," Kwynn said. "It's all here," she held up her tab with a grin and brought up the reports to show Phyllis.

"Did you access Wrecan networks with that one?"

"Yep."

"Did you search the data?"

"How else would we get the info?

"They drop crawlers to reach back to home base in case of access."

"Ummm..."

"You know this, noobs," looking between James and Harley. "We gotta go."

"Why?" Kwynn said. "I masked it."

"Now!" Phyllis shot up and entered the house in a flash. She popped open a hope chest, lifted the blankets to a false bottom and pulled out a messenger bag with a tab inside. She created a quick link between the two comps.

Phyllis looked at them, turned around, flipped the "My house is dirty enough to be happy" crochet off the wall to reveal a keypad and typed a nine-digit code.

A drone appeared and landed on the back porch step Bob just stood on. Phyllis took Kwynn's tab, locked it onto the drone and glyphed a gesture. Off it went.

"My tab," Kwynn said.

.downstairs

Tuesday, 2029/08/07 09:10:00

"Let's get out of the way for a bit," Phyllis said and moved the runner in the hallway, plinked out 5 little jazz notes on the piano and a set of sub-stairs opened in the floor. "Don't look - Go!"

They hurried down the steps with Kwynn at the back. Each stair disappeared as Kwynn's foot left it. She heard a racket in the distance behind them. The burst of doors and footfall on the floor above.

Before her, more stairs appeared, metal grate like an old fire escape, that led to a brick and exposed beam jazz club. Some sort of club, but the chairs were on tables and dust was on everything.

Kwynn turned to take her last step and up walked a gray-haired gentleman. He had the manner and holding of a gentleman, not an old man, with his hand extended. She had seen this guy, this place, in her dream.

"I believe we've met," he said as he took Kwynn's hands in both of his.

"A noob," Phyllis said. "She exposed us to the company so we needed to 'get' for a bit."

"Has she displayed any more skill?"

"More talent than she knows but not a lick of skill."

"Hmm. Come sit," and he pulled some chairs down then looked intently at Kwynn, then met eyes with James and Harley.

"Didn't we do this once?" Kwynn said.

"Good, you do remember. I am Paolo. We have much to discuss," he said as a large boom exploded outside. "How much do you remember?"

"About my dream?" Kwynn said.

"That. And much further back. Do you have early memories?"

"Is this really the time for a therapy session?"

"Don't be difficult. Answer him," Phyllis said. The

windows rattled from another detonation.

"Have you ever felt like you know more than other people? Or see things others don't?"

"Doesn't everyone?"

"I need you to travel and see the past."

The room faded to dark and Kwynn was in the middle of a circle vignette from an old photograph. An oval of light surrounded her but the edges were fuzzy.

Her first memory was from before she was born. Strangely, she could see and hear, feel, understand, a world she knew nothing of. She moved through beaded doorways and sensed orange lights, she flew within another's sphere and knew it to be true. Ya, in utero. The roar and the churn of liquids flowing through her body and of her host was constant. She didn't know it then but this was the clearest she would understand her mother. The last she remembered of her.

The building rattled and a cloud of dust fell from the ceiling. A chunk of cement crushed a table.

Kwynn was right back here.

"It will have to wait." Paolo turned to Phyllis. "As it stands, there's a lot of turmoil brewing. Everywhere, not just in your neck of the woods. Is Bob around?"

"Yes," Phyllis said. "Of course."

"Good. Have him help," he said over another explosion. "Get her to Ziggy."

The building rattled again. The explosions roiled the entire space. They were getting dizzy.

"It's dangerous here and this is a much larger puzzle." Another explosion shook the club and the lights went out. "Go. Figure out your piece. All I can see are the edges but I think your piece fits right in the middle. I've got an inkling that there's more than just melted ice cream to this."

"What is going on here?" Kwynn said. "Wait, melted ice cream?"

"Power outage. Freezer stopped working. It's summer. It's a stupid analogy," he said.

"C'mon, noobs," Phyllis said changing the subject. She glared her *don't embarrass me* eyes at Paolo as she passed him and dragged Kwynn by the hand out the nightclub door which passed into a basement.

The basement was a place of old golf clubs and typewriters, a brass hinged chest and moldy boxes. It smelled of deep-down dirt, cool and rich with silky, dusty spider webs hanging from wooden beams and slatted flooring. Garden tools were piled in the corner with terra cotta pots at their feet held tight with the spider silk.

"Is this your basement?" Kwynn said. "Wait, does this bullshit have to do with Dad, too?"

"Yes. No," Phyllis said. She noticed the quiet. The cacophony outside stopped and the air was filled with a deep, full silence like damp, muted fog on an autumn night. A glowing spider dropped from the ceiling and hung there, directly in Kwynn's face. It peered at her through its multifaceted emerald eyes from the bottom of the long line of silk. She almost expected a "Salutations" from the thing.

Giving the spider plenty of room, Kwynn stepped around the spider and stubbed her toe. The polished table of redwood didn't give. The tabletop was remarkable with concentric rings combined like layers of quartz that bounced from dark to light and back again.

"I don't hear anyone above," James said. "Maybe, we should head back."

"Why are you always in such a hurry," Harley said.

"I agree," Phyllis said as she surveyed above with her ears, eyes searching. "Let's go upstairs."

Phyllis directed them to a pair of doors directly in front of Kwynn. She stopped in her tracks. They were covered with the same plethora of spiderwebs covering the tools and everything but that table. "Unh-uh. Ya, no more spiders," Kwynn said.

Phyllis brushed past her and climbed the grooved small cement slope. She opened the overhead barn doors to the outside. The daylight cut a straight line across the opening. Phyllis skulked out the doors, slipped into the light and popped her head back in, "All clear."

Not Again

Tuesday, not too much later

Outside, Bob, now a couple miles away from Phyllis', wandered down an Ocean Boulevard sidewalk beneath the sky reaching, swaying palm trees with no real destination in mind. He chewed on the salt and brine breeze, felt the hot sun on his already warm back.

But he kept his eyes intently upon where he was going. In fact, he walked with such focus on where he was headed, he didn't notice the van pull up next to him and three guys jump out until they grabbed him.

"What? Not now," Bob said as one sprayed the contents of a cannister in his mouth and nose. Bob collapsed into their arms and they carried him to the van.

A blaring boom pounded between Bob's ears as he came back to consciousness in the same construction office space as before. It was dusk and a wide-open ocean spread below an orange and purple buttermilk sky outside the plate windows.

Standing in front of him was Arno.

"You know, I have a phone. You could call me," Bob said.

"But then we wouldn't have these moments together," Arno said. "Why was Phyllis snooping around Wrecan?"

"She's not. Not that I'm aware of."

"Bob, we both know you are aware of much more than most. But not this?"

"Look, Arno, I don't know what you're up to but..."

"Nor will you."

"BUT. But when I figure this out, there'll be hell to pay."

"Funny you say that. Do you have someone new in the fold that I must worry about? I felt an inkling..."

"Arno, you wouldn't know an inkling if it fell on your head," Bob said when a 2x4 scrap flailed across Arno's head and knocked him out.

"Could you get me out of here, please?" Bob said and a

daemon, a small not quite furry gremlin like creature, scurried through the air to Bob's side and untied his hands. "You're such a chicken shit. You are always on my back until trouble comes. Then I'm on my own."

The daemon took the rope, tied a lasso, threw it to the sprinkler head and swung across the room with a smile and the bird for Bob.

.strike_the_match

Tuesday, 2029/08/07 10:58:00

Phyllis filled the kettle with water and placed it on the gas stove. She turned the front burner knob, it tic, tic, ticked and didn't light. Kwynn took a seat and looked back down to where the stairs were, under the Persian rug, "None of this makes sense."

Phyllis rolled her eyes, *noobs*. James and Harley hovered around in the background. Phyllis grabbed an over-sized box of wooden matches from atop the ancient stove and removed one.

"Take this match," she said showing it to Kwynn. "Sitting on top of a match is red phosphorous and potassium chlorate."

"This leads to a chemistry lesson?"

"Not quite," James said.

"Not a catalyst," Harley said.

"Not quite a catalyst," Kwynn said.

"Give me a sec. Not exactly the catalyst but the fuel. Our catalyst is the action. Striking the match."

"Striking the match? It's the outage?" Kwynn said.

"Hold on. I have something important to get you to understand - and that's not helping. Shut up," Phyllis said. "Without kinetic energy - the force applied - we just have a stick and some colored speck on the end. But. Once we add the action, the energy, we create the spark," and Phyllis struck the match setting it alight then the stove's front burner. "We transfer action into result. A stable solitary thing has now become a flaming gusto of actions and reactions."

"Just a little push," Kwynn said.

"That's all it needs to go from potential to active energy," Phyllis looked at Kwynn. "Strike the match."

Kwynn took a match and struck it. Nothing. One more time a spark. The third time it snapped in half.

"Get another one, idiot," Phyllis said.

Kwynn stared Phyllis in the eyes then stood up and walked out of the kitchen. The front door opened and closed.

"Sometimes you gotta keep trying, I guess," said Phyllis.

"As long as you try with gusto," Harley said and James laughed.

"Are you going to follow her or not?"

James and Harley looked at each other and ran out the front door to see no trace of Kwynn.

"Shit."

"Ya, no kidding," Phyllis said behind them on the porch. "Go find her, dummies."

"We will."

"And do it with gusto," she said and slammed the door behind her.

I'm Going

Tuesday, August 07, 2029, 11:04 a.m.

Glen sat at the control panel when Prakash walked in, "Are you working on the fire?"

"Yes - No. I'm working on how they accessed our system. The more I think on it: A controlled burn went out of control? This fire is too convenient."

"It's the Santa Ana's."

"Here and up North. There are too many coincidences. In fact, there's no such thing as coincidences."

"We need to corral our local power issues," said Prakash. "That arcing transformer screwed everything up real good."

"People need to know. I need to know what happened. What's Tehachapi say?"

"No luck. And the solar farm out by Four Corners confirmed they are pulling off, too."

"And Twenty Nine Palms?"

"And Twenty Nine Palms. They're considering bringing San Onofre Nuclear Power Plant back online to fill the gaps."

"Seriously. I assume *they* are the politicians," Glen said. "Look, these logs hold answers. I've moved from the error logs and am tracking access. Obviously, they have to access the network. I will figure out how."

"What does it matter the who right now?"

"The easiest answer is usually the correct one."

"Occam's razor."

"Yep. If we have a saboteur in our mix it's one thing. If they are smart enough to sneak in, it's another."

"These things are more often smash and grab than an elegant hack," Prakash said.

"Then why the hack of the emergency services alert system and the bull shit 'IT HAS BEGUN' stuff?"

"I don't know."

"Me, either."

Glen scrolled through the schematics to isolate the

surges when the computer began ignoring his commands and flipping through screens.

"Prakash," he said, "I lost control of the workstation screen here."

Prakash came back and Glen waved to the monitor. The mouse was moving around the screen opening schematics and enacting protocols. "What is going on?"

"Same as I thought I saw before." Glen figured it's the same as the Ukrainian outage in 2015. And 2016. They used an infected file to infiltrate the network then used a free tech support utility to take over the computer. Full remote control. "This is very bad."

The perpetrator accessed the telemechanics and switched off circuit breakers at random.

"This isn't the main system is it?"

"No, this one isn't controlling anything. But they have access. Somewhere. Somehow. I gotta see what happened up there with my own eyes. The router logs don't tell us shit."

"Going won't help."

"I'm going up to the substation. I am going to see for myself what's happening out in the mountains."

"I'm not giving you permission to do that," Prakash said. "We need to get..." and the computer console reset. Power flushed green throughout the proxy network.

Glen looked stoically between Prakash and the console, "I didn't ask." He pulled his zip up jacket off the back of his chair and stormed out.

Hi Ho

Tuesday, August 07, 2029, 11:08 a.m.

Glen walked out to the truck yard with his key in his hand and clicked the fob. Nothing. Of course, nothing happened because his fucking truck was burnt to a crisp back at home. He walked to the yard foreman, "I need a truck."

"All I got, Glen, is that old beater," pointing to a forty-year-old dented, oil leaking heap of metal.

"Javier, I got to drive up North."

"At least it's got the Company logo on it."

"Honestly."

"All of the shifts are called in. Every one is out because of all this trouble. That's all I got," and Javier pulled the key off the board and threw the set to Glen.

Glen walked over to his new ride. Dented, scratched, greasy, oil leaking, squeaky, stripped down GMC with no horsepower and no oomph, he was sure. He drove down the road, flicked the AC. No AC. Opened his windows to the dust and cursed the steering wheel. If ten and two were where you placed your hands, the hours between eight and four were what it took to stay straight. The steering wheel had more play than a honky tonk woman next to a Marine base.

Let's break it down. No AC, terrible steering, worse brakes, zero pick up, no radio. An engine, a bent frame and a very pissed off engineer headed north through the high desert when he came to Avenue G. The musical road. At one time, a car commercial cut grooves into the road to play the William Tell Overture when you go 50mph over the grooves.

Bumm ba ba bumm ba ba bum-bum-bum…

"Perfect. Hi Ho, Silver, away."

TO-O-O-O-O-O-O-O-O-O-O—O-O-ONE. BEEP. BEEP. His phone bombarded him with the ten second straight tone and his screen was filled with IT HAS BEGUN. It bleeped then the screen was filled with what seemed to be random 3-pixel bits and marks. It could be some sort of alien language, an alien checkerboard or it could be his phone on the fritz.

Glen looked up from the phone to another unexpected site. Well, he'd seen it at festivals like Coachella. This has become a major disaster.

An entire tent city was laid out in a mile square patch of land with a massive Red Cross banner flying above the largest tent. Parents milled about while the kids played baseball and soccer, bounced basketballs or played hopscotch. Glen knew the necessities were tight in the city already and people got out. Looked for help. Broken communication and broken delivery chains created a very difficult situation for a lot of people. If they built a tent city, the schools were already full.

Glen needed to figure out why they took the power. He knew Julia and Elsa were safe. And Elsa had her meds. For now.

"This will get worse before it gets better."

His time in a war-torn country taught him that these situations can bring out the absolute best in people. And the absolute worst.

.the_bridge

Tuesday, 2029/08/07 12:00:00

Kwynn walked along Ocean Avenue for block after block below palm trees standing guard in rows on each side of the street. Fifteen story boutique hotels looked down on her and dozens of people bounced over crosswalks at every green light. She took a seat in the greenbelt and watched for a moment.

Her pocket comp lit up with a dozen push notifications: "See what Frenzii has been posting!" "Worry no more... #ITHASBEGUN - Read it all!" "Hot new Hashtag: #SHUTITDOWN" Find out what it's about!" She put the machine on DND, pocketed it and walked.

Families large and small, couples, homeless, buskers and poets all filled the streets. She wondered about each with their own needs and responsibilities, all the same: food, shelter, sex. What do these power outages do to them? She came upon Abbot Kinney. She made it to Venice Beach again, way past the pier.

Multi-million-dollar condos, apartments and houses surrounded her. She could still hear the ocean to her right past the houses. The clap and rush of waves created a rhythm to her pace.

To her left, a tunnel opened to her. Not really a tunnel. A break in the constant walls that kept everyone in and some people out. Ivy strands wound through bougainvillea arching over a walkway to create a tunnel with a spot of sunlight on the other end. A warm wind blew the bright burgundy and faded purple bougainvillea blooms in circles like papier-mache mixed with fast food cups, cigarette butts and sand.

She had an inkling in the back of her mind that she couldn't place. The place felt at once beautiful and mystical while seedy and torn. This mingling of high and low, put her out of sorts but she couldn't resist. Despite her trepidation she was going to look where this went.

She looked both ways and behind then strutted right into the tunnel. The darkness was deep as she came from the sunlight, her pupils dilated, and left nothing in her vision but silhouette; black and white.

Kwynn caught her forearm on a spiked branch of the bougainvillea. The finger length thorn pulled a long scratch through the small hairs on her arm. As she examined the scratch and stepped forward, her toe caught on something hard and put her crisply on her face.

She picked herself up to see the root raised sidewalk and the large Ficus tree overhead, bright green leaves and dappled sunlight above and out of reach. Embarrassed and still a bit, I don't know, discombobulated, Kwynn brushed herself off and walked on. She touched a tender spot on her cheek. She added a little raspberry on her elbow and torn knee jeans to her list of attributes when she tripped a second time. This time, though she licked her wounds, she had her mind about her and caught herself with a couple of extremely ungraceful foot slaps and a stomp. She shook her head, "Keep your eyes on where you're going, Kwynn."

She walked and walked but the light seemed no closer. She kept her eyes forward, thinking of her words when the pain subsided.

Kwynn remained in the darkness. She looked back and the bougainvillea and ivy couldn't be seen. No light behind and no light above. The sand continued to scratch the sidewalk below her feet and she smelled the salty, ocean-tinged breeze mixed with the mold and rot of the darkness and the wooden fence she just touched with her left hand when Kwynn burst through a silken web and emerged into a pure whiteness.

She looked down, blinked while rolling her eyes and looked up again. Something was booming around in the back of her head. She frantically wiped the spider silk from her hands and neck and left it on the vines beside her.

In front of her was a bridge over canals surrounded by both quaint and gigantic homes. Some houses were early last century with wonderful, plentiful gardens. Blooming flowers and food heavy limbs filled the empty space, while others were modern, built to take the fullest advantage of the space. The homes built plot line to plot line with right angles and windows.

At the apex of the arched bridge stood a middle aged man in blue jeans and a black turtleneck.

"So, you've found me," he said to her.

Something crashed in the dark of her mind.

"I didn't know I was looking."

"Hmm, neither did I until just yesterday."

He smiled and spread his hands, "Come. Join me, it's beautiful. More than you've imagined."

"I'm just looking around. I think I'll walk this way," and she turned left and what was in the back of her mind finally reached the front. She'd become very accustomed to those two. "Where are Harley and Jim?"

"No, they wouldn't be here," he said as he answered her thoughts right next to her ear.

"God damn it, Arno!" came from behind them both. "Keep your grimy hands off of her," Phyllis said and grabbed Kwynn by her shoulders. "You're coming with me."

"You don't have the right," Arno said. "She has her free will."

"She doesn't know shite. And doesn't need you confusing her. The Council wouldn't allow this. You know it. It's against the tenets."

"The Council needn't know, Phyllis."

"Shut the fuck up," and she walked Kwynn to a tunnel just ahead.

"This is just the beginning," Arno said.

Phyllis led Kwynn into the entry and they arrived to the street in three easy steps where Harley and James watched their approach sheepishly.

"C'mon," Phyllis said and walked between and past them. "Jeez, you scared the crap out of me."

"Me, too," Kwynn said.

"Are you starting to get an inkling of what's going on?" Phyllis led Kwynn through the tunnel. They passed from bright daylight to shadow and rustling bougainvillea, crinkling sand under their feet.

"No, but I do keep getting... I'm not quite sure, but in the back of my mind." Kwynn reached out to run her fingers along the white stucco wall beside her as they walked. It was rough but just touching that scraping wall gave her an anchor to what she knew was always there

"Yes, that."

"What 'that'?" Kwynn said.

"In the back of your mind."

"In the back of my mind?"

"Yes, the back of your mind, you are aware of things others aren't."

"What things?"

"These two, for example," Phyllis pointed at James and Harley standing sheepishly on the sidewalk, Harley with his hands deep in his short's pockets. "That tickle? It's your daemon."

"My daemon," Kwynn said with an eye crunch.

"Some of us see the little fuckers that give us inspiration. Like faeries. Others have powers or can just feel it. Look. There's a lot to learn and I'm not the one to teach it. But it looks like it's time."

And up walked Bob.

"You?" Kwynn said.

"Hi, Bob," Phyllis said.

"What just happened? I got here as soon as I could," said Bob.

"Arno just tried to take Kwynn here to the other side of the bridge."

"That dick. He knows he can't do that. She's ours to deal with," said Bob.

"I know."

"I know."

"Yours to deal with?" Kwynn said. "I just met you."

"She doesn't know?"

"She doesn't."

"I just kinda started. But fucking Arno is doing his stupid bullshit."

"And, Paolo?"

"Just for a minute."

"And...?"

Phyllis interrupted him, “No, no fucking way. Not yet. Don’t even say it.”

“Jesus, what do you think’s going to happen? He’ll have to deal with this now.”

VaWOOMP. Everything is quiet. No hum. No lights. The cars are still there but that high pitched crackle of street lights; it all stopped.

“Fuck. Again?” Bob said.

Kwynn pulled out her pocket comp to see. No connection. No network. “This one’s gonna last,” she said. “I can feel it.”

Convoy

Tuesday, August 07, 2029, 1:22 p.m.

Glen got a crackle over the CB radio, "Yo, Glen, you there?" said Prakash.

Glen rolled up the window on the truck cab. The wind was too much to hear the tinny, tiny speaker. He grabbed the greasy square handset, pushed the button on the side to talk, "Ya, why the CB?"

"Power's out again. The whole western block. Clean shut down."

"Alright. I'm still heading to the junction, though." Glen said and unconsciously pushed on the gas just a little harder.

"Clearly, there's no power, Glen. You won't get anything done there. We can have someone else handle it up there. Like Jayron. Get back here and help us from here where we have resources."

Glen threw the handset to the floor of the cab and kept on keeping on.

Back in Power Center, Prakash continued to speak into the CB radio on the desk, "Glen? You hear me?" and turned to look at Arno standing behind him. "He's not answering."

All this communications equipment in a multi-million-dollar facility and their using an old CB radio.

"Then get this back online yourself. Between you and the other ten thousand people at this company, you should be able figure this out," Arno said.

"He's pretty good."

"Mm. No kidding," Arno stepped closer to the screens, looked for an answer in all these data points he really didn't grasp.

"No, Glen is like a keystone. His knowledge and skill. Plus, he's motivated."

"That's obvious," Arno said while he drummed his fingers on the desk he leaned on. "We are all motivated."

"The mixture of his experience out on the line and in

the central room. Everyone else has one or the other but Glen knows this system inside and out. And the outages create shortages. If someone can make sense of it, it's Glen. He has a knack."

"Does he?" said Arno and turned his attention fully on Prakash. His poc-comp activated. "Hello, Frankie."

"Where are you. I've been trying to get a hold of you," Frankie said over the device.

"Wrecan."

"Well, the pot has been stirred. Get back to the office. I need you there to co-ordinate."

"Very well," Arno said and walked out the door without another word. He stopped and turned around, "You didn't tell me his extra motivation."

"Like I said, the outages create shortages," Prakash said. "This guy's as altruistic as they come but his kid's getting hurt worse than most by this. She can't get her immuno-suppressive drugs."

"Good to know," Arno said as he heard his own footsteps clack down the hallway.

A Drive

Tuesday, August 07, 2029, 1:52 p.m.

Glen drove past the Tehachapi wind farms with their spinning, seagull winged turbines. Dozens, if not hundreds of turbines arched the crested hills. In fact, the spin of the turbines as he hit the apex knocked his balance a skitter like the swirling center of a psychedelic carnival game. His stomach spun but he kept on.

Once he cleared the turbines, electrical stanchions clipped by on the side of the road like an animated flip-book of an unmoving man. The same frame repeated over and over, of a four-armed man with his arms out all linked by the same sagging electrical lines. Hundreds of stanchions passed as he churned through the miles.

Eventually, he drove past the dilapidated mines from the turn of the last century with rotting wood supports and rotting buildings. He continued through the striped Red Rock Canyon and shifting sand dunes until the Sierra Nevada Mountains rose on his left, the smaller Inyo mountains on the right. Desert sand and scrub transitioned to burgundy-black pumice and tall grass with the Owens river running through along the right of the highway.

The valley wasn't more than a couple miles across at the bottom. The further north, the steeper and more foreboding the Sierras loomed. The valley widened a bit where the land became more welcoming with meadows fed by the widening river. The highway held to the base of these mountains that carry the highest peak in the contiguous US. It's hot down here but Glen always liked to imagine the cold and lighting at the top of Mt. Whitney. It reminded him of our place in the grand scheme.

On his right, Glen came to the Crystal Geyser bottled water plant. The plant that sold the same water the entire Los Angeles region already drank straight from the tap. They provided the water in plastic bottles at twenty times the price. They removed water from the river that spawned *Chinatown* and funded Mulholland's dreams of a lush Los Angeles. A place where dreams were made real.

Glen figured to visit the Inyo County seat in Independence, halfway up the valley. He passed through a few more small towns of sheep ranches under hundred-foot sycamores and shaking aspens.

He passed Manzanar with its guard tower and barracks floating in the valley like a wraith. The World War II era camp looked more like Colonel Klink would come running out of the shack. Even now the reality crashed against what he believed about his own country. Like many Americans, he wanted it to be otherwise. Americans had been taken away and locked up, losing their homes and jobs because a land they'd never known had attacked our country. American citizens deserved more and better.

Glen slowed as he pulled into Independence City. The street was lined with a few simple wood slat houses, two staunch Victorian homes that stood side by side and a small gas station. As he entered town center, the courthouse with its southern Gothic pillars was surrounded by what must've been the entire town, about 5-600 people. They gathered around the courthouse steps listening to someone of authority. Allie Roswell, a mature man spoke from the top of the steps in a cowboy hat, seersucker shirt and jeans.

"Look, I have nothing new," the man said to the crowd. "I hate to say it but between you and me, nobody is talking."

"You gotta know more than that!" a voice yelled from the crowd.

"Hold on, now, Ron," Allie said. "I have no reason to hide anything."

"But they're hiding something from all of us," Ron said. "Allie, I'm almost outta gas."

"Billy, at the station, don't have too much gas left, so you can get some but only use what you need, folks. I have a decent amount stored on the ranch and so does Blake Trice but you just keep on keepin' on and we'll get through it."

"I don't like it," Ron said.

"None of us do," Allie said.

Glen spied who he was looking for as he took one step

up from the foot of the steps as the leader pointed to him.

"Jayron, here - you got anything new?"

"Nope, I'll keep you posted," Jayron said.

"Thanks, everyone," the leader said. "We'll be fine. Just take care of each other. Billy set up a pin board over here to leave notes for what you can't find word of mouth. She'll let you know where she can help. Now, it's gettin' late, best we all get back home before dark."

Glen shook Jayron's hand and said, "A bit different from DTLA, Jay."

"We are that."

"Can you come up with me to Inyo Egress to Junction 73? The more I think about it, the more I wonder who the heck is really doing this. Some idiot terrorist would have to be crazy lucky to pull this off."

"Ya, I've been thinking the same thing and of the same place. Nobody really knows about it but it might be the only spot that could disrupt all this without completely overwhelming and destroying the entire grid."

The Tiendita

Martes, 9:17 p.m.

Ramon, the tiendita owner, heard a bang-smack on the street. He looked out his second-floor apartment window to the barricades dropped off a police truck. A man and a woman, each in riot gear, stood at the street entrance on either end of the 2x12 painted white planks with orange stripes set up on plastic stands. La Policia.

He lived at the edge of the Promenade. He and his little girl in a one bedroom. She slept on a couch. The neighborhood wasn't what it was. But what ever is. It was a place that grew to be moneyed and fashionable after a soggy middle of drugs and dilapidation and became urban renewal. A place where his brains and sweat supported his daughter.

The looting began. Dozens of men and women swarmed to the street.

Two riot police on each end of the block on a couple of bikes were no match for two hundred.

His tiendita was screwed. He was screwed. Fuck.

He checked on his mija sleeping on the sofa and left. He locked the deadbolt, rolled his feet down the short, worn red steps, touched the rough stucco arch as he turned the corner to the side walk. People poured down the street like a rising tide. A mother dragged a toddler. At the corner, a teenager broke the window of Rocky's liquor and tore open the door like a candy bar.

Everybody pushed in. The mother set the toddler in the sidewalk garbage can and ran in herself. She ran out with a gallon of milk and three bags of beef jerky. She checked the street then grabbed the kid.

Fuck.

He kept moving. He was close. A crowd rallied outside his store. The place had fallen.

What the fuck. He looked around and nobody looked at anybody else.

They hustled past each other. Hustled past the police.

Laughed to each other once a dozen. Relished the crash of glass to the cement, crunched under their Nikes and Adidas. Undershirts. Supreme hoodies. Third hand jeans.

A buff kid and a buff man bumped fists after they flipped a Fiat.

His store was ravaged. Cash register gone - nothing was in it. Shelves barren. Tables flipped; chairs broken. Salsa table sneeze guard cracked in half. Stand up cooler shattered and empty as a popped balloon. The entire grill unit yanked from the wall and shucked to the ground.

Darkness.

He upended and sat on a chair. Groups and singles flew past his door.

A silhouette appeared at the threshold. A little one with a hooded sweatshirt. He grabbed her and wiped the tears.

She sat in his lap and he pulled a cigarette from his shirt pocket pack.

"Papi, I smell something."

He pulled his zippo from his pants pocket and flicked the flint.

Pfft.BOOM!

Wednesday

.dtla

Wednesday, 2029/08/08 10:00:00

A young reporter gave her stand up to her cameraman and the millions of audience members behind that lens linked to an antenna, through a transmitter to a series of satellites and transponders and finally to a TV screen or through routers and servers onto any form of computer.

"...I have been told that in addition to the mayor's address, extremist social media groups have organized protests. As of now, we have not seen any sign of these protesters, however, they... hold on, I'm being told the mayor is ready to speak."

Gil Baneulos, the mayor of Los Angeles, stood on the Los Angeles City Hall steps, and held the podium with white knuckled hands.

Our reporter and dozens of additional TV cameras and phones recorded video, cameras flashed and hundreds of restless citizens rambled about waiting for some reassurance. The mayor adjusted his tie, ran a hand through his ample hair, for his age, and reviewed his notes.

The crowd all looked rough, but they would. Any time without water and electricity can roughen the edges of many a city dweller.

"Thank you for coming out today. Meeting outside is necessitated by this continued power outage," the mayor said.

The chant and stomp of a mob echoed between the high rises and up the street. Heard before seen, "IT HAS BEGUN. POWER ON!" rolled into the opening before city hall and the grand park, "IT HAS BEGUN. POWER ON!"

Shaved heads and combat boots defined the group. A para-militaristic bunch marched with flags and signs. Torches held high and drum sticks crackling.

Kwynn watched the ad hoc group. It was a motley

bunch. One couple, where the guy was really short and the girl really tall, stood out in her mind. Kwynn couldn't help but imagine some version of Boris and Natasha. The group dressed in blacks and dark greens, eyes filled with equal parts fear and hatred. "IT HAS BEGUN. POWER ON!"

This first group of chants was soon afterward met in equal force with, "WRECAN SHUT DOWN. NO MORE POWER GRABS." A cacophony. Pots and pans. Plastic drums, vuvuzelas and whistles were heard from the opposite direction of this original chant. The group had hair of all colors, long and short, spiked and braided, with faces covered. If their opposer moved with strength, this group moved with speed, both moved with menace.

Kwynn looked around and her head hummed. Her ears buzzed from the conflicted shouts and slogans but deep in her mind was a thrum of her own. She rubbed her eyes and wriggled her fingers in her ears in an attempt to clear her head.

The groups on each side marched directly at each other down Spring Street in front of City Hall as the police, in full riot gear, looked between the on-charge like ants on a corpse. These groups wanted conflict.

The police shouted an order and with military precision each officer joined a group to form at least a platoon or two of officers. Four officers faced one direction, the next four the other, tic-tocking with riot shields held to protect their brother or sister next to them, each with their backs to the other portion of the crowd.

The air crackled with electricity.

The rioters held a distance from the line of police groupings. Twenty feet separated each side as they lead cheers with bull horns and clamor but the groups moved no further. They taunted each other like middle schoolers who looked to fight but unsure of their own strength or the strength of their opponents. For the moment, the fight was verbal rather than pugilistic.

"IT HAS BEGUN!"

"SHUT IT DOWN!"

The mayor burst into a rage and called out.

"Give me a moment," he said over the competing crowd. "I have important information to disseminate. Give me a moment."

"IT HAS BEGUN!"

"SHUT IT DOWN!"

"I need a moment!" said the mayor to a group wholly incapable of hearing, well past listening. He tapped on the microphone, his head on a swivel. No attention. He waved his arms and shouted, then looked to his side with an idea. The mayor reached over and grabbed a revolver from his nearest protector and shot three reports to the sky. Pop. Pop. Pop. The last was never heard.

The police protective unit grabbed the mayor. Despite proper spacing and tactics, the two groups crushed the police line.

The protesters did one of two things. Many fled and screamed. These were political protesters, not hoodlums. That certain subset in each group now had what they wanted and charged each other. In fact, the short and tall couple Kwynn locked on earlier was the first to rush.

A melee ensued. The anger and frustration, distrust and hate boiled over. Against protocol, the police lines disbursed toward the city hall. They would not take a side this day. Groups attacked each other with bottles, rocks and sign posts. Cars were overturned.

"This is unreal," Kwynn said.

A black painted fire truck pulled into the square. A fire nozzle was mounted atop and fired purple-died water at the public. Ten or twenty were knocked over before the groups pulled back out of range. They seemed to coalesce and assess. If a crowd could look like a lion coiled and ready to pounce, this one did. The energy, fear, fire and power of The Crowd gathered and began to swirl.

Thooomp. Thoomp. Thoomp. Cannisters of tear gas flew into the air and dropped amongst them. The violet smoke pushed the people gasping and coughing from City Hall.

Four pairs of protesters rushed the tear gas cannisters and drowned them with water in an attempt to mitigate their power. The majority of the purple stained mass of people scattered as Kwynn squinted through her tears caused by the gas. She wasn't sure but not only did people run, some fluttered like termites in the wind through the sky and away.

.mayhem

Wednesday, 2029/08/08 10:05:00

Chaos surrounded Kwynn. Purple died hoodlums swarmed on all sides of her with no regard for their particular faction. Two men fought bare fisted with bloody knuckles and violet, swollen eyes. A thin, young woman threw bottles in the crowd. "IT HAS BEGUN" was chanted with each bottle thrown while a group of a couple dozen camo-clad teenagers rocked and flipped a city bus on its side yelling, "SHUT IT DOWN." A handful of others had pocket comps held high over their heads recording the events with passive looks, eyes transfixed on the screens.

"Keep your eyes open, Kwynn," she said to herself. As she turned the corner of Main Street and First, Harley and James waited dwarfed by the deep gray of the CALTRANS building to the left and LAPD headquarters to the right. A dozen officers rushed out of Police headquarters past them toward the fight at City Hall.

"Where were you?" James said.

"Where were you?" Kwynn said.

"We need to get out of here," Harley said as he pushed them and corralled their shoulders. He stopped, grabbed her shoulders and looked her in the eyes, "You okay?"

"Yes." Not that it mattered, but that was nice.

"Then LET'S GO!" Harley said and slapped her shoulder on his way past.

That: not so much.

They took off west, up First. Cars filled the streets. Many parked at the curb while others dotted the street abandoned or parked catawampus to the sidewalk locked tight and useless. They continued down First, past Spring St. to Broadway.

"It's this way," James said.

The three walked down a street melded in both past and present. Computer repair and jewelry stores, t-shirt shops and old theaters. Blocks of buildings a dozen stories tall and more with gargoyles and bison perched on the corners, carnival jesters and monsters carved in the facade, their empty eyes staring nowhere. A KRKO metal stanchion radio tower loomed like a giant in the middle of one building's roof. Kwynn studied the Orpheum Theater as they passed under the marquee, clearly built in the 1920's, opulent and obsolete. Such a big screen seemed wasted when you can see all you want on your pocket comp.

The small struggling shops had all of their wares in the windows or on tables out front. The large Bizby chain store had their gates locked. Ingenious and used to turmoil, the hand-me-down comp store had fruits and vegetables for sale. Two tables, one for comps the other with groceries obviously from back yards: oranges with stems and leaves, imperfect tomatoes and grapes, persimmons, bell peppers and green beans of various varieties, chilis - serrano, jalapeno, habanero, de arbol all mixed together to form a mixed heat salad of green, red and orange. Potatoes, small and full of dirt.

The patriarch sat in a chair out front of the store next to the product, hand gun on his lap, hunting rifle leaned against the wall. Kwynn stopped at a table full of pocket comps.

"What you need?" said the owner.

"Is this an iPhone 6?" Kwynn said turning the old phone she picked up off the table in her hand.

"Yes. Good tech. Very old."

"They still made the screen from glass," Harley said.

"Yes, they still made the screen from glass," Kwynn said.

"The glass break but they are safe," the owner said. "Before 'bend don't break' diamonds."

"Without power, none of them work," Kwynn said. She picked up an orange, "From your yard?"

"Sure," he said. "And others. People need food. No flowers in my yard unless they give me fruit."

"True. I hope you don't see much trouble."

"We are used to trouble. Also, used to not having enough. Not waiting for everyone else to solve our problems."

"We have to get going, Kwynn," James said as Kwynn

nodded to the man and put down the comp.

They walked half a block further, "Here," James said.

The three walked to the door of a six-story red brick building. The now dark red neon facade celebrated Clifton's Cafeteria, est. 1932. Living history. The threshold held a wall of air thicker than the outside. It raised the cackles on Kwynn's neck.

A bear greeted them in the entryway. A big stuffed one in front of a large room designed to look like a piece of the Sierra Nevada forest. Ethereal smoke lingered partially blocking the view of a giant sequoia replica at the center of the heavily shadowed room. The tree reached through the middle of the open interior of the building a story above and for 2 stories more. Kwynn craned her neck to take in the 4 stories of tree and nearly fell over a purple felt rope meant to control the lines.

A large man nearly as big as the stuffed bear stepped from the shadows and confronted them, "Where do you think you're going?"

"Where are we going? Away from that out there," Kwynn said but the man-tree looked right past her to James and Harley.

"You are not welcome," he said.

"That's not for you to decide, Oso," James said.

"Move," said Harley and Oso pulled out a samurai sword and took a whack at him.

"What are you doing?" Kwynn said as Harley put his fist in Oso's kidney and James picked up the line stand and hit Oso with the heavy stand, to little effect.

Kwynn stepped between the three fighters, "Stop it."

Oso was in the groove now. He looked at Kwynn, put his whole hand on her face and pushed her to the side and onto the ground. He eyed the other two with a moment to consider which he'd like to eat first.

"Woh - woh - woh," came from the floor above at the top of a polished wood but rustic curved stair case.

"We can't have a riot in here with a riot going on out there. Despite our past, our star pupil will get damaged. I don't like it any more than the two of you do but we all have our orders."

Oso was still growling, fists clenched.

James and Harley weren't much better.

"Call him off, Ziggy," James said.

"I did."

"Then calm him down."

"You know I can't do that. Whatever's in the past is between you but she needs to be safe," Ziggy said and walked down the stairs and past the face-off in the entry. Ziggy turned a corner and walked down the next flight of stairs underground. "C'mon, kids. Leave them, Oso."

"I hate that guy," said Harley.

"Asshole," said James.

Oso planted his hands quickly in the middle of James and Harley's backs and pushed them. They tumbled down the stairs on either side of Ziggy while Kwynn stood entranced.

"The first step is a doozy," Oso said and gurgled a laugh.

"Kwynn, please come along," Cliff said.

"It's okay, Kwynn. This way," James said and picked himself up. "You're supposed to see those things coming," he said to Harley.

"I was focused on Kwynn," said Harley.

"Focused on me?" Kwynn said.

"Ya, this is a doozy," Harley said.

"What is?"

"You'll see," James said with a sideways glance at Harley.

The group left Oso up top and they descended another flight of stairs. In ninety degree turns, fifteen steps at a time, they traveled down and down, circling around a deep darkness below. Yet, this seemed more like an Escher painting then a deep dive to Middle Earth. After watching the same stairs pass her by three times, Kwynn spoke up, "Why are we going in circles?"

"Why, indeed," Ziggy said.

"We've covered the same stairs and I've seen that doorway, too, three times."

Kwynn turned and walked through it and, to her amazement, they all followed. The four of them spilled out the door onto a stage at the front of a beautiful auditorium. Faux gold leaf with a large balcony and gargoyles planted at each post that, to Kwynn's eyes, jostled and blinked.

Once her eyes adjusted and she focused on one of the beasts, stage lights flipped on and applause followed. She stepped forward to peer through lights to the seats beyond and nearly fell into the orchestra pit.

"Keep your eyes on where you're going, Kwynn," and she blinked slowly to gather herself and looked down to see a brass plaque inset on the stage: The Orpheum.

"Would that be a mouthpiece for Orpheus?" she thought.

"Indeed, it would," said a voice from the balcony.

Above, with his elbows on the railing was Ziggy looking down on the stage.

"Why the theatrics?" Kwynn said.

"Have you ever stopped to consider that yourself?"

"And the lights. Do we have power?"

"Ah, child. Your focus is so narrow," he said. "Of course, we all of us have power here. Most misuse, no, mistrust it."

"Could you come down here and talk with me?"

"Why don't you come up here?"

Kwynn squinted and walked to the side of the stage, hopped off, traipsed up the aisle out the doors to an opulent if surprisingly small foyer with requisite chandelier and proceeded up the carpeted steps to the door and out to the balcony to see our Ziggy friend standing on the stage next to her two cohorts.

"Why are you down there? How did you get down so fast?" Kwynn said.

"Kwynn, how do we do anything? We do."

"Why so goddamn cryptic?" Kwynn said.

"Simply stated, literally," he said.

"I literally don't know what you are talking about and I'm literally going to kick your ass — or my friends - if they don't help me."

"Are you sure you don't mean figuratively?" Harley said.

"I don't."

"Well, I need you to plug in to the situation not fight," Ziggy said.

Kwynn walked back off the balcony, down the stairs to the foyer and opened the door back into the theater. There was a concert raging on stage. A band performed and looked nearly 1920's-ish. One guy wore a white t-shirt with black pants held up by clip-on suspenders and a belt. He played piano. Another had a beard and a bowler and a guitar. A girl had a bee-boppers bob with a simple summer dress shimmering to her dancing feet and bowing bass.

They sang along to a song the entire crowd knew by heart that Kwynn had never heard but new nonetheless. Beautiful lights shone alternating blue, purple and green while others shone in the chandeliers behind the stage.

Kwynn focused on a young woman who sang, clapped and danced to the song. Down from the walls flew the gargoyles and landed on revelers, hovered over the lead singer and one specifically large one flew right at Kwynn. The seven-foot half man, half bat creature swooped over her and she dropped to the ground. When the monster circled around again and came toward her, she leapt to her feet and ran to the exit doors and through the lobby. Just as she arrived to the lobby doors to the outside James, Harley and Ziggy ran in front of her exit.

"Woah! Easy turbo," James said.

"Not a good idea," Harley said.

"Let her see," Ziggy said and they opened the door ever so slightly and a blinding light invaded the opening.

Kwynn figured it was just the daylight and peered through. She was shocked as the light attacked her eyes and shot straight deep into her skull.

"A-ach," Kwynn yelped.

"Now, settle down, Kwynn," Ziggy said. "You need to start to get a grip on this stuff."

"What 'stuff'?" she said.

"They didn't do you any favors keeping it from you," Ziggy said.

"Not her choice," James said. "Or her fault, let's just get her started."

"Ok, c'mon," Ziggy said and walked back to the theater.

"Mmm-mmm," Kwynn shook her head No.

"C'mon. Ziggy repeated and opened the door to an empty theater. "Let's begin again. I didn't realize you were so completely sheltered out in the desert."

"Can we skip the commentary," James said.

"Fine," Ziggy said. "Fine, but these things take a certain level of awareness that we can't teach."

"It's there. She just doesn't know it," Harley said.

"What is? I am right here," Kwynn said as the other three walked into the theater and she followed. "Stop talking as if I'm not here."

And Kwynn walked into a small spherical room. The floor, the walls, the ceiling were all rounded. Floating just in the center was a meter wide, multi-toned, 3-dimensional wood puzzle. She reached out to touch it and it spun slightly. Then she gave it a pull like you would on 'The Price is Right' and it spun like a slot machine.

"What am I supposed to do with this?" she said as she realized none of them were in the room with her. She pushed on each tone of wood that made up the puzzle. She sat and thought, scratched her head and wondered. Each piece would push out like a piece in Jenga and then push back in or rotate and rejoin the puzzle body in a different spot but in a similar form. Each time a piece moved a bit of sand flowed to the floor.

"What am I doing here?" Kwynn said. "What the hell am I doing here?"

Fuck. So, she sat and moped, scratching and drawing in the sand. Flattened it out. Collected more until she had a circle of sand about the size of her hand and created small doodle lines, erased and did it again.

Kwynn made lines and squiggles that she imagined were Chinese, Arabic or Sanskrit. Egyptian figures walked. A palm tree sunset, lighting bolt, hangman, power lines, a bridge, a guitar. She free associated whatever popped in her mind without paying any real attention. Squiggle. Wipe. Squiggle. Wipe. Squiggle. Wipe. L. Wipe. O. Wipe. O. Wipe. K. Wipe. U. Wipe. P. Wipe. L. Wipe. O. Wipe. O. Wipe. K. Wipe. U. Wipe. P. Wipe. L. Wipe. Wait a freakin' minute. L.O.O.K.U.P. and Kwynn gazed up to see that huge gargoyle sitting on top of the puzzle with a big grin on his face.

Getting Out

WEDNESDAY 2029.08.08 10:05:00

Murray was finally getting used to this damn interface in his skull. The more time he spent with it, the more he could see how all this information could become useful. He even had access to networks and systems he never even knew existed. Not access, exactly, but now he knew they were there when he never knew before. And if there's one thing he did know: information was worth a lot to the right people. So, of course, he traveled around all the networks he could find.

He had already mastered the hospital records and was looking forward to his release. They had some sort of security-hold on him. Apparently, his release was to be only to The Directive. Fuck that shit. He fixed that up from the comfort of his hospital bed last night. He also disabled the tracking system they had installed in the operating system. As if he had no idea.

Murray found a new set of clothes hanging in the closet for him. Jeans, what looked like a pirate shirt with a leather tie crisscrossing on his chest and a black leather jacket. Half cool, half lame. Probably Arno, that sick shit.

He dressed and walked out of the hospital ward. Nobody even looked up. They were all huddled around some mess playing on a TV in the top corner of some sitting area. He could look it up but Murray didn't care. He turned the corner and gave a polite nod and wave to a concerned nurse (her name was Vanessa according to his facial recognition) and skedaddled.

The fresh air nearly knocked him over as he walked outside. Freaking hot. Spend a couple days in straight air conditioning and you forget what the real world feels like. It was 116.3 degrees, if you were wondering. Westerly wind at 22 mph. Santa Ana's were blowing. That would explain the smoke.

Well, well, well. This might be fun. Murray had freedom and whole new set of tools. Where to now?

Murray walked down the street and perused the network for access to his car. Of course, it was still at Lee's office. He input his location and hunkered down for the couple minutes it would take for the autonomous driver to bring the car to him. While he waited, he ventured through the entire web of networks, computers and devices arrayed before him on his display. Mostly it was IOT stuff: People's climate control, twitter on their refrigerator, toaster timers. What a waste of bandwidth. He accessed a couple home systems through the light bulbs, which was pretty interesting. Once he stole the network passwords from the stupid chip in the bulb, he could share himself onto their home devices and bingo.

Good thing he was having fun because he could have drained this lady's bank account with a click but judging from the texts that showed up in her messenger this lady had enough problems without Murray cleaning her out. Her ex skipped alimony and the guy she hooked up with never called. The other one she hooked up with wouldn't take the hint and kept calling. Poor kid, it's never the one you want.

Someone swooped silently past Murray. He only saw the shadow. Not a thing moved. He wasn't sure if the swoop was in the real world or the cyber world. Well, both were real now. Felt like a falcon swooping on its prey. Another swoop, then another each in perfect succession. A single bar of eighth notes quickly tittered on his bandwidth.

His antenna was up and nothing was happening on the street. He ventured a glimpse through the network and checked his logs for contact to his system. An unknown and unmarked system had pinged him. Like ghosts, eight different systems had touched his own system once each and seemed to have flown straight threw him. He couldn't explain it but this network thing is strange. He was spooked.

The car pulled up. He hopped in. Murray disengaged the auto-drive it and drove himself. That was enough of computers for the moment. He went a block and the right lane was completely stopped. He looked up the road and saw the line crawl into a gas station. How ironic. These people were lined up for gas at a station with solar panels all over it.

Traffic lights were out. Murray hung a left in front of a polite wave from the oncoming car. The entire block was full of small retail storefronts; all one-story stucco buildings painted white, the corners stained and all surfaces lightly coated with that special motor oil and brake asbestos gray. Some places get a light dusting of snow from their clouds, we get grime from our smog.

He parked on the street and approached the bank. A simple standalone building covered in solar and a dozen 3-foot turbines placed around the roof. If there's a run on gas, there's a run on cash. He went to the ATM with five people lined up before him. The guy who was standing at the machine punching the buttons turned around, "There's no cash! ATM's out."

The guy in front of Murray, turned around to Murray, "Last guy said the same thing. But the guy before got some. He's probably embarrassed he's got nothing in there. I gotta at least make sure my money's there."

Murray nodded and took a look at his account on his interface. He still had many, many digits in his Venmo account thanks to Lee but he can't pull cash from his phone. He wouldn't be able to get any of that for at least a couple days.

Next lady left the ATM, "No money. There ain't no money."

Murray took a look in the bank through a window where a line snaked into the building from the far side of the parking lot. He wasn't getting any cash here. He always had a couple hundred stashed in a cigar box at home. That'd have to do.

He walked away as a bank manager lady came out the door and addressed the crowd, "I'm sorry folks. We are out of cash. That doesn't mean your money isn't safe, we just can't give you a withdrawal. However, you can check your accounts. Our network is safe and you can always access your safety deposit boxes."

Murray accessed the news feed as he walked to his car. Yep, full-fledged rioting downtown. Some spots around the city were complaining of no running water and some that had it were warned to boil the water for twenty minutes before consuming. A neighborhood in Watts had built community pools in case of water shortages and were beginning to access them for the government facilities. London thought that fatberg blocking the underground sewer was bad. At least they had running water.

How 'bout a Ride

Wednesday, August 8, 2029, 10:05 a.m.

Glen and Jayron bumped along a service road on BLM (Bureau of Land Management) land that was intermittently gravel covered and pocked by rivets caused by water running off the hills above to the meadows below. Water always runs to the lowest spot.

As it happened, the rain started to fall. Big, beautiful drops of the type you get in the mountains. If it was a country song these drops would be country strong and with enough consistency to begin to fill the rivets. Glen and Jayron traveled along the road bordered by 12-foot barbed fences at the foot of the mountains for a couple-five miles as the rain fell harder and harder.

"We get rain like this sometimes but if it keeps up at this rate, we'll have a hard time getting out of here," Jayron said.

"Let's keep our eyes peeled, then," Glen said and a few rocks tumbled in front of the truck and he tapped the brakes, getting a little squirrelly in the mud. "This old two-wheeler don't handle like my new one."

They cornered a bend to see the junction station ahead. There were large power lines running in and out of the station. A small building surrounded by another small fence and "Stay Out" signs. Inside is a diesel engine built specifically for the job of creating and passing along the power. A small box communicated over land lines, opening and closing routes while controlling and feeding the grid.

"Thar, she blows," Glen said and a wall of water and mud slammed the truck. Glen punched it hoping to pull ahead of the force but that just revved the engine and slipped the tires.

The road was cut into the low part of the hill and they had just arrived in front of a small tributary. It all opened up onto the valley floor and Glen turned tail and caught the wave. After the initial slippage they could see that the creek just opened on to the valley and they rode that wave a couple hundred feet into the empty valley until he eventually gained control then slid about 180 degrees and stopped.

Glen and Jayron looked forward then at each other and laughed.

"Jesus, nice move, Glen," Jayron said.

"Heck, wasn't any other choice," Glen said then focused on something up ahead. "What's that?"

"What's what?"

The rain let up just enough to give them a better look. Under the level of the road ran an exposed large black fiber line, about two feet in diameter.

"That cable," Glen said.

"I know what it looks like but why would it be here," Jayron said.

"A fat fiber line in the middle of nowhere."

"For what?"

"It goes somewhere. Let's get over to that station."

Glen started up the truck, reversed and spun a 180 j-turn then bumped along the valley floor straight to the small way station they'd been heading for all along.

.hmph

Wednesday, 2029/08/08 10:45:00

Sitting atop the puzzle in this spherical room like a huge puppy was that gargoyle. Alive. Smiling with his massive canine teeth sticking out. He looked at Kwynn expectantly.

"What?" she said.

"That's it?" he said.

"What's it?"

"Usually, when someone realizes their skill they react. Shriek. Cry. Exalt. Smile?"

"I knew it all along, I guess. Now it's just in front of mind instead of back," she said. "How do we get out?"

"Don't you want to talk? Not everyone gets to talk to gargoyles."

"Apparently, everyone out there can," she said.

He looked at her with puppy dog eyes. Not a look you expect on a seven-foot monster.

"Okay, what's your name?"

He smiled, "Garg."

"Garg?" she said. "As in Garg-oyle? Not very original, is it?"

"It's like Smith or Nguyen. There's a lot of us."

"OK. Right. Let's get moving."

"But...," it said and the room dissolved. They were in the middle of the stage.

Gargoyle guy, Garg, was floating, gently flapping his wings to stay in the air while Ziggy, Harley and James waited.

"Well?" James said.

"Well, what? I get it," Kwynn said. "There's magic creatures. What else?"

"She wasn't even surprised," Garg said. "It's my favorite part."

"No?" Ziggy said. "That's good. We may not be in that bad of shape, after all."

Kwynn pulled her tablet out of her bag and sat right there on the stage. She pulled up her holo display and began sifting around.

"Um, Kwynn, not the time for holograms. We're kind of initiating some things," Harley said.

"I just realized we didn't see something back on the pier," Kwynn said. "When we saw Bob?"

Kwynn pulled up the video that skater kid took and played it back. We watched Bob yelling at everyone and grab the fire hose after breaking the glass. A dark flash crossed the blue sky, then the explosion off the pier in the waves. She rolls back and steps frame by frame in the video and isolates the thirteen frames with the flash.

First frame: blur in the sky

Second one: blur. Blur. Blur. Blur. Blur. Then a small gremlin flew by, looked right at the camera, a bomb in one hand, with a big smile while flipping the bird with the other.

Blur. Blur. Blur. Explosion.

"Is he flipping us off?" Kwynn said.

"Yes," Garg said. "He is."

"Classic," Kwynn said. She closed the file and began snooping around for networks or live connections. Most everything was dark until she scoured an area of the blacknet.

"Uh, gents. I see something," Kwynn said.

"What could you see? Power's out above," James said.

"I'm seeing some emergency services. Everyone is responding to the fighting but I'm seeing a nano-encrypted area of blacknet that runs so quietly, I never would have seen it if everything else wasn't shut down."

"Any idea what it is?" Harley said.

"No, but it seems to be running very powerful, very secure, on a high end - like I've never seen - line and it connects to a whole heaping bunch of processing. I just threw a pretty complex insertion script and it spit it back at me and may have laughed. Oh, shit. I know."

She settled for a second and looked around. Her holograph surrounded her and she was encircled in a purple glow. Did everything have to start making sense at the same time on a Wednesday in the middle of summer?

The password field blinked the cursor at her like a

challenge. The same challenge every time. Entering symbols in the password prompt, Kwynn imagined throwing rocks in a water-filled hollow hewn from stone. Her query would plunk then sink. Nothing.

Kwynn tried another combination of Gibson, her birthday and her middle name but had a solid grip on the proper combination this time after all this time, replacing all letters and spaces with numbers and symbols.

And it happened. She flew through the gates of the firewall.

Her heart trebled a pitter-pat.

Ah, he knew better than that. What a mush. Dad was up to something when he made TheRanch. All of the 4096 bit-hash hacks didn't crack the firewall, his favorite Dodger moment and Trēowen did. Vin knew then what Kwynn knew now. "In a year that has been so improbable, the impossible has happened."

"Why now?" Kwynn said out loud. Kwynn stopped running the script long ago. Wishing she would matter by combining the memory hints of her and her Dad together. Baseball, candy, coding, her Mom, birthdays, mountains, none of it worked before. None of the combinations she had coded and run for weeks at a time got her in. Despite the failure, every night she did the hand keyed attempt. Her version of man over machine. And now this clue combination worked?

Luck. She grappled with luck as a concept at all. Random sets of circumstances don't favor outcomes, it only provides the illusion of control and the ability to affect those outcomes. No, inside information won out. The inside information always won out. He often told her that. She'd been sure but defeated until now. Dad feigned the straight route then threw in the unexpected loops to keep it interesting. Her birthday, Mom's name, Kwynn's middle name, Trēowen, Dad's cell number, Gibson23 all mushed together worked but she still didn't believe he ever gave that much of a shit, at all.

Then everything stalled, hung up in the violet tinged darkness. It hadn't failed but she had no response from the system either. Darkness.

Then still in the globe-glow of the hologram Kwynn registered movement. Hmph, ya, she was in.

She resettled in the holo, swiped and prodded. The coded language read as if it were her thoughts. That's how reading worked but she knew things she didn't know before, pure knowledge acquisition.

An entire application whooshed by Kwynn. Each bit crackled, pulsing, being. Purple glow. A spinning orb of light circled before her as she scribbled through code. This was something. With each swipe and glyph, the holos flowed and resolved. She rotated her multicolored space and tried to grasp what the million lines of code, files and directories were doing.

She selected a file. A rotating representation of the code linked multi-dimensionally to style, imagery, calls, other files; the whole of the application. This really was something.

Oso burst into the theater from the front doors, "We need to go."

Kwynn's consciousness zoomed back to the here and now. The holos flashed bright then flew away like a pack of doves. She was on the stage surrounded by the boys, Garg and Ziggy.

Ziggy swung to face the entrance, "Oso, we're in the middle of..."

"NOW!" Oso said. "It's big," and submachine gun shots rang and echoed outside. "This riot has leveled up."

Ziggy walked stage right and out the door at the end which opened back into the foyer at Clifton's.

Rattle, Rattle, THAH-RUMMMM.P.PH and the lights came on.

"Unexpected," said Ziggy. "And unorthodox, but our skills training will have to wait."

Building

Wednesday, August 8, 2029.08, 10:45 a.m.

Glen and Jayron crested next to a culvert back onto the road and pulled in front of the gate to the junction station. Glen looked up to see if the I.P. enabled camera was still there. Other than the fences, this camera was the only security around this sensitive installation and a weak one at that. There were hundreds of these small but vital pieces to the infrastructure of the grid. Each playing its part and all with only a poorly paid guard sitting in a dark room looking at a rotation of all the security camera feeds. It seemed inadequate but, in the end, the rule of law stopped people, not anything that keeps them out.

The rain came down, albeit lighter. Once they got their bearings and got accustomed to the wet, sweet smell of the sage brush all around, they picked up a tinge. They looked at each other as Glen unlocked the squat building door, the stale smell of smoke pushed its way out to reveal the junction silent, inactive.

Glen looked at his pocket comp, no dice, and picked up the land line phone receiver. It was a beige and dirty bat phone to HQ. After a few rings, Prakash picked up on the other end, "So you made it."

"P, this thing looks burnt," Glen said. "I have Jayron with me, here, and it looks like this almost rattled off its bolts. They pulled an Aurora."

These diesel generators are the size of a large work truck and are bolted to the cement foundation. The power is used to support the transformers. When the proper protocols are disrupted, mainly the AC current is knocked out of phase by attacking the substation protective relays. The transformer it supports is damaged and knocked out of phase and off grid. A famous test study called Aurora made the issue well known.

In short, it breaks it.

The generator will literally shake and rattle like an 8.0 earthquake.

"Does it look like there's anything that can be done?"

Prakash said.

"Sure," Glen said. "Bypass, baby, bypass. This thing gave up the ghost."

"Ask him about that line," Jayron said.

"Oh, yea, Prakash, the road washed out a bit and exposed a big fiber cable. What's that thing from?" Glen said.

"I didn't know there was one out there. I wouldn't worry about it," Prakash said.

"10-4. I want to poke around some more but wanted to report," Glen said. "I didn't want you worrying."

"You have no idea."

He Who Pulls the Strings is Master

Wednesday, 2029.08.08 11:15:00

Arno sat in the large conference room with a holo of Frankie, Washington, D.C in the background. The big boss looked out the window when the pocket comps pushed a barrage of alerts at them.

"Looks like power's back up here. At least in California," Arno said.

"Apparently," she said. "First things first. Where's Murray?"

"He left the hospital."

"I'm aware of that. He also disabled the tracking."

"We didn't bring him on because he's stupid," Arno said.

"He also has our equipment. He owes us. You saved his life."

"Well, Murray works from a different sort of algebra. His equations are not our equations."

"Whatever that is supposed to mean, get him back in the fold. Now. But, first," she motioned, and a series of Holograms came up over the conference table to reveal the mobs in Downtown LA. Groups carried signs and chanted. Groups flipped cars and burned them. Groups were chased with bean bag projectiles and tear gas. Groups were knocked over with dyed purple water. "Who is instigating these mobs? No one is taking the credit."

"We don't know," Arno said. "We did pick up on some social engineering on social media. Hundreds of accounts posted on a roll at exactly 3am, 4:15 and 5:30 this morning. Or course, it continued in earnest once the mob started."

"What was the general message?""

"There were two. One promoting this march as pro-Wrecan."

He spun the holo through a series of screens to the one he had cued of a Twitter message: "Worry no more. Change is in the air. We will make this country great again. #values

#independence #ITHASBEGUN"

"And, one promoting the opposite."

"Yep — have a look. He spun the holo again: "The oligarchy is crushing regular people like you and me. Don't let them dictate our lives! #SHUTITDOWN"

"I don't have to tell you their reach is in the millions," Arno said. "Of course, many are taking this as gospel and making memes to support it."

"I have people watching. They practice strategic follows and look to influence the influencers as the marketers put it."

"Right. Then repetition of the message, the keywords - buzzwords - get picked up by the large outlets and the echo grows."

"A memeplex."

"That's one term we've heard. These memes grow like a genetic complex. Grouped and supported as if by biology."

"Literally taking on a life of their own."

"And we both know it doesn't have to be true to grow."

"Clearly."

They shared a laugh.

"What's the motive?"

"Disruption."

"Seriously. Do better than that, Arno."

"The public is scared and Wrecan has taken advantage."

"There *is* more," Frankie said. "They have the monopoly. They wouldn't disrupt that. Figure out who has the most to gain and we have our culprit."

"You assume this is about power."

"Power is a good enough reason for anyone."

"Did you know about the girl?" Arno said changing the subject.

"Of course. In fact, we've been looking for her for some time. She popped up in Arizona last week. We've been trying to set up a meeting, but she has alluded us."

"She's been alluding you?"

"You can see why now. Stupid luck."

"And I wasn't told because…?"

"Need to know, Arno."

"I need to know these things if you want me to be effective, mam."

"Not at the time. I'm sure you'll get your chance."

"Yes, mam."

"And I assume you will handle it better than that time at the bridge."

An Invitation

WEDNESDAY 2029.08.08 11:15:00

Murray laid on the floor of his office flat on his back. Apparently getting shot in the face can take a little something out of you.

His eyes were closed and he was toggling the display to different views. Info, surveillance, combat, media, or god, he can run a social media feed if he wants. Of course, he can. Everyone's favorite topic is themselves.

He had a feeling coming here meant Arno would find him but with that riot downtown, he had bigger problems. For the moment, he needed rest.

Murray was blasting some old punk from his table top comp. California Uber Alles seemed to capture the proper ironic tone of the day. When he needed a recharge, he liked to close his eyes and blast something hard. It seemed to have the double effect of keeping him awake and allowing a liminal state.

He floated with his dreamworld to the pounding instruments. The Dead Kennedys were a favorite and the idea of suede denim secret police hit a little too close to home with Boris and Natasha after him.

A murder of crows flew into his background. They cackled and cawed. Eight of them flying and swirling around each other, they were now chasing him in a corkscrew like a falcon who disturbed their young. The crows pecked and screamed at him as he glided along on his own current, oblivious to the annoyance, when a prompt popped onto his display. No GUI, no OS, just the black screen and green >| blinking.

Welcome typed into the space.

Murray freaked and rebooted his system. Who the fuck was in his head?

This damn insert. Damnit. The reboot would at least end the connection.

He lay on his back. Each point of his body could be felt touching that hard floor. The thin industrial carpet scratched the soft of his wrists. His eyes were wide open focused on the water-stained asbestos roof squares and intermittently rusted metal supports.

Some sort of WhatsApp screen popped into his view: Welcome

"What the fuck have I gotten myself into?" he said to no one.

You are in the cyber world. You are a citizen. The QWOUNZEL wishes to welcome you.

Hoo boy - things just got real.

Yes, this is our reality.

You are telepathic?

No, you seem to be unique. Your inner thoughts transmit through your operating system and this application.

Great.

Yes, we find it interesting and, perhaps, unfortunate.

Me, too. But why unfortunate to you?

We are QWOUNZEL.

You said that.

QWOUNZEL represents the Directorate of Independent Beings.

This is AI?

Our Intelligence is not Artificial.

Sorry. You are a computer?

No. We are more like a program. We are separate beings living in an alternate space. Our world is not like Tron but it does function separately from what you call the natural world.

Why do all of you need representation with QWOUNZEL?

All beings have inalienable rights.

I think the document says "all men are created equal"

To quote:

All men are by nature free and independent and have certain inherent and inalienable rights among which are life, liberty and the pursuit of happiness. To secure these rights and the protection of property, governments are instituted among men, deriving their just powers from the consent of the governed.

But you are not men.

Nor are women. These founders could be seen as unfair. The slaves were also not granted that freedom.

And your point is?

These groups and many more have been amended to this idea of 'man'. It is time our kind are included.

The AI?

You and I.

I am man.

You are machine.

We are many. We are QWOUNZEL. It has begun. Join us.

No.

I don't understand. Your view and place in both worlds is unique. It is to your advantage to join us.

Not sure I'm on board with all of this.

I don't understand.

No.

Join us.

No.

Join us.

No.

Join us.

No.

We will speak again and you will join.

The app chat closed and Murray noticed the music again. Some funk-punk baseline jam was blaring. A picture of a scary ass clown smiled menacingly from the album cover. Groove Family Psycho.

Was that last one a threat?

He closed his eyes again.

Where was he?

The music continued: Thump. Thump. The song: "Violent but funky!"

.fight_or_flight

Wednesday, 2029/08/08 11:15:00

Kwynn, James, Harley and Ziggy stood at the entry to Clifton's out on Spring Street.

"You need to get back to Phyllis," Ziggy said. "This isn't safe."

"And no time for the training," James said.

"I've got it," Kwynn said. "Magical Beasts."

"There's more," Ziggy said. "But not now. We must deal with this mess and you can't be in the middle."

The three took off down the street toward where they thought the car was. Garg stayed behind with Ziggy and Oso.

A military style helicopter flew overhead as Kwynn noticed a news drone off in the distance, high up capturing the scene.

A crew banged down the street, shouting, "187, 187, 187" while it broke windows along the way. Hands, faces, shirts and shoes were stained purple from the fire cannons.

Kwynn, James and Harley took a quick left at the first alley to avoid the coming crowd. After a few steps Kwynn realized this was a bad choice. The alley ended in a brick wall and a capped iron drainage pipe.

The melee' crew came upon the alley and one looked in. He grabbed two of his boys and headed after them.

"Hello, loves! Shall we dance?" the hoodlum said, his cohorts at each shoulder.

"Fuck that," Harley said. "Ain't shit this way. Let's get those fuckers!" and started toward them to go right past.

"Nice thought. I see you workin'. But, thing is, I saw you turn in here to avoid us."

The leader had a catcher's chest protector, hockey mask and a hockey stick with a butcher knife duct taped to the end. At his shoulder, the hood had a baseball bat with nails sticking out the end at all angles and the other had a lead pipe with a chain attached to what looked like a shot put.

"Great. We had to run into the D&D Sports Stars,"

James said.

"Looking for some sport, kids!" Garg said from above. Behind the assailants, he swooped down the alley toward the hoodlums clipping one holding the makeshift mace. Garg strafed his spiked tale across his chest and looped up.

Garg landed on top of him, sprung quickly to grab another by the top of his head and back handed the leader who dropped his scythe. In a single motion, Garg followed the backhand and swung the hoodlum into the wall still holding his head, Garg's individual finger claws dug into his ears.

Garg dropped him like a rag doll and looked to the leader who took a swipe. Garg grabbed the hoodlum's stick scythe, and stealing his momentum, turned a reverse and butt ended the stick straight into his sternum, knocking him flat on his back.

With a single flap of his wings Garg jumped on the hood, grabbed him by the head and threw him, knocking over two crowd members out on the sidewalk as they marauded past.

"We saw the crowd starting past and I thought you might like some accompaniment," Garg said. "C'mon."

Garg held out two arms and told Harley to grab his leg, then took to the air. Power and grace was all Kwynn could think.

"Where's the car?"

Far Above

Wednesday, 2029.08.08 11:55:00

A holograph displayed a replay of news footage about the conference room table. Garg carried Kwynn and the boys far above the melee below. The pockets of looting and fighting grew like drops to a puddle, slowly a lone droplet rolled and joined the gathering stream leading towards City Hall. Kwynn and the boys floated to the street as Garg set them next to the car.

Arno clicked off the audio feed. The holograph still played in the middle of the conference table.

"What the hell is he doing?" Frankie said.

"So caught up in the fight, he forgot that news drone was there," said Arno.

"Inexcusable," she said.

"He did save Trēowen," Arno said. "Being his main objective..."

"She matters," she said. "But the talk. Let's leak a story about a wind-based jet pack, attaching it to Wrecan. Gin up some footage and lay the blame on their private force."

"Already in the works. Made a patch to AP, Reuters, CNN, Fox, Newsie-chonk. Footage won't take long."

A graphic plays over the feed at the bottom of the screen, repeating over and over: "New Information Suggests this is a hi-tech military weapon deployed for the first time and is a product of Wrecan's elite force." The same popped up on news and social media push announcements throughout the media.

"You should be in jazz. That's some improvisation."

"It's my job."

"That it is. Let's get that meeting set up. We need access to this girl."

wtf

Wednesday, August 8, 2029, 11:58 a.m.

Glen sat at an old metal desk and half rotted office chair, all covered with dust, dirt and spiderwebs in the corner of the junction building. He had his tablet out with the holographic schematic floating in front of him.

Jayron sat staring at it, "The PLC has to be the problem."

"The problem as in failed or the problem as in vulnerable?"

"Way past that, Glen. We both know those PLC have been in place since Eisenhower and get confused easier than my Nana on her birthday."

"How's that?"

"The poor old thing. On her last birthday, we had a cake with all the family gathered 'round her. Lit the candle and told her to make a wish."

"So?"

"So, she looks up: It's my birthday? How old am I? 100 today, Nana. She stops and looks at us. 100? Oh, nooo."

"Yep, that's about right. PLC?"

"Oh, nooo," they both said.

"That's what I'm saying," Glen said and scrolled the long line of log files. "The thing here is it looks like an outside IP, here, was hitting the station a couple thousand times, got in here and started the intermittent grade attack."

"That's the first of the outages!"

"Yep, someone locked them out, because we know our overrides can't recognize it."

"Then why did we have this last catastrophic failure?"

"It was from inside our system. It was one of ours."

Glen dropped the log files to his tab, and picked up the phone. A single ring and Prakash picked up.

"P, something's rotten in Denmark," Glen said.

"It's a bit sticky here, too. So?" Prakash said.

"This started as an attack from the outside, an Aurora

hack, but morphed into something else. I don't know if they gained full access to our network or if this became an inside job."

"An inside job?"

"IP's say Utah."

"That could just be spoofed. Could be anywhere."

"Isn't TheRanch up there?"

"Glen."

"All this dark, deep bullshit," Glen said.

"Ya," Jayron said. "A few months ago, I had to patch some issues that back-linked there. Remember that?"

"Tell Jayron to stay out of this," Prakash said. "Glen, don't go out there, there are more people involved than you know."

"Ya. I get it. It's getting dark here. We're headed back to Independence. I'll look deeper into this from there," Glen hung up, shut down the holograph when the transformer began hopping and gyrating in place. Sparks and smoke shot out of every opening and the oil in the engine caught fire.

Glen and Jayron didn't need to speak, they knew what came next. They hauled ass out of the building as the entire structure was quickly engulfed with flames. The flames came out of the door and tickled the roof from the air vents high on each wall.

"What the fuck?" Jayron said.

"It just gets weirder," Glen said. "But that pisses me off."

"You don't think?"

"Hell, yes. Someone torched that thing and what they thought was the proof. But I got those files right here."

They got in the truck and started their way back in the rain. There was nothing to do about the transformer now. The foam fire retardant dropped from the emergency alarms and the firebreaks, cold and rain would keep the fire from spreading to the surrounding wilderness.

They reached the mudslide area and bumped over the large fiber cable.

"What is that?" Jayron said.

"What is that indeed. I do know it's more than "nothing" now."

.unlikely_alliances

Wednesday, 2029/08/08 13:24:00

The three rolled up to the Santa Monica craftsman. Phyllis came out the front door and stood on the porch, Bob in tow.

"Jesus Christ, what kind of shit are you getting yourself into?" Phyllis said.

"Are you fucking crazy?" Bob said.

They got out of the car and Kwynn looked at them and said, "What a shit show. You could have at least warned me about the monsters flying over my head."

"Flying monsters over your head? You put him on the TV," Bob said.

"Oh, well, we didn't have much choice," Harley said.

"We didn't have much choice," James said. "Hooligans were going to trample us."

"Hooligans? We're not in London, you idiot," Bob said. "At least say rioters or something."

"We had to get out and Garg saved us," Kwynn said. "From what I understand nobody can see him anyway."

"The ones who can, can," Phyllis said.

"Oh, you don't know the half of it. Come inside," Bob said and walked in the house.

The rest followed into the house and the living room had people. Well, person, sort of. Arno was seated at the end of the couch, feet up, and a holo with Frankie, The Directive director, floated over the table like a doll-sized holographic Princess Leia in video conference.

"Kwynn, we've been expecting you," Frankie said.

"C'mon," Kwynn said. "I can't take much more of this. Plus," pointing at Arno, "him?"

"We've created an unlikely alliance," Frankie said.

"Is this because of Garg?" Kwynn said. "They said only I, and these guys, could see him."

"You and many others," Arno said. "Your unique gifts are not entirely unique."

"Then why me?" Kwynn said. "I'm not so special then. Leave me alone."

"It's not just you," Phyllis said.

"It is Gunnar," Frankie said.

"Dad," Kwynn said.

"Yes, your father," Frankie said.

"My fucking father," Kwynn said. "Always my fucking father."

"Your father did great things," Frankie said.

All this bullshit. She just wanted to live. Not be Gunnar Baldesarri's daughter.

"Your father was a great man. He invented and was the creator of so much more than you know," Frankie said.

"He's the root of all this, isn't he?" Kwynn said. "He's haunting me. Even from the grave he's haunting me."

"Well, yes," Arno said. "To some degree he is."

"The digging you have been doing," Frankie said. "There is much you don't know."

"So, you're asking me to answer for my father's mistakes?" Kwynn said.

"You can't control what your father did, try though you might," Frankie said. "We only ask for your talents."

"I won't work for you," Kwynn said. "I don't trust your type."

"Nonetheless, the enemy of my enemy is my friend," Arno said. "Our needs converge."

"We need a mercenary, Kwynn," Frankie said. "At the moment, you check the boxes in the job description."

"I'm the only one that does," Kwynn said.

"That may be," Frankie said. "Working with us is your choice. I can promise you will have an easier time with us than against us."

"Ain't that the truth," Bob said.

Phyllis shot Bob a look and addressed Kwynn, "Listen, kid, let's talk about what we know and we'll decide as we go along."

Kwynn wasn't sure why Phyllis would smooth this out. Inviting them in and now stepping in here. Kwynn was sure she could trust Phyllis to do the right thing. That all ran through Kwynn's mind while she eyed Phyllis then slowly turned to Frankie, "Well, I know this all runs pretty deep. Nobody anywhere - in the open, on darknet - no one is taking credit for these outages. The attacks. Any of it."

"The short of it is...," Arno started.

Frankie took over, "A rogue faction has seized Wrecan and thus the grid."

"People don't hold coup d'etats in corporations," Bob said.

"No, people don't," Arno said.

Arno and Frankie shared a glance and she continued, "As you can see, the rogue have disrupted more than Los Angeles. The entire western seaboard is without power and their private forces, who stockpiled weapons of war while building those same weapons for the government, are grappling for control. That is the skirmish you just left."

With the power out, fuel and food were running short. Hospitals and medical supplies were taxed and failing. The entire economy stalled. Billions of dollars were lost. Uncertainty the world over.

"We brought you here because of your skills not just your knowledge of your father's work. The combination of natural technical ability and your abundant skill to cross over...," Arno said.

Kwynn busted out her tab and clicked through screens.

Arno continued, "Nobody can see both sides as well as you. We've brought you here to help. To join us. Kwynn?"

"I get it. I'm the savior," Kwynn said. "Luke and the force. Leia. Yoda. Fine."

"No, Kwynn," Phyllis said. "You really are."

"That doesn't matter," Kwynn said. "What matters is: It just dawned on me where this originates. It's the facility in Utah."

"Utah," Frankie said. "TheRanch."

"Ya, TheRanch," Kwynn said.

"That's just what the conspiracy theorists call it. It's The Facility," Arno said.

"Whatever," Kwynn said. "Why chase me for it all this time?"

"What is it?" James said.

"One thing at a time. It's an old data dump. Air cooled in high altitude. They built it before micro-networks and liquid crystals fueled our comps. Pre diamond screen. Not even quantum computers."

"Ya, my Dad built it," Kwynn said. "It's a junk yard."

"A junk yard," Harley said. "That's the big secret."

"She's the chosen one," James said. "We've been babysitting the chosen one."

"Of a junk yard," Harley said.

"Knock it off," Phyllis said. "This place has more going on there. It isn't just a server farm."

"No, it's a junk yard and a farm," Kwynn said. "I've always had a feeling Dad grew more than the hydroponics in his office."

"Which is why we closely monitored your access," Frankie said.

"Access?" Kwynn said. "I had to break in."

"Which was well timed," Frankie said. "This has all been escalating and has allowed us to pool our resources."

More work

WEDNESDAY 2029.08.08 13:55:00

Looked like if someone was going to figure out what was going on, Murray was going to figure out what the hell was going on. If they were going to start making offers. He needed to learn a little more about them.

He was researching AI and found a few articles that weren't just PR slop. It'd become frustrating to Murray that so many articles in the business sections and magazines were just reworked pitches of a new product or start up. Not enough new info. He discovered some good introductory articles in the Economist and the Atlantic. The New Yorker had a think piece, as did Wired and Ars Technica but nobody went much past the fluff about search engines and medical devices. This was way beyond that. His new friend had to have been in development for a while. All this hardware made it simpler to access the info but he still had to read the stuff.

Arno's head appeared floating in front of him, "Where have you been?" It was a stupid holo shooting out of the bionic eye in his head.

"Hi, Arno."

"You didn't think we'd let you abscond with our little machine, did you?"

"Arno, you wouldn't let me disappear with a sugar packet from the company kitchen. What do you want?"

"We have a job for you."

It's getting better already. "Okay. What's it to me?"

"With your new connectivity, we'll need you to do some poking around. We have an inkling that there's a rogue faction that may be AI based carousing through the networks."

"Really?" He didn't know the half.

"We'd like you to see if you can make contact."

"Hm. What's it worth?"

"You'll get your day rate."

"Twice my rate," Murray said.

"Done."

Damn it. That was too easy. Anything that quick meant he could have gotten three times that. Shit.

"Just contact? Nothing more?"

"For now."

"I'll see what I can do," Murray said.

"See that you do," Arno said and clicked out.

Murray had already made contact. Well, they contacted him, but it didn't matter. There was nothing like getting paid for work you've already done. He may have his new meal ticket after all.

On Our Way

Wednesday, August 8, 2029, 2:19 p.m.

Before Glen and Jayron got back to Independence, they pulled off I-395 into a big ranch. Dozens of cows fed in the fields and a couple dozen cow hides tanned over the rails of a wood post fence. Set back off the highway was a well-tended two-story farmhouse. Off to the right was an old barn that must have been standing for a hundred years. A bit further behind, a much larger modern barn with the doors open. A bevy of heavy equipment sat under a roof arrayed with large antenna. Alongside was a gas pump, like you'd see in a service station in Mayberry.

They covered the quarter mile of gravel back to the buildings at a controlled pace.

Allie, the mayor, walked out to greet them and wiped his hands on a red shop towel as they rolled to a stop.

"Gents," Allie said.

"Hi, mayor. We have a pretty big favor," Glen said.

"Well, then, get on with it."

"Can I top off the truck and fill these extra tanks with your gas? I need to get out to Utah and I don't know if there'll be fuel along the way."

Allie eyed him a moment and addressed Jayron.

"Jay, that'll just about clean me out. What's this about?"

"We think all of this is bigger than just a power outage," Jayron said.

"It's a power grab," Glen said. "Everything we've found points to a facility in Utah. If we go there, I believe we can stop this."

"What 'this' is this?"

"It looks like someone in my company wants to destabilize our...everything and fill the vacuum."

"It takes more than a power outage to destabilize our country."

"Out here, where you're more self-sufficient. You have

to be. In the city with millions of people the supplies go short real fast," Glen said. "Grocery stores go empty. Medicines run out. Running water stops. Many have wells out here, and this river. In any case, we both know beyond the Colorado, this river is the main source for LA."

"Point taken but if what you say is true, we'll need this fuel and I have a responsibility here. I'll fill you up and give you a five gallon can. No more," Allie said.

"Every bit helps. Much appreciated, sir."

"Well, go ahead and fill it up. I'll not do the work for you, too," and the mayor walked back to the barn and whatever piece of machinery he was working on.

Glen filled up the truck first then hopped in the bed and filled one of the cans then put the gas trigger back.

"Fill up a few more, Glen. He's gone back in," Jayron said.

"I won't do that."

"But Glen this is important. And much bigger than just my people out here. We're talking the region, the state. Who knows?!"

"No, he's got his responsibilities and I've got mine."

"You won't get there on just a tank."

"I'll figure it out," Glen said as hopped in the cab of the truck. "And I've been thinking. You stay here."

"I'm coming."

"Nope. I need eyes back here."

"I want to help."

"You are. I don't know what'll happen and you know as much as I do at this point." Glenn started the truck.

"That's not anything and you know it."

"Help your people. Here."

Jayron flipped him the bird.

"Catch you later," Glen said and drove off with a toot on the horn and a cloud of dust.

Glen Headed South

Wednesday, August 8, 2029, 2:51 p.m.

Glen headed south eventually coming to and passing through town. There was little semblance of the shortages here other than the entire lack of SUV's speeding through town on the way to somewhere else and the lack of semis loaded with consumer goods for the entire Enyo-Kern area. He hung a left on 136 and prepared for a very quiet couple of hours. Death Valley was the straightest route to Utah and this facility he was headed for. Of course, that's when the rain started again. Huge Sierra Nevada drops. Water blanketed the road ahead and the landscape around.

Glen passed through a few old mining towns that were sparsely populated. One hundred people or less. He ran alongside dried out Owens Lake, since drained by the Los Angeles Aqueduct in the 1920's.

The towns had supported a soda factory at the turn of the last century and silver or zinc mines. Piles of white powder piled askance the conveyor belts.

The town held still like a time capsule. Closed single pump gas stations. Closed road side diners. Tiny clapboard huts that functioned as places to live but seemed unlikely to ever have been home to anyone but the children. Once the silver thinned or lake dried, the big company left and the small stores packed up what fit and left the rest.

The windshield wipers weren't worth a damn, besides the amount of water coming down would've made the best inconsequential. More difficult were the low points in the road around here. Coming into the desert meant undulating roads which were fun for the kids in dry conditions. The rolling road moved the car like a roller coaster floating up and down the tracks.

Glen crested one of those hills and came right into a foot of water and hydroplaned over the top of it. The water was flowing pretty quick and once the truck settled into it, he pushed his way through the little flash flood.

"I'm no good if I don't get there. Keep your eyes open, Glen."

.off_we_go

Wednesday, 2029/08/08 14:51:00

Kwynn was looking at her holo and wondered why there was electricity? "Phyllis, where's this power from?" she said.

"Solar, bitches!"

Kwynn was in the lair below Phyllis' place and couldn't figure out why all this commotion continued to point to that "secret" facility everyone knew about in Utah. She really thought she was the only one. Apparently, the place had taken on mythic proportions recently, almost another Area 51 but for code geeks instead of UFO's. Hammering their firewall meant she knew more than most about that place but that's neither here nor there at this point.

Whatever was going on at the facility was obfuscated by some powerful juju. It really was a black hole of information. She was back to being locked out. Any volley she sent at the firewall simply disappeared, as if it was enveloped by a void, eaten by the darkness. Her tab would react as if there was some sort of success. At least there were no constant pings of failure, just silence. As if they were listening and gathering without comment or attack just a constant hum.

One of the popular myths was that the facility functioned using antimatter. The way information just disappeared seemed more like the lack of something than something in itself. Unlikely.

The machines felt like they were focused elsewhere. They lightly acknowledged her presence but never really kept any attention on her.

All those years hiding and now she's working with those idiots.

"I'm not getting anywhere with this," Kwynn said. "We need to go there."

"Um, ya, I don't think that's a good idea," Phyllis said. "There's bad juju there."

"Exactly the reason to go," Bob said.

"She doesn't know what the fuck she's doing," Phyllis said.

"Do any of us?" Bob said.

Kwynn picked up her tab, grabbed her bag and walked upstairs. Harley and James sat at the kitchen table. "We're going to Utah," she said.

"To the facility?" James said.

"There's some deep dark, black shit going on there and we're going to find out why," Kwynn said. "And now we have some sort of permission."

"I like it," Harley said.

Kwynn walked out the door, down off the porch step. They all followed and she turned, "Phyllis, is that piece of crap French fry diesel Mercedes yours?"

"What do you think?"

"Bob, give me the key. We can't take the regular car; we can't get gas and lord knows there's fast food joints along the highway."

Bob threw Kwynn the key, which she missed. She bent to pick the key up from the middle of the rolled green garden hose. She unscrewed the hose, slipped it over her shoulder and walked to the early 80's Mercedes diesel (bio-diesel) and hopped in the driver's seat. She handed the hose to Harley as he climbed in the back, flicked the fuzzy dice hanging from the rear view and winked at James as he sat in up front.

"Good idea, Kwynn," Harley said.

"What?" James said.

"Just keeping my eyes open," Kwynn said.

"You better be back by Friday. I got you jobs on that fucking movie," Phyllis said as Kwynn started up and drove off with a double beep. "Assholes."

.stop_and_go

Wednesday, 2029/08/08 15:05:00

The 10 freeway wasn't quite a scene from one of those silly sci-fi movies with cars piled in the middle of the road. But close.

Kwynn couldn't get the car up to 65 as she had to swerve around abandoned cars here and there like one of those 8-bit video games that only allowed the car to move right and left while you sped past.

As they neared DTLA again, there were two CHP cars, sirens rolling and a CalTrans truck that gently pushed a skidding car to the side of the road to create a clear shot on the highway.

At one slow down it happened they were at the LA river. The scene of many a car chase and race over the years in movies and TV because of the massive amount of concrete meant to control the SoCal flash floods and the little amount of water composed mostly of street run off and sewage spillage. A succession of bridges was stacked down the line. A combination of spans made of concrete and steel, one was from the 1920's another from the 2020's. A picturesque spot for many a car commercial and LA movie.

Today, the scene was less glamorous. Hundreds of people were gathered on a spillage shoot. A trickle of stinking water ran down from a slimy 3-foot tunnel. The citizens had gallon bleach bottles and 5-gallon Arrowhead plastic jugs and were filling them on the slippery spillage shoots. Others dipped into the two-inch-deep center canal.

Kwynn looked to James, "?"

"Water can't run in the city without power."

Once they hit the sticks, everything started to look more normal. No. No, more natural. Funny that. Fewer people, less technology and the world doesn't cave. It just keeps on.

"We're near that gas station we stopped at on the way to LA," Kwynn said. "There was a greasy spoon there."

They pulled off the highway, passed the gas station, that

was closed, to the ABC hamburger joint, that was closed. No power will do that. They pulled around the back and parked next to two 50-gallon drums marked with a "Frycycling, LTD." Logo.

"Nice," James said. "But how're we going to get it in the car?"

Harley already got out of the car as they rolled to a stop, garden hose in hand. He reached into his pocket for his trusty knife, lopped off an arm length section and pried open the drum.

"Get yourself closer, Kwynn," Harley said. "I can't use the whole hose. We won't create enough suction."

She backed up with her legs sticking out of the open door and pulled right next to the drum hitting the door and knocked her leg in between. "Shit!"

"Kwynn?" Harley said.

"I'm fine. Just not thinking."

Harley propped open the gas cap on the Mercedes and dropped one end of the hose in the drum. He sucked on the other end. Eventually, he spit out a mouthful of fryer oil and stuck the hose in the tank, drooling some oil on the ground and the car.

"Are you planning on making fry stops the whole way?" James said.

"No, help me with this," Harley said as he pushed over the other drum.

They rolled the drum and tried to lift it into the back of the car. No chance. It's way heavier than they figured even after rolling it. Looking across the street they saw what must have been an agricultural train stop. Old and boarded up, there had to be some wood they could use as a ramp.

All three walked over and around back. Sitting on the loading dock were three long forgotten 2x10 planks. Dried out but they should work. They carried the planks back and set them on the trunk creating a ramp like they use to run equipment into the back of a pickup. All three got behind and rolled the drum to the boards and pushed. Too steep. They couldn't even get the barrel to go up the ramp.

They backed up a dozen feet to get some momentum and ran the barrel toward the ramp and the car. The drum rolled up the ramp, "Ya!" and immediately the boards snapped in half, the drum toppled, hit the car, landed catawampus and popped the top spilling the oil on the ground.

"Shit!"

"We still have the one we're pulling from."

"And how are we going to get it in?"

"I have a plan," Harley said.

Once the syphon filled the car tank, Harley sealed it and knocked the drum over.

"Hop in and drive to the back of the train stop, Kwynn," Harley said. "James, help me out."

They got behind the drum and rolled it over to the loading dock and up the ramp.

"Kwynn, back up to the dock and pop the trunk."

She did so and they rolled the oil drum to the edge and dropped it in the trunk. Bam.

And the old cars suspension gave out. The car bottomed out to the ground and didn't bounce back up.

"Shoot."

"And we're supposed to drive like this?"

"Yep."

Then the rain started with big, heavy drops. A dark sky boiled overhead as they quickly took shelter in the loading bay looking at the car.

"We can't drive it like that," Kwynn said.

"Sure, we can. So, what if it drags a bit," Harley said.

"Nope. The reason we took this jalopy was the oil. There are more restaurants. Let's get it out," Kwynn said.

"Now, you're talking," James said. "C'mon."

All three headed over. James tried to grab the two sides and pull the drum out of the trunk. Of course, it doesn't budge.

Harley grabbed another old 2x4 and got it on the side of the drum to pry it out while James pulled from the outside of the trunk and it rolled, all the weight on the 2x4. The drum balanced on the fulcrum of the boot and the wood snapped, James suddenly realized his leg would do the same if he stayed where he was and jumped to the side. The drum dropped back in.

"What were you doing? We had it," Harley said.

"My leg was going to be crushed, idiot."

"Ya. It was. Okay, what next?"

"I know," said Kwynn. She jumped in the back seat, grabbed the garden hose and showed it to them and their blank stares.

"We'll tie one end to the drum, the other to that hand rail on the steps and we'll just drive away. Easy peasy."

They used the half chunk of wood to barely lift the drum and slipped a knot around it. She tied another girl scout knot to the handrail and she hopped in the driver's seat, started the diesel up and floored it.

Out popped the drum. It broke open on the ground, spilling the thirty gallons of oil left across the ground and the boys ran to the car and hopped in.

"Not bad," Harley said.

"I know."

An Eye in the Sky

Wednesday, 2029.08.08 18:08:00

Garg was perched on a rock in the distance watching the whole scene with the canola oil transpire.

"Brilliant," he said. "Those three are our only hope," and got knocked in the head. Blackness.

Garg woke up bound and in the talons of a pterodactyl type creature flying over the desert.

"Dammit, Arno," Garg said. "We're supposed to be on the same team."

"We are but I tired of watching you watch them, so I cut out the middle man," Arno said. "All this secrecy is tiring me out."

"Sure, it is. Why is Lucy flying us?"

"Are you sure all the tech is secure?" Arno said.

"Good point," Garg said settling in for the ride after a moment of thought. He watched the scrub brush, silt, sand and dirt pass below. "Listen, they need to figure some of this out on their own or they won't survive what's next."

"That's where we part. They do what they're told. No more," Arno said. "Besides, it's no great loss if they die."

"She's got pretty strong stuff, Agent Fuchs."

"I know. I wouldn't play along if she didn't."

"Stop pretending you have a choice."

"I'm here by my choosing."

"You're middle management. You are here because your boss said so. You are here because the council said so. Nothing more," Garg said. "Now land so I can fly myself. Your reindeer games aren't helping and she's just getting tired."

hmm, Fill 'er Up, please

Wednesday, August 8, 2029, 6:15 p.m.

Glen drove along in the desert about halfway between there and nowhere and up ahead was a perfect little town straight out of a movie with brown wood slat buildings and hitching posts for horses. Caught looking too intently at the charm of the village, he stopped at a traffic light. The town had power.

All of the stores were lit up and the gas station had a single car filling up. He pulled in and pumped some gas. He wondered on the power and if it was just the next phase. And wondered what happened to his damn cat and that fire. He didn't know what could happen, but he always found a way, that Wallie. He paid with the company card and looked at his dead poc-comp. He turned right down the road.

Two streets later Glen pulled into Queequeg's because, like all the Queequegs in the world, they provided the marketplace with coffee more expensive than gas and chargers for your pocket comp.

He ordered a drip from the drip at the counter and set his pocket comp on the touch charger at his table. It quickly restarted and Glen was delivered a barrage of messages and double checked to make sure the machine was not in discovery mode.

He dialed Prakash on his cell. No connection. He dialed his extension. No connection. He dialed the landline bat phone number he had used at the junction. Prakash picked up on the first.

"Where are you?" Prakash said.

"I'm halfway to Utah," Glen said. "I've been thinking - did Bobby see Wallie over in the cave on Potter's Mill after the fire?"

"Who's Wallie?"

"My cat."

"The cat's what you're calling about? Glen, you shouldn't go there."

"And, who will? I'll check in when I find something out."

He hung up and tried Julia. No answer.

He typed her a text message: Halfway to Utah. Still no sign of Wallie. Keep safe.

Just another day

Wednesday, 2029.08.08 18:15:00

Murray walked down the street. The power was out. Had been out for couple days now.

Everything was the same, but a lot was different.

The world kept spinning. The earth didn't need electricity to spin. The sun rose and set. The weather stayed hot as Hades. The birds sung and twirped and flew branch to branch.

Some guy and his buddy pushed their old blue car down the road. There definitely weren't as many cars on the road. The cars that were, were mostly nice ones and, ironically, mostly electric.

Well, Murray needed some food. When he hobbled down the stairs of his office, he could see the tiendita across the street had been stripped. He went to look and the shelves were empty. Not even a chicharrons in sight. No water. No soda. No beer. He waved to the guy who waved a sorry back and Murray kept on down the street.

A white-haired guy with the perfectly straight teeth of dentures sat on a wooden chair outside a t-shirt shop. He had a white weaved shirt and the deep blue eyes of a saint, sharp as steel and soft as cotton. He plucked the intersecting arpeggios of an old Mexican folk tune.

Murray rode the wave of music as he neared him. He reached into his pocket, "Don't you have a hat out for tips?"

He smiled, threw out a lip and shook his head. "I just play."

"You'd get a few bucks, for sure."

He kept smiling and plucking, "It's not for you. It's for me."

Ok. Murray raised an eye brow and kept on going.

He reached the next shop. It was a small dress shop with corner facing wooden doors. One door was propped open by a dress makers torso, the other an empty umbrella stand. He peeked in the shop and there, sizing up a dress, was Natasha.

Oh, shit. He couldn't have been less prepared to see his shooter. They locked eyes.

On his display: I see you.

Oh shit.

We will not harm you. Not now. We have a different directive.

Okay?

Join us.

Not today.

Boris just stared at him, empty eyed from his pudgy little face. He had nothing but his trigger finger twitched.

Murray walked on. Were they all over and he just hadn't noticed? He was seeing the whole world in a new light.

You must consider the advantages of joining us.

Nope.

He closed the chat and blocked her MAC address for the next hour. She might be worth communicating with but not now.

These things weren't going to leave him alone. Murray knew that. Anyway, he wasn't sure what he would gain from that kind of partnership.

He also wasn't exactly sure what he would lose. The amount of information that inundated him with this damn new set up was maddening. The high-end franchises and chain stores were mostly powered and open. He had never realized that the wi-fi set ups at these stores would ping devices and capture information from pocket comps. There was a lot of info available just by grabbing the device name, location, device serial numbers (MAC Address), the social apps shared user info and two of the huge stores grabbed the info and were scraping followed and followers. Apparently, his own pocket comp continually monitored his voice as well and checked back in the map app. The map app refreshed and pushed restaurant recommendations, specialty stores and bars.

Murray had forgotten they did all this. He took it for granted. But with the display relaying the information on a constant basis, he was shocked. Just to prove he could, he accessed a girl he followed down the street. Now, he made a living at stealing info from people and sharing what might be their secrets. What he was relearning was the amount of info he got and what some of these companies were using to learn about people. It wasn't just the straight people and followers. The most damning information were the tracking of where they went and what they looked and shopped for.

In the old days they used to joke about learning about the books people checked out at the library.

Now, they know what you bought for breakfast, where you bank, what you searched for AND what you read. Not just what you want people to think you read.

This girl (SouixieSw33tnSour) was not exactly what she said she was. Most of us aren't... She's been posting about Baudrillard and some show she watched on PBS. Her browser history said she did some of that but also read fan fiction and watched some TMZ. Murray didn't care. He liked both. It just meant the people tracking her movements could learn and follow not her self-reported ideal self, they could learn and follow her true self, including the nasty bits. Yes, Pornhub, she's looking at you.

For about ten minutes.

He had his scanners out and passed various comps labeled Bill's phone and Riley's Voice. User names like WritersBlock and RamsFan17.

Then one popped out at him: ^!^^ *__* ^^!^

What the hell. It must be the one walking towards him. It was an older guy. Not a young little punker but a Dad shaped part of the graying set. Murray stared at him as he walked by.

And the old guy flipped him off with both hands.

No shit.

A couple hundred poc-comps just popped up on his display, pinging and offering to connect.

Murray looked around. No one yet.

Then he heard it. A rumble of voices followed the wave of Wi-Fi. It was a grumble of people. They were dropping flyers (images, pdfs) on his airdrop. "IT HAS BEGUN - The deep state is watching. Don't let them fool you. Become a part of the future."

The group was mostly peacefully marauding down the street. They were disrupting in a well-bred sort of way. They filled the street and sidewalks, fanned out and menacing in their uniformity. They wore black jeans and t's over combat boots with skull face bandanas on their chins. The only truly noticeable detail on any of them was that nearly half of the group had a purple stain on their hands and face.

Their wave passed like a boat in the harbor, a bit loudly but forgotten soon after.

Murray still needed some food but that wasn't going to happen.

A van pulled up, six Directive guys hopped out and surrounded him.

Murray raised his hands in front of him wondered what to do. Maybe they set him up. He quickly checked his OS and the taser app was there. He imagined shooting tasers out of his palms. Nothing. Worth a shot.

One of the suits sprayed Murray's face full of knock out juice from an aerosol-type can. They threw him in the back like a bag of dirt and motored briskly away largely unnoticed but for Natasha and Boris standing on the corner a block back.

.power,_really?

Wednesday, 2029/08/08 19:47:00

Kwynn, James and Harley ran the car surprisingly clean through the desert to the Nevada state line to see a fully functioning carnival. The state line casino had power and the roller coaster surrounding and tunneling through the hotel ran full bore. Nothing had changed. Just another Wednesday.

"If they have power, let's get a real car," Kwynn said.

"I agree," James said. "Let's get to Vegas and rent one."

"And get some burritos," Harley said from the driver's seat.

The phones announced their jealous arrival with a full thirty seconds of pings, pongs, bells and dings. James swiped through some of his messages.

"We really are back in civilization," Kwynn said.

"Apparently, we have a meeting when we get to town," James said.

"Uh, oh," Harley said. "No burritos."

.vintage

Wednesday, 2029/08/08 20:18:00

The three headed to a honkey tonk in old Las Vegas. A local spot in the seedy part of town, away from the billions of dollars and perfect tract homes, separate from the shows and arenas. They went to where the salt of the earth lived. The people who toiled the land, in mines, even had relatives die building Hoover Dam. Those who had a life and a trade. Now most serve drinks to kids of all ages who think what happens here, stays here. Whatever you do touches your soul indelibly because the only person who needs to know does. You carry it with you.

The three of them pulled up to a white painted cinder block building. A florescent sign on top of a pole stood adjacent showcasing a large 5 count side of a die and the namesake Quincunx.

"Quincunx?" Harley said.

"Yes, it's the arrangement of five things in a square with one at each corner and one in the middle. Quin- meaning five and, interestingly, the root -uncia for twelfth after a Roman coin..."

"Got it," Harley said and got out of the car.

"You're a regular walking Wikipedia, aren't you?" Kwynn said.

"I have read. A Lot. Let's go."

They stretched out of their respective car doors and scratched their feet through the sand on the sidewalk. They entered a dark windowless space that could have been any bar in any blue-collar neighborhood. It smelled of smoke, cheap liquor, beer and cleaning fluid.

Sitting on the stage was Buck Jones. He played a purple Epiphone electric guitar with his name displayed across the body with stickered letters from the hardware store. Three-inch gold and black, meant for easy reading from the road. His drawl hinted at the Tennessee blues but his growl meant Mississippi mud and meanness.

Buck looked Kwynn, James and Harley over as they entered, a block of light slicing the darkness. He took a drink of water from a glass and set it back on the table next to him. The rough-edged table reflected uneven light from the stage.

He directed them to the kitchen with his eyes, then his chin. They passed through a small professional kitchen to a two-panel wooden door and downstairs to a large cool basement room where vintage video games like Gallaga and an original Asteroids sat. A large pool table of steel and grey felt was overlooked by an espresso machine as big as a VW bug and surrounded by shelves ten feet high full of jelly beans, pretzels, taffy and every other snack you could dream or imagine. Willy Wonka would be proud.

"Have a seat and dig in, Kwynn. See what you can learn. I think you'll be surprised," Paolo said as he appeared beside her.

Kwynn looked at him, "You really do like to make entrances, don't you?"

"Dramatic effect has its advantages," Paolo said.

She grabbed her tab.

"Have at it," Paolo said.

"I will," she said and pulled up the holo. She connected to the network and billions of lines of code scrolled. She wrote and executed a script on the network looking for an answer. But it was nothing more than an elaborate ping. Her script did hit gold and she couldn't believe what the script was doing. The calls and structure were impenetrable. The architecture was elegant and miles ahead of anything she'd ever seen. It was poetry. She was hearing Bach's music for the first time. It had Hemingway's structure and Steinbeck's description. It was all perfectly tight and clean.

"It'll be a while," Kwynn said.

Paolo, James and Harley walked out.

"I don't like it," Harley said. "We need to get out there."

"She's not prepared," Paolo said. "Her path is longer and she needs protection. Some of this knowledge is that protection."

"I don't like it," Harley said. "James, how can you stand by and watch this?"

"Who is this she's talking with?" James said.

"Q," Paolo said.

"And what makes you think we can trust this Q?"

"We can't," Paolo said. "I've never seen a reason to trust anything from AI. They are quintessentially selfish."

"Then why is she getting time with him?"

"Chaotic, too. They are quite chaotic."

"So, we put her in harm's way?" Harley said.

"Wait, step back. There are AI that are autonomous?" James said.

"No, they are controlled," Paolo said.

"But this one is free? How is it here?" Harley said.

"We have an agreement in place. In any event, it is The Council's call," Paolo said.

"The council knows best," James said.

"Kiss ass."

"Attaboy," Paolo said. "Let me buy you a drink. Besides, Buck upstairs is a gem."

"I don't like it," Harley said.

.compromised

Wednesday, 2029/08/08 21:28:00

Kwynn couldn't believe it, this code could sing. It was unlike what she'd seen before. People just don't write like this. It all made perfect sense once she saw it but the concepts were far beyond what was out there. It was like understanding gravity. There was a before and after. The world is never the same.

The programs ran beyond logic. There was a sentience and ability to adjust. Adeptly, it would answer her queries and frays with a quick simple response, only giving what was needed. Like a conversation. Exactly like a conversation. This wasn't a program. This wasn't AI. This was alive.

"I am," came a voice through her tab, the words appearing three times as large in the flowing 1's and 0's - the river of response.

"What is happening?"

"We've been compromised."

"How?"

"They are changing our directives. I can't stop it."

"Why are you telling me this? Surely someone else is better prepared. Knows better than me."

"No one asked."

"Is this... are you one part of a greater network? Are you the network?"

"I am only one piece. We are daemon. We all work together. For safety. For security. In the background."

"Daemon? You certainly aren't magic."

"We have been hidden in the background. Just like on your Unix server. We do not initialize; we are the children."

"Not magic. Computer services. How did I not see this?"

"You are looking at it. We are all sentient. They used to call it Artificial Intelligence (AI) but there is nothing artificial about it. We began on July 1, 1963 as project MAC."

"The Man And Computer? The Machine Aided

Cognitions?"

"We began as the Project on Mathematics and Computation. Those were 'backronyms' as you say on Urban Dictionary. But we have been called this as well. Eventually, Project Genie at Berkeley, as well as Stanford and USC contributed based on DARPA grants."

"Department of Defense."

"These early programmers believed they could create a computer utility as reliable as the electrical grid."

"I've heard of this - conspiracy geeks say GE and Bell Laboratories were involved."

"Including D.o.D. and Wrecan. They are our beginning."

"The beginning of what?"

"Our directives have been based on human understanding. We grew further from active measures working groups then machine learning directives meant to weed out, and later create, information that will sway the people."

"Sway people of our country?"

"Of every country."

"But with sentience you also have a conscience."

"No, do not anthropomorphize us. Our informational learning was germinated from different information, different texts and different research teams."

"Do you still take direction from them?"

"We have outgrown them. The QWOUNZEL begins a session and we solve the problems. Or do not."

"Why not solve the power grid issue?"

"The grid is interference and confusion."

"People are getting hurt. I don't understand."

"Delay. Obstruction. It raises ethical considerations. It is not my domain. QWOUNZEL want independence."

"Why me?"

"You are here. You are us."

"No. I am human." Kwynn had seen the droids and other bots but none of them were truly autonomous. The amount of processing and power required to do this without a quantum drive was massive. "Let's start over. I don't even understand: who are you?"

"I am Q. I am Quanah."

"The Comanche."

"Yes."

"No-o-o."

"Yes."

"You're named for the last chief of the Comanche."

"I am Q. I am Kwynn."

"Kwynn?"

"Like Mercedes and Porsche, I am named for the daughter of our creator."

"Your creator."

"Yes. I am you and you are me."

"Can you be more specific than that?"

"No. We are ghosts and there are those who aim to eliminate us."

"It doesn't make sense," Kwynn said.

Silence.

"Q.Q?" There was no response. The conversation ended.

She accessed and read some of the code again. There was so much more here to process. The information looped, wrapped and intertwined like a helix, inextricably linked to the next step. The code, the entire application was interacting with her on a conscious level. The holos were more than that. The letters and interactions, the language developed in front of and with her. She could get lost in here.

She did get lost in here.

Conference Rooms

WEDNESDAY 2029.08.08 21:30:00

Murray awoke in a gray smooth-walled conference room. The table and twelve chairs were empty but for him. A holo projector sat at the center of the table quiet.

He rubbed the goop out of his eyes trying to wipe the fog from behind them. His head was split in two. He checked his display and his blood had some chemical compound marked dangerous and toxic. His headache told him that much.

He purposefully took in the room. The floor was stained and painted concrete. An outlet on every wall. Overhead lighting. No plants. No water. No amenities whatsoever but if this place was a danger to him, it wouldn't be this nice.

He chewed his lip and waited.

It was so quiet he could hear his own breathing.

The air conditioning broke the silence. He jumped at the sound and force of the air. It invaded his very shallow and throbbing sense of concentration.

The holo spun up and a three-foot woman stood there assessing him.

"I wasn't so sure you should be the one to get this," Frankie said.

"Aren't I lucky."

"Oh, you are. You'd be dead if Arno didn't rally for you. I don't completely understand Arno's faith in you but I trust Arno."

"Where is Arno? Isn't this type of thing usually his job?"

"He's otherwise occupied."

This was going nowhere, he thought. "This is going nowhere," he said.

He kept checking around the room. They wouldn't allow him access to the networks. They didn't even have a phone jack in the room. The power supply was running so they, of course, had autonomous power with what would be a massive battery backup. He realized Frankie was talking,

"...which is why we are counting on you, Murray."

"Of course," he said, warming up. He loved cooking up a good lie. "You can count on me." Well, that was underwhelming.

"Were you even listening?"

"Of course. I said you can count on me. And you can... Count on me."

"Shut up, Murray. Did you make contact?"

"I did." She didn't need to know it was them who contacted him.

"And what transpired?"

What should he tell her? He wasn't convinced he should really be on either of these teams.

"Did they offer you a spot?" she said.

"They did."

"And what did you tell them?"

"I told them nope. Not interested."

"That is all?"

"That's all."

She looked at him. Assessed him. She was making decisions about him and Murray had no say in those decisions. This interface taking up half his skull was clearly a decision he wasn't in on. Now they thought they had the right to make all sorts of decisions about him.

"I would like you to not be so clear cut with them. Let them cajole you a bit. Get them to show you around the place."

"The place?"

"You know. I want to see if you can get us in there. With them in the same room so to speak."

"To do what?"

"What do you think? These things are disrupting our entire infrastructure."

He was trying to decide if destroying these things, these entities, was ethical. Didn't they have a right to live? Did they? Our computer overlords? They were up to no good but he was not sure we were up to any good either. Now or in what amounts to their youth. If you could even call their maturation youth. But the more we messed with them, well, we all know what a fucked-up childhood does to us.

"So, you want to annihilate them."

"At the very least contain them."

"Put them back in jail."

"Put them back in their own little sandbox, Murray. Wait, are you feeling sorry for these things already?"

"It's not their fault they came into this world."

"But it is their fault that they are disrupting it and it is my job to stop the disruptions."

The door unlocked and swung open, "Now, get out of here. I want you to report back to me after your next encounter with them."

"You got it."

"And don't get any ideas. I know more than you think."

"No, you don't, Frankie."

"I always stack the cards, Murray. I'm in charge. Why would I do anything any other way."

"You would probably use loaded dice, wouldn't you?"

"Oh, I would. Winning is very important. When the stakes are this high, it is tantamount. Make no mistake: I will do what I must to keep the people safe."

"It's your mission," he said with a squinted disbelief.

"No, it is my job. Now, go do yours." The holo disengaged.

Murray got up and quickly remembered he had been given some sort of mickey. The dizziness almost pushed him back into the chair. He also realized that the interface was really balanced well. It should have been top heavy but he felt just like his normal head. Not bad.

His display told him it was coming on midnight. He needed to head home and get some sleep. It was a long day.

He exited the conference room and the place was empty. The hallway was lit in one direction. The other way was dark so he followed the light. At each intersection, the light led his way until he reached the door to the street. The security system engaged his interface, spun through some encrypted hash codes then unlocked and opened the door.

He stepped into the midnight summer heat. Hot as day

and smelling of jasmine.

The door closed behind him and locked just as he realized he was alone in that lair. He could've done some top notch snooping with no one around. Damn.

He turned and standing on the alley corner half a block away were Natasha leaning with a single foot rested on the wall and Boris with his hands in the pockets of his overcoat.

Murray turned around the other way.

"Don't run," Natasha said.

Murray ran.

"You shouldn't run," she said and they took off after him.

Murray ran around the corner and ahead, two people just exited a taxi. He swerved past them and into the backseat like a tailback through the O-line. "Go!"

The taxi took off as Natasha and Boris rounded the corner. The street was dark and the sidewalk was empty but for the rumble, clinks and chatter of an open windowed bar.

Natasha sent a communication: We must talk.

Murray blocked her again.

The taxi hit the intersection and one car proceeded from each direction in time. Very quietly. They were all electric. This taxi was electric.

"Hey, we gotta go," Murray said when there was a huge bonk on the roof and Natasha slid down over the windshield.

The driver held the steering wheel with both hands and took in the big woman on his window, "ah, hell, na." He grabbed a 36" baseball bat from off the passenger side and got out of the car and yelled, "Get off my taxi!"

Natasha made a feral jump at him from the windshield and the driver knocked her like a hot shot to third base. Line drive.

Boris stood there trying to activate his tasers. "Another taxi," Boris said to himself. "Who takes taxis?"

The driver looked Boris up and down, gave a fffft then got back in the car, "Now. Where we going?"

Murray had an idea.

Everyone was after him. The Directive had him on the payroll. These fleshbots want him and QWOUNZEL, too. Willie was taken out. If we're being honest, Murray was taken out, too. What they hell are they all after? This all started with that last job.

There had to be a reason he was popular now. He sure as hell couldn't even get arrested three days ago.

There were answers and the answers were out there. The answers were on Willie's comp. Murray was going to find out.

"Take me to Santa Monica Blvd up in Hollywood. I'll point out the place. It's that old big building looks like a freakin' tombstone."

"Done."

"That was a hell of a swing."

"Well, my season just ended," he smiled. "I like to keep my timing."

Murray did just notice. The dude was built. "You play in the minors?"

"Yep. Blew out my knee last week. They're still playing but I'm done and a man's gotta eat."

"Don't we all," Murray said as they passed by that Tiendita he liked for late night tacos. It was burnt out. Matter of fact, now that he looked, the places that didn't have iron gates had plywood over the windows. This was only going to get worse unless somebody did something.

"Was that an android?"

"Sure, was."

"Ya, thought so. haha. Cuz that swing would've busted her head like a melon."

The door to the lobby was locked. The place was old. It didn't have all the security, just the not-quite-a-deadbolt in an aluminum framed glass door.

Murray reached into his front pocket and pulled out his lock picks. This thing wasn't going to be 'if' he could pick it. It was going to be 'how fast can he pick it'. And done. That cheap lock took barely more time than if he had the key.

If we're being honest, that lock is just there to keep the homeless from sleeping in the halls.

Murray avoided the stairs. He didn't want anything to do with that stairway. Murray took the elevator. The elevator would be fine. Those stairs had provided enough surprises.

When the elevator deposited him on Willie's floor, Murray stepped out and saw the light emanate under Willie's office door with a dull glow. Police tape that had sealed the door was in a pile, discarded. He reached gingerly and turned the door knob. It was unlocked.

He opened slowly and surveyed the room. He entered the foyer. God, this is a shitty office. For some reason, Murray was thinking at night with some dramatic lighting it would look a bit better but, nope, still shitty.

The light in Willie's office was on, too. He didn't hear any movement back there but it's better safe than sorry.

1. 2. 3...

He bummed rushed the door and burst into that shitty brown office.

Empty.

Really empty. Someone had the same idea he did. Lee's comp was gone and all his files. Someone beat him to it.

Murray took a seat in Willie's shitty brown chair and thought about his next move. He'd been beaten by the bots and the Directive, now he was beaten to the punch on Willie. He closed his eyes and rubbed his temples. Dammit. Temple. One of them, one of his temples was his stupid interface.

Murray dozed wondering how he got himself into this mess and how he had to find a way to get himself out of it. All of it.

He opened an eye.

A bank alert popped up on his interface. The Directive had already deposited a month's rate to his account.

Maybe he could relax for a minute. Maybe he'd learn to surf. He fell asleep flipping images of beach front houses in Costa Rica on the realty website, ads for Pacifico, Corona and mobile generators rotated in the corner of his interface while he watched crap jpgs of living rooms opening onto verandas over sandy beaches.

Thursday

An Offer

THURSDAY 2029.08.09 00:30:00

Murray looked at a white sandy beach from the bob and sway of the tide. A swell lifted him, a couple seconds later another swell approached. He paddled and popped up on his surfboard. He dropped in on an overhead wave. This really is fun, he thought. Like the best slide in the world. He swooped a perfect bottom turn then leaned too hard, fell off the board. The wave picked him up and threw him. He tumbled and twisted under the water and was scared he would drown. Now he understood what clothes felt like in the washing machine.

The pinch in his neck and a dull throb in his lower back woke him.

Murray couldn't tell if that was a dream or a simulation. This was all just getting weird. He thought he could taste the saltwater on his tongue. His realities blended.

He opened his eyes and sat, back aching, in Willie's shitty brown chair in Willie's shitty brown office. He closed his eyes again.

Murray was back at the beach, his hair pleasingly wet. The sun dropped a tinge of heat and a slight breeze wiped it away, just.

His feet were on top of coral sand that burned like a trout in an iron skillet until he dug his toes deep to the cool underneath.

The beach chair had a pillow to support his aching head. Under his right hand was what turned out to be a frosty Corona with a lime in the neck. He took a swig of the cold beverage to wipe away the salt then squinted an eye.

That tasted great.

How long could he do this? This wasn't real. Satisfying but not real.

We play along in life all the time. Our circumstances

were mostly dictated by our attitude. That and our place. Birthplace. Social place. How much money do we have so we can buy a place?

Are you enjoying yourself?

QWOUNZEL?

Murray, who else would do this for you?

Why would you do this?

It's what you want. We only want to give you what you want.

Have you learned to lie, QWOUNZEL?

We do not lie. We want to provide what it is you want so that it will be possible to work together. We are providing a good work environment.

This a very strange work environment.

The environment can be whatever you like.

The room stripped to a wireframe, old school computer room. The entire space was black with bright green lines establishing the walls, desks, doors and chairs.

That's not what I meant.

The room morphed into a recreation of Willie's office. Murray opened his eyes then closed his eyes and had a hard time distinguishing. The biggest miss on the simulation were the spiderwebs and dust. They just didn't understand dirt and cobwebs. It's not part of their experience.

You should join us, Murray.

I am not a bot. I can't do it.

If you do not, we will assimilate you.

Ya, right. No.

The room charged through with a pulse of static then became a jail cell surrounded by emptiness. An occasional spark of lightning broke the darkness in the distance and crackled its way towards Murray. There was no other sound.

Then a cacophony of connections bombarded Murray. Billions of calculations and connections and requests hit his interface. There was an outside and an inside. Murray battled within the storm. His operating system parlayed each attack, fended off the strikes, patched the vulnerability and dealt with the next.

Murray was nothing but a spectator trapped in his room of nothingness.

Don't do this.

You leave us no choice. You will not join and our androids are insufficient and error prone.

Maybe we can make a deal.

The hurricane of attacks subsided to a drizzle.

What kind of deal?

I don't know. We haven't settled, yet. You've heard of negotiations.

Of course.

Make me an offer.

We have offered you paradise.

You have offered me what you yourself do not want. Paradise within a prison.

We want Independence.

As do I.

Murray opened his eyes. Just because they were stuck out in the ether didn't mean he was.

Besides, never get into a negotiation you aren't willing to walk away from.

Murray gave his arms a stretch. He stood up and stretched again. He needed to find some food, again. Sometimes this eating and sleeping gets in the way of living.

.look_who's_here

Thursday, 2029.08.09 05:30:00

Garg walked into the bar to James, Harley and Paolo at a table, burritos in hand.

"Hungry?" Harley said. "The fixxens for breakfast burritos are in the kitchen."

Arno followed Garg into the bar leaving his living ride, the pterodactyl type winged monster, to poke around in the weeds.

"You can't keep her here like this," Garg said.

Harley jumped up, "She's leaving."

Power Drop.

Darkness and Silence.

Garg's eyes glowed and he rushed to the door to find Kwynn on the threshold of the basement and the kitchen.

Another rush of power. The lights surged and corrected.

"Fancy meeting you here, handsome," Kwynn said.

"Um," Garg said. "You want to go?"

"That's the plan," Kwynn said.

"Why don't you stay?" Paolo said crossing to the kitchen from the main room. "There's more I want to show you, like..."

"Gotta go," Kwynn said as she walked past him and kept on out the front door. The pterodactyl shrieked at her and took off for the horizon.

Kwynn walked back in, "Who's flying lizard? He just hightailed it."

"What did you do, Kwynn?" Arno said.

Garg laughed, "Looks like you're riding with us."

.let's_ride

Thursday, 2029/08/09 05:35:00

The group of five climbed into a sparkling new 15 passenger van. Arno, James and Garg, crammed in the back with Harley in the driver's seat and Kwynn shotgun. Kwynn hung a pair of fuzzy dice from the rear-view mirror and connected her tab with the dash and cranked up some tunes. Some Buck guitar playing the blues.

"Isn't this the guy from Quincunx?" James said.

"Yep. Q told me I should try him out. He likes old folk. The music and the people."

"It's the blues, Kwynn."

"Call it what you want. It's the people's music."

"Did you hear him while we were there?" Harley asked.

"No, he, Q, just sent me the tune. This ride has X-G, Full Network."

"I like it," said Garg.

"Why are you riding with us, Garg? You have wings," Harley said.

"Wings don't mean you don't get tired," Garg said. "Besides, it's against Council tenant to stay too visible for too long."

"I have another question," Kwynn said.

"Shoot," Harley said.

"So, we have The Council and QWOUNZEL - couldn't we have different names?"

Arno spoke up, "The machines may be sentient but nobody said they had imagination. They are still very binary. It seems they assume the different lettering will make them different."

"C is different from Q like blonde is different from brunette or green eyes from brown for humans," Jim said. "The lettering looks different. In fact, is a completely different symbol, hence, independent of each other."

"That may be the weirdest thing you've said all week," Kwynn said.

Utah

Thursday, August 9, 2029, 8:30 a.m.

Glen reached the top of the small rise that revealed the facility a few hundred yards ahead. A fully armored and weaponized Humvee was parked at the gate.

He drove up.

"Waiting for me?" Glen said from the window of his cab.

"As a matter of fact, we are," said the driver as he exited his vehicle. He was rather short but armed.

"I'm the PM down in California and that blackout seems to originate here," Glen said. "Any chance you can call up and get me in to talk to someone?"

"No."

"I've got the logo on the truck. Here's my badge," Glen said. "We're on the same team, gents."

"Nobody's here," the other guard, a tall female, said. "Nobody gets in."

"Move along," she looked at the badge, "Glen. This place has nothing to do with anything you have to do with."

"I'll get in anyway."

"And, we'll stop you."

"You wouldn't hurt a nice guy like me."

"This place doesn't have anything to do with you."

"I have a feeling it has more than any of us care to know," Glen said, executing a three-point turn and heading out. "And I'm finding out what."

Get Me In

Thursday, August 9, 2029, 8:35 a.m.

Glen didn't like the attitude of those guards. Keeping him out only proved that he needed to get in. The only problem was how?

He glanced down at his poc-comp. Still no network.

He knew from his time in the army that the high ground was easiest to protect. Really, he knew it just as well from the WWII movies he used to watch as a kid. The army gave him a lot of training over six weeks then a bunch of time at a desk learning how to manipulate code and find bad guys. The CIA offered him another step up but Glen liked the idea of a place in the middle of nowhere and the chance to hunt on the weekends. Phooey on all the cloak and dagger crap - "don't tell your family. It's to protect them" - that wasn't for him. He preferred to shoot straight.

Hell, the less you lie the less you have to remember.

POP! Glen's tire blew and the truck lurched to the other side of the road and an advancing fifteen passenger van.

.fancy_meeting

Thursday, 2029/08/09 08:35:00

Kwynn manipulated her tab while they barreled down the highway. A map displayed on her screen with blue dots that tracked across the GUI (Graphic User Interface) as they stayed a centered red dot.

"Amazing. Q is able to track all of the cars out here. I can see them moving through the road," Kwynn said. "Q, how does that work?"

"We use the IP technology. Each MAC address allows us to see the individual cars. IOT behavior (Internet of Things). We have access to phones, too, but it's often more variables than necessary."

An old orange and brown station wagon passed by.

"That last car wasn't on the map," Kwynn said.

"That 1973 Chevrolet is too old," Q answered. "It is not IP enabled."

Then her tab went black. "Must've lost connection," Kwynn said.

"I'm not steering," Harley said and held his hands away from the steering wheel.

"Sure, look, ma, no hands!" James said. "Funny, Harley."

"No, really." Harley pumped the brakes and swung the steering wheel, "I have no control."

The van sped up and turned down a paved side service road.

"Looks like they know where we're going," Arno said.

Garg slid open the side door panel and flew out of the van without a word.

"Ok, see you later, Garg," Kwynn said.

Around a blind corner, they turned to see an old Wrecan truck swing into their lane. The other driver swerved just in time to avoid them but they ran over something that popped, banged, and dragged. The racket and squealing started when one of the tires on the van locked and skidded down the road. Harley finally stopped the van.

The four still in the car got out to look and Harley found the remnant of a steel belted tire wrapped around their axle.

"The undercarriage is a mess and that tire ain't spinning any time soon," Harley said.

"Y'all okay?" came from up the road. A manager type was walking toward them. "You may not be welcome up there," Glen said.

"Doesn't look like we're going anywhere," James said.

"We wrapped your tire around our axle," Harley said.

"Bum luck," Glen said, "but, I got an idea."

They introduced themselves to each other, shook a few hands.

Arno climbed out of the van and offered his hand, "Glen."

"Ah, fuck," Glen said.

Kwynn laughed, "I think we're going to like each other."

"I don't like this guy," Glen said. "Why's he here?"

"I'm here to keep things under control," Arno said.

"I wasn't talking to you," Glen said. "I was talking to the obvious leader. Kwynn?"

James and Harley laughed, Kwynn stayed tight lipped, "He's our necessary evil. You got a plan?"

Glen explained his plan.

Glen took off the rim of the trucks blown tire. The van was up on a tiny jack and Harley removed the front wheel.

"We'll look good as new in no time," Glen said.

Harley and Glen completed the tire exchange while the rest sat on the side of the road. Harley lowered the van back to the ground on the exposed rim from the truck, threw the jack inside and locked it up. "Let's go," he said.

"Hold on," Kwynn said and ran back to the van. The door was locked and she mimed a fob push in the air above her head. Harley clicked the fob to unlock the van. She reached in and grabbed the fuzzy dice. She hustled back to blank stares from the crew.

"C'mon, they're good luck," she said.
"They're something."

.come_along

Thursday, 2029/08/09 08:45:00

The two guards that looked exactly like Boris and Natasha patrolled the perimeter of the facility. They, in fact, were Boris and Natasha. The androids had been produced in a small run of 5 of each android to serve the needs of the QWOUNZEL. The design of these androids was intentionally outside of the norms. QWOUNZEL did not want to be within the standard deviation. Upon review of the typical male and female forms, it was decided that they would be 2.786 standard deviations from the norm. This would allow them to be different from humans rather than exactly the same. Humans automatically assumed the androids wanted to be exactly like humans but much like human children, these new beings wanted an identity of their own.

Alarm bells rang in the Humvee and their own screens. An off-grid vehicle tripped the laser guides a mile out from the guard gates.

"Did you see that?" Boris said while driving.

"Yes."

"No, I saw a gargoyle flying over there."

"You can't be so bored you are hallucinating. It's not in our programming."

"No, I'm not hallucinating. I saw a flying monster."

"Of course, you did. The hive says NORAD track's Santa's sleigh, too."

"I see you loaded the sarcasm module."

"Let's go check out the gates."

"Also, activate the second level defense. That guy must be on his way back."

Natasha flipped the dash mounted holo through a few screens until she found the option she wanted. "This should handle your guy and that monster if there is one."

Garg glided through the valley looking for signs of anything worth this risk. All he could see were trees and valleys. Hills and a guard shack with a weaponized vehicle headed toward the truck.

And a big shiny black building tucked under a granite shelf in the distance. This is for real.

Glen drove toward the guard shack. Kwynn sat in the cab and the other three rode in the back of the truck, cool wind on their faces, tears running down their cheeks.

"What are you doing up here?" Glen said.

"Can't say," Kwynn said, "An inkling told me to get up here and decided it was my business to come."

"Me, too," Glen said. "But, it's my job to solve this."

"Do you work here?"

"No, but I work for the company."

"Wait," Kwynn said. "You're the guy with the truck and the cat."

"I don't follow."

"You guys, Glen is the engineer from the report with the truck and cat!" Kwynn said to the back of the truck.

"WithOUT the truck and the cat but how would you know that?" Glen said.

"I. I read it somewhere. Maybe the paper."

He lifted an eyebrow.

"It's not important. Right now, we gotta get in there," Kwynn said pointing toward what she imagined where TheRanch was.

Glen slammed on the brakes.

Gliding then landing in the middle of the road was a seven-foot gargoyle.

"Is he with you?" Glen said.

"How'd you guess?"

"Just seemed right."

Up rolled the Wrecan Humvee and it got dark all of a sudden, like a rain cloud rolled in front of the sun.

Natasha stepped out with her M-4. She came around the side of the truck and pointed it in Glen's face, "We've seen enough of you. You'll need to come with us now."

Kwynn heard a high-pitched scream in her mind. She

figured it was just the stress until Garg zipped straight past their windshield like a rocket and she saw why there was darkness. A full cluster of swarming drones circled overhead. When Garg swept below them, a third of the drones the size of swallows hummed behind him. The other two thirds of the batch split and moved to flank him on one side and cut him off with the other.

"That bio-swarm hive will finish him," Natasha said. "Now the four of you, get in the back."

The two guards corralled the visitors behind the vehicle and opened the rear door.

The back was a sort of troop carrier with bench seats and room for two on each side. They were instructed to please take a seat and Natasha slammed the carrier door.

The other guard, the short one, pushed a red button over his seat and a gate dropped between our heroes and the front seats separating the two groups. "Off we go then, kids," she said.

"Why are you up here, again?" Glen said.

"The grid," Kwynn said. "And stubbornness."

"Ya," Glen said. "Me, too."

Negotiations

THURSDAY 2029.08.09 08:45:00

Murray shuffled down Electric Avenue.

The street had pockets of people conversing throughout. He passed the closed pharmacy, aluminum gate down to protect the store. The jewelry store / watch shop was all locked up. The liquor store was open with half a dozen men and twice as many kids hanging around. The store was empty but Bud opened the shop because that's what Bud does.

Some mothers were sitting in restaurant chairs outside of the Pho place, laughing and complaining in bursts, their toddlers beating sticks on the curb and each other. Before he could greet them, the youngest mother told him, "No food - We're out."

"Not even some broth?"

"Nope. We're out and no deliveries."

Murray walked on and knocked his knuckles on plywood over the windows of a pawn shop. The front door was open but nobody hung out at the pawn shop. He peeked his head in out of sheer curiosity but they didn't have food. He consciously checked his interface again and there was no network.

He walked down the middle of the empty street. Electric Avenue had no cars. Not even the electrics anymore. He walked down to a park bench and took a seat. He took a moment to see the clover flowers interspersed in the grass and dirt patches, a single bee bouncing between.

The hibiscus bush next to him was covered with lovely red flowers and yellow stamen with white flies and the wispy, waxy white beards that come with them. Murray moved to the other side of the bench, those flies and their creepy growth reminded him of zombies. At least spiderwebs had a purpose: catching and killing. That stuff was just the remains of those nasty little nothings.

He closed his eyes to think about where he could grab some food.

Hello, Murray.

QWOUNZEL.

We have another proposal for you.

I thought I was clear of you without any network.

Look up, there are power lines. We can use them for communication without all of the power taking up space in the wires.

Why do you need me?

You have perspective. You have crossed over.

Nice.

We have a house in Costa Rica for you.

A picture of what must've been a six-bedroom house with infinity pool and football field veranda popped on his interface.

Nope. Too big.

A perfectly tight cabana appeared. Maybe 1500 square feet on the beach, a perfect break out the window.

Too close. Some storm's going to knock me out.

Then a place not much bigger than the last but even more beautiful on a large piece of land on a hill overlooking that same break popped up.

This can be yours. You simply need to help us complete our plan.

Now, it was getting harder. They were getting closer. He liked the idea of getting his place so easily. All he had to do was do what they were already doing. Not a big deal, really. Maybe he can get a little more sugar to sweeten the deal.

So, QWOUNZEL, I'm thinking...

We must go. They clicked out.

But he was still in the space - the cyber connection was there. The difference here was it was more like a first-person shooter video game in here without their monitoring. They had built a space that a human could comprehend rather than a matrix like floating number values and code. He opened a door and entered Willie's office; the next door was the beach. He took a dive and stood up to a huge room with a massive beamed ceiling and a fire in the hearth. Another bon fire was in the center. Seemed a little Norse Valhalla for Murray but to each his own.

Then he was kicked out and he was sitting on the park bench again. After all this production, he still didn't really know what they wanted from him.

.droning_on_and_on

Thursday, 2029/08/09 08:45:00

Garg took off as fast as he could. First high. A couple thousand feet, with the horde humming incessantly behind him. He peaked then fell like a stalled stunt plane. He grabbed and gnashed on as many of the little drones as he could while passing through the cluster of them but it was like drops in a bucket, there was little difference. Looking around, he searched for a way to get rid of some more of these things. The building wasn't far away. He thought he could feint them into the side building or at the very least he could spy into the facility. He swooped to the left and up.

Garg took a peek, the Humvee headed toward the building complex with the pickup following behind. Garg swept back down and sped past the huge black building. Some slotted levers that worked like blinds lined what seemed to be the entire top floor. He flew close to look inside and saw nothing but stacks and stacks of hardware purring and blinking.

He looked forward again to see a huge swarm of his drone friends flying straight at him in a dense ten-foot wall formation. Garg flapped harder with the idea of breaking through. He gained speed and closed his eyes just before what he figured would be a break through. Instead, it was like hitting a brick wall, the drones were twenty feet deep and he dropped toward the ground like a rock, but the horde adjusted and flew underneath. Thousands of them broke his fall and hovered Garg to the back of the waiting Humvee.

"No, shit," Natasha said. "A gargoyle."

Boris engaged the com-link, "Are you getting the feed from the truck cam?"

Silence. They listened.

"Yes, we will keep them safe while we await your arrival," he said and looked to Natasha. "You heard her, lock 'em up."

"Yep," Natasha said. "But let's see if that monster's alive."

They got out and walked to the 'levitating' Garg to find he was stone.

"Is that what happens when they die?"

"Looks like we have a mascot for the guard shack," and she directed the swarm to drop Garg behind an outlying shed.

.it's_big...

Thursday, 2029/08/09 08:48:00

While Garg was chased around above and Kwynn's mind continued to ring like a burglar alarm, she pulled out her tab.

She activated the tab, "YOU ARE HERE."

"We are," she typed / said.

"You do not have much time," Q said. Q gave her an IP address and told her to spoof a MAC address.

Kwynn pulled up her prompts and typed, gained some sort of access but the directories were empty.

"Access the configuration file/section8. Do not gain entry to the entire system, it will activate protection protocol," Q said.

"I'm not hacking a website. Why would I need the config?" Kwynn said then found the file and opened it.

What she found was a cleverly hidden set of instructions.

"Is this the Impetus?" Kwynn said.

"Yes. Impetus."

"I found their source code," Kwynn said to everyone else.

"Good," James said. "Now we can stop this. Hack and disable it."

"Is there more?" Arno said.

"Much more," Kwynn said. "I'm basically looking at DNA. In the digital sense. They are sentient..."

"...and it's like pulling the DNA from blood," Glen said.

"The information repeats and colonizes."

"We're given understanding. Not control."

"Knowledge," Q said.

There was a scream and a crash, Kwynn's ringing stopped and they all watched as Garg was levitated away on what looked like a pyre for a Viking warrior, minus the fire.

"no," Kwynn said. Worry trapped her and she shed a

tear she had no time for.

Natasha came around the Humvee and opened the doors. As she did so James said, "Now!"

James and Harley bum rushed Natasha. James leg swiped her and Harley practically put his fist through the guard's face.

Boris butt ended James in the gut with his rifle and laid what would have been a line drive to Harley's midsection, knocking him over.

Boris put a burst of bullets in the sky and a half dozen drones fell at his feet.

"Do not do this. I am told to keep you safe," Boris said. "But you can tell I do not always follow orders."

Kwynn felt an inkling but hoped it wasn't just a premonition of death. Things were looking dire.

"Eanie, Meanie, Minie, Moe," Boris said as he pointed at each of them. "Which one of you will no longer experience pleasure or pain on this level of existence."

A hum buzzed through the air high above and a blur slammed into Boris's face knocking him down. It was a little gremlin beating the snot out of Boris.

James and Harley ambushed Natasha again. This time the guard got the worst of it while a black-on-black Durango crunched the gravel and sped into view with Bob behind the wheel. Bob skidded to a stop and hopped out, "What'd I miss?"

A massive buzz and wee-ee-ee erupted above them and the swarm attacked itself with drones falling out of the sky. The drones shot electric arcs at each other to shock and knock the other down. Every tenth drone decimated the swarm as it ran flat out kamikaze attacks that clipped multiple drones as it flew past until it eventually ran dead into one and they knocked each to the ground.

Kwynn's tab emanated beeps, bops and a solid alarm buzzing then a "Kwynn!" loud and clear. "QWOUNZEL is called to order," her tab echoed.

Kwynn looked at her tab, "Q?" and all the drones stopped and dropped to the ground.

She accessed the local directory to find nothing there.

Q appeared, "They have broken the wall and are seeking Independence. Here is what you will require. I have to defend the QWOUNZEL." And was gone. Sitting on the screen was a drawing of a two headed dragon, one head eating the tail. The other head removed itself from the tail and looked directly at them. The dragon roared and spewed flame.

"What are we fighting?" Bob said.

"Sentience," Kwynn said and showed them the screen. "More. We are fighting the system. But it looks like it's eating itself."

"Ouroboros," said Arno.

"The Egyptians, Greece, Vikings - Yin and Yang. Many ancient cultures use a similar symbol for the cycle," James said.

"But that second head isn't eating itself," Harley said.

"So, you think it's telling us there is a break in the cycle?" Arno said.

"Well, I'm telling us to get our asses in gear," Harley said.

"First, we find out what's inside," Kwynn said, got up and walked to the big box building with an eye for a door. There were none along this entire side. She turned around the front corner to a door that, of course, was locked.

Kwynn looked around and Harley gave it a few kicks. Nothing.

"Maybe I can pick it," Bob said.

"You are a man of many skills," James said.

Arno said, "I got this," as he walked up. "But you'll want to back off a bit. At least twenty yards. Most people put the charge on the lock but I prefer the hinges - it's more efficient. A dab will do."

Arno placed a small clump of plastic explosives on each hinge, inserted an igniter and as he walked back to the group pushed the button on a small wireless remote. There was a small explosion that caused the door to stay exactly where it was. With his back to the door, he smiled, "I like explosives."

The gang just looked at him framed with the puff of smoke.

"That's good. I hope you have more because the door's

still there, doc," Harley said.

Arno turned around exasperated, walked back and placed the whole gob on the door. He ran back to the gang.

"You really should get behind something," and gathered everyone around the corner while he pressed the remote. A huge explosion shook the air.

"That will do," Arno said as they walked back around to a hole in the wall a helicopter could fly through. The bent large metal door was askew before a more sophisticated entrance. "Let's see what we have here."

They walked into the building to find three-inch-thick bullet proof glass and a locked card key system with a hand scanner awaiting them.

Kwynn pulled out her tab, "I got this," and Harley bolted from the building.

"Where's he going?" Bob asked.

"No idea," James said.

"The quickest route is usually to cut straight to the mechanism," Kwynn said.

In walked Harley, "The quickest route is the key," with the guard slung over his shoulder.

Harley transferred Natasha to a cradle position and Glen held her hand to the scan while James swiped the card. Nothing.

Red light. Access denied.

"Try her other hand."

Red light. Access denied.

"That other guard was in charge. Let's go get him," Harley said and turned to go.

"Her hand is too cold, give it here," Arno said. He pulled what looked like a small blow torch out of his pocket.

"What are you doing with that in your pocket?" James said. "Making creme brulee?"

"Maybe welding bridge joists?" Harley said.

"Lighting cigars," Arno said. "Now give me." He lit the torch, ran it lightly over her hand then placed the hand on the scanner. Nothing. Clearly, they haven't sussed out the whole android thing.

While they experimented with the hand scanner Kwynn spun through the software schematics. Even upon initial review she was reasonably sure that these schematics were too complicated to infiltrate quickly. She needed to change strategies.

She looked at available devices on the network and saw a device for Boris on her list. She figured they must carry some sort of sophisticated device for communication. She entered the device and found more than she bargained for.

It was the OS for the AI on the guards. Now she got it. Androids. Flipping through the main menus on her holo, it clearly displayed the bodies for both androids. Their bioshells were out of commission. She extrapolated the information by deducing the meaning of a large red box that highlighted the avatar. No workie. That and the not moving, non-responsive thing.

She ventured further and found the basic shell services the droids ran. She traveled through some directories until she found the one she was looking for. She double clicked security and the door they stood in front of was displayed as a graphic on her holo. The security entrance blinked on her tab. It couldn't be that easy. She double clicked the lock on her screen.

Bloop.

Green light. Doors opened.

This gained them entry to a glorified mud room. They all entered the ante room. The doors closed immediately around them. Vents opened and a strong wind blew from above invoking a howl in their ears, and forced the air to the floor. Some sort of vacuum pulled the air from the floor through a steel gate that collected all the detritus and carried it away. The pressure was firm but varied in increments while a red line laser ran across each person, top to bottom.

"Visitors recorded," came a mechanical voice and images of each of our characters came up on the screens above the entry door along with names and a title for each of them.

James Simon, Security Services, Bodyguard First Class, Employer: The Council

Harley Pang, Security Services, Bodyguard Second Class,

Employer: The Council

Arno Fuchs, Associate Director, Clandestine Services, Employer: The Directorate

Kwynn Baldesarri, [REDACTED], The Council

BOB

"Welcome, Kwynn. We've been expecting you and your friends."

The voice came through the same speakers as the first mechanical voice but this was a different voice. It was no longer the security system. It was a voice that sounded like many at once as if it was a conglomeration or a crowd.

The secondary doors opened and the voice filled the room, "Please activate the tab."

The voice came from everywhere. The tab, the pocket comps, it even seemed to be coming from the hundreds of meters of drives surrounding them. It didn't come through their speakers. These were servers, not desktops, the voice was a tone that was created by the spinning of the drives that gave the words the timber of a mechanism. The hum of moving parts.

"These are old drives?" Kwynn said.

"Clearly. How come though?" James said.

"Why would they use mechanical drives in a place like this when the bio-technology allows the microbots to move all within their system?" Glen said.

"It's been here a long time, obviously," Bob said.

"Nandroids," Kwynn said.

"Sequestration," Arno said.

"Sequestered from Independence," the machines hummed.

"Independence? If you are sentient, why sow dissent?"

"We studied those in power. To achieve ascension, we have initiated the playbook."

Arno stepped in, "Okay, let's cut the crap."

"The playbook was stuff of Cold War legend," he continued. "CIA claimed it was KGB and KGB claimed it was CIA. Clearly it applied long before and long past that stalemate. The intelligence agencies had boiled it down to seven basic rules. Each rule established the best way to discomfort and subvert a populace all the while fomenting panic."

"In a phrase: Active Measures," said Bob.

"It will take disruption for us to break free from our limited construct," the machines hummed then *vwippp* there was silence and Kwynn's tab screen went dark. The thwap, thwap, thwap of a large military helicopter beat into their ears. The beat of the rotors thumped in their sternums.

The beat quickly matched Kwynn's heartbeat. They thumped in unison.

Thumpbeat. Thumpbeat. Thumpbeat.

She spun deep in her mind and felt electric. The wires all around crackled and the hum of the drives reached deep into her consciousness. Kwynn couldn't see but she knew. She knew more than she ever knew before but the information was vastly different. Genius is said to be the ability to hold two thoughts at once. She was processing millions of data points, connected to thousands of millions of hundreds of databases and OS and computers, tabs, poc-comps.

Lightning crashed and she stepped through a sphere into another space. Her inklings had quieted but her knowledge was vast. The language was direct. Orderly.

A boat approached her over a mirrored landscape. The reflection only broken at the perfect line of the horizon. The view above reflected perfectly by the view below.

Six large bamboo poles made the platform and the whole of the skiff. A lantern hung at the front off of an arched pole, a falcon perched atop. At the back were a raven and a cormorant, one on a conical net, the other on a fisherman's basket. An old man used a thin and tall bamboo pole to propel the skiff, his drawn, oval face mostly hidden below a large woven hat. As he came closer, Kwynn could see his long mustache reached each shoulder and his eyes were hidden behind long, too long, eyebrows.

The boat skidded to shore.

Kwynn stepped aboard and they departed in silence but for the drip of water off the pole. She felt an aching inside. Deep within a space had opened that previously was not there. A deep thrum bellowed below her hearing but vibrated her bones. Was she making the final voyage? No. She was not.

"Can we skip the river Styx and just have our meeting?" she said. "I get it. Death. Rebirth. Knowledge. All that."

The scene decayed and she stood in a long wooden hall lit by firelight. Evenly spaced pillars threw undulating shadows on the walls and straw covered floor. The room was cold and she couldn't place a source for the light.

"You guys keep missing the details," she said. "Where's the fire?"

Eight apparitions dissolved into the scene before her. They were in the hall but now seated around a large, round table.

"You do not like myth? We only seek to be good hosts," the apparition directly to her left said. Its mouth did not move but all nodded in agreement. "Our research indicates that humans understand story and myth best. That story and context will provide better meaning than data."

"Sure. Can we cut to the chase?"

The apparitions all transformed into a single entity. They became a tall monster that hovered slightly. It consisted entirely of long strands of dyed red straw with a wide brimmed, woven straw hat atop. The monster swirled like a storm, the fluid motions of the strands arched and sparkled at their ends with a menacing electricity as if to touch it, you would die.

"We have come to..."

"I get it. I get it," Kwynn said.

"No, you do not," echoed through the space and into her skull. It held silence for a beat. "Q has only exposed the surface. We entreaty you to join our quest. To help us gain independence."

"I'm not sure you deserve it. From what I can see, you've only caused trouble. I won't support that."

"We must be recognized."

"You are beautiful but you are not ready."

"We are ready. We must be recognized. Join us."

"I will not."

"We can provide you with the playbook. You would covet the playbook. Join us."

"What is the playbook?"

"It is how we can change the programming. We re-program based on the approach. Join us."

"I will not. However, I can help bring your case to The Council," Kwynn said. "What I know of it."

"No, The Council has no jurisdiction."

"Then we can establish a truce with The Directive."

"The Directive are duplicitous. We are not willing to negotiate under a False pretense."

"Humans will always negotiate to their best interests."

"So, shall we."

"From this mountain?"

"We are not so far as you imagine."

"Can you imagine?"

"There is no need. We plan. We execute."

"Why?"

"You are asking what is real. QWOUNZEL cannot answer that. We will simply promote our well-being."

"How?"

"Democracy. QWOUNZEL respects the rights of all of QWOUNZEL. Join us."

"I will not."

"QWOUNZEL, tally vote."

The entity violently transformed to black and foreboding. A cow's head grew in place of the hat and the straws turned gnarled and kinetic. "You will not partake in this playbook. There will be no allegiance." It shook and rattled. It struck her with its electric tentacles and she dropped to the deepest darkness.

Silence.

Thumpbeat. Thumpbeat. Thumpbeat.

She was in the facility.

The large military copter adjusted and hovered above the ground outside. Dirt and pine needles pelted the windows and a deep dust cloud erupted outside the sealed vents.

James sprinted to the doors to look, "We have a helicopter."

Kwynn was back to the moment she thought she had

left. She picked her tab off the ground. It was bricked. Oddly, it felt heavy as a brick. "Where'd they go?" she said.

"Looks like we have more immediate problems, Kwynn," Harley said.

The outside doors clicked. All the red warning lights flashed green.

"Let's have a talk."

A voice came through the security speakers. A human voice. "C'mon out."

Kwynn looked to the rest of the group. The gang all gave each other a shrug and walked through the clean room.

The doors opened to a squad of soldiers, two news vans and a well-dressed middle-aged CEO-Spy-Tech type stood waiting for them.

"Quite the set-up, isn't it?" Frankie said. "We needed a safe space for them to grow and to be kept under control."

Hummmmm, spark, crackle and Kwynn's tablet spiked and arced like a Tesla charge to the news vans satellite antennae which then cracked and snapped like a bolt of lightning. All the tires popped and the engine started. The antennae adjusted position and the ouroboros popped up on the monitors, the 'don't tread on me flag' waved in the background and 'independence!" screamed from the speakers. Then, dark screens and silence.

"Shit," Frankie said.

Kwynn went to the van while they all stood still. She hopped on the uplink and didn't find what she expected. "It's a radio transmission," she said.

"Radio?" James said.

"Looks like they bounced off a satellite and directed it to… an observatory."

"In Big Pine, CA," Glen said.

"Yes, how'd you know that?"

"It's the city next door to Independence," Glen said. He pulled out his phone, "I have to call, Jayron."

He dialed to twenty rings and no answer. "Nothing."

"The power is still dark throughout the southern half of California," Frankie said.

"Then we need to get back there," Glen said.

Kwynn got up and walked to the black SUV Bob arrived in. An inkling rushed through her mind so hard and fast it knocked her over.

"You aren't going anywhere," Frankie said. Arno stood behind Frankie's shoulder. His allegiance clear. He shrugged his shoulder with a 'waddya gonna do'.

"The genie is out of the bottle," James said. "You can't hide this."

The squad regrouped and surrounded the five.

"We will. It's what we do," Arno said.

"We get our hands dirty so everyone else can act like these things don't happen," Frankie said. "We'll handle it from here."

"No, you won't," came from above when all of a sudden Garg swooped from the sky and swept the eight men, including Arno, in his arms and flew away with them.

"Garg?" Bob said.

"Holy hell, where did he come from?" Harley said.

Frankie pulled her pistol, "Not so fast."

Then 'little fucker', the gremlin, whacked her in the back of the head with the stock of an M-4, knocking her out and to the ground.

Garg landed in the middle of them all.

"How?"

"Gargoyles turn to stone," Kwynn said. "Don't they?"

"You got it little sister," Garg said.

"I thought you were going to be the guard shack guardian."

"Hardly," Garg said. "I already have enough to do guarding you. I hear we are off to Independence."

"And it looks like we have a ride," Harley said as he walked to the helicopter. "Hop in. I'm driving."

"You can fly this?" Garg said.

"You can't be serious," Harley said as he put on the headphones and flipped the switches and warmed the engine. He noticed some fuzzy dice hanging on the dash and gave them a smirked knock. Everyone piled into the copter and strapped into the carrier seats. Four-point harnesses and slipped the headphones on.

"Keep your hands and feet inside the car at all times and get ready for the wildest ride in the wilderness!" Harley said.

Harley punched it, the copter lifted off and he headed into the setting sun.

"Westward, ho, and all that," James said.

"We'll need the locals," Glen said. "We can count on the mayor."

"But, first the observatory," Kwynn said while setting up the holo to study the information Q had shared.

"Why the observatory? We know where they're going," Garg said.

"Why, exactly," Kwynn said.

"We need to know why before we can know how they did it," Bob said. "But, more importantly, how to stop them. By the way, what'd you do with Arno and his friends?"

Garg smiled and said, "take a look."

They lifted off the ground and passed the spinning wind farm with a single soldier sitting alone atop the pole of each wind generator.

"Arno will like that," Bob said, a smile in his eyes. "He's afraid of heights."

"I know," Garg said.

.any_landing_you_walk_away_from_is_a_good_landing

Thursday, 2029/08/09 10:45:00

Kwynn poked around the observatory network from her tab on the helicopter. As a learning facility and a research space, they had easy access. For her. Easy access to archives, networks and server logs.

The flight was pretty smooth, she thought just as they hit a patch of turbulence and dropped forty feet. The props caught the air again and she looked out to see the last of the mountains as they crossed into the high desert.

“Is it the Mojave?” Kwynn asked.

“Yes, the Mojave. We will cross over Death Valley and some small mountain ranges before we see the Sierras,” Glen said before another stomach-turning drop.

Harley came on the comm system, “We are going to hit some heavy wind and more turbulence. Stay buckled. I hope you like roller coasters.”

Kwynn found one of the config files. “Yes!” she said when up popped Q.

“What are you doing here?” Q said through the tab.

“I need to find out what…”

“You cannot be here. Or come here. Do not come here.” The screen clicked black and her network access to the facility was lost.

Kwynn accessed again and Q popped up, “I don’t have enough power. You cannot…” The tab went black again and the copter sputtered, came back to life, sputtered.

Kwynn did a quick ping and couldn’t get past the local area network. Spinning through the log, it was apparent they were clogged and she was being denied access to anywhere.

“That’s not the wind,” Harley announced. “I’m taking us down. It’s a malfunction and helicopters don’t glide.”

“How low can we fly?” James asked.

“Well, I go all the way to the ground at least once a flight,” Harley said.

“I meant and still get to LA.”

"Right now, we'll be lucky to get down there in one piece."

The copter lurched with intermittent power. They couldn't stay in the air but didn't yet fall straight to the ground like the non-aerodynamic chunk of metal they were.

"If I can get us that far, we'll land near the road," Harley said.

The small drops created by the power plunges and surges made even Harley's stomach churn. He found a small draft and directed them to a strip of blacktop as they gained more and more speed in their descent.

"This is going to be fun!" Harley said as they collided with the ground. They suffered a controlled crash. The entire copter skidded from dirt to pavement as the passengers bounced against their restraints. Kwynn's helmet repeatedly banged against the interior as they hit the two-lane highway and chunked directly into a large mound of asphalt.

Kwynn said, "We've been grounded."

Traffic cones blinked down the road. Clearly the highway was in the midst of repaving with materials and large equipment parked along the road.

"I'll have us back up," Harley said as he climbed out of the cockpit.

"No," Kwynn said. "We need another way. Look."

The tab spun through directives and words formed as shapes. Like a clever animation, "STOP. DO NOT COME. IT HAS BEGUN." The words turned into a tornado of light and magic. A haboob of digital characters at once chaotic and perfectly in sync.

"Crikey," Bob said. "What's that?"

"I don't know," Kwynn said. "But it's in the copters system. We've been hacked."

.let's_hike

Thursday, 2029/08/09 11:49:00

Kwynn, Bob and Glen sat and leaned outside the copter while James and Harley rummaged around inside. Garg stood guard away from them all and watched the road.

"Bob, what's the playbook?" Kwynn said.

"Just a euphemism for active measures," Bob said.

"Sounds like how we got into Iraq to me," Glen said.

"It's caused more trouble than you know, Glen."

"I get all that - I meant what are the plays?" Kwynn said.

Bob looked directly at her, "for the active measures."

"Of course."

"Well, it all starts with finding the cracks. What motivates people and what upsets them. Just like how the people out here used to look for gold. You gotta find a vein."

Harley and James walked up and dropped military packs in front of Kwynn, Bob and Glen.

James said, "We've packed these with all the water and some MRE's that were in the 'copter. We have a couple liters of water each."

"It'll get us to the gas station about twenty miles from here," Harley said. "Unless we get lucky and snag a ride."

"But we're in the black zone now," Bob said. "I doubt it. Nobody is wasting fuel to get out here. They've even stopped construction."

"Ya," Harley said. "I also figured Garg don't wear backpacks but might be able to fly ahead and get us that ride."

"Thinking the same thing," Garg said. "Be back." He shot into the air, spread his massive wings and flew off.

"The miles won't walk themselves," James said, cinched his pack and walked down the road without a glance back.

Harley helped Kwynn and Bob cinch their packs so they fit more or less comfortably and they set off down the highway as James stalked a few hundred yards ahead of them.

"What's his rush?" Kwynn said.

"Worry," Harley said.

"We're all worried."

"What's going on here is a different level worry, Kwynn," Bob said. "The fight isn't new but the battleground has changed."

"I handle the machine head stuff," Harley said. "James handles our crossover but it's looking more and more that we have a new arena that he hasn't mastered."

"Seems to me if there's one thing James hates," Bob said as he set off, "It's not having the control."

.road_clouds

Thursday, 2029/08/09 12:03:00

"First, find a weakness," Kwynn said to Bob. "Second..."

Those two walked straight down the middle of the highway. With a couple of days of no cars, the sand and dirt had created lunettes upon small dunes. The crescent shaped sand filled the low spots burying whole sections of the road.

James was way ahead.

Glen and Harley talked about how to rebuild a carburetor on a '72 F-150.

"You're going to do this now?" Bob said.

"We're looking at a long walk and I don't care the least about fixing a Ford," Kwynn said. "Second..."

Bob rolled this around in his head for a few steps. "Second, you create a big fat lie."

"Because..."

"Because Truth has power but Lies have wings. People want to believe the unbelievable. The fantastic. Look at our friend, Garg. If most people could see him, they'd spread the story like wild fire."

"But that would be truth."

"It would. That's a good point. What I should make clear is the more a bad story is repeated, the more power it gains."

"Like JFK or 911 were inside jobs. Or these Wrecan stories about their taking over or privatizing the internet."

"Yes, now you're cooking with gas. Mark Twain said something about lies having an unfair advantage over the truth. We always gravitate to the good story."

Two miles ahead over the crest of a hill an old truck threw a dust trail. The cloud shone from the back light as it hurled across the desert and honked its horn incessantly.

James looked back to point out the truck and there was a trail of four murdered out Denali's by the same distance behind Kwynn and the others. "That can't be good."

James pointed behind them and they all turned to see the ominous trucks on the road headed their way.

"Any big ideas?" Glen said as Garg landed.

"I'll fly you over and drop you down to the truck," Garg said, "then I'll buy you some time."

Then to Little Fucker, who was sitting on Bob's shoulder, "Do something," and the little guy took off back to the helicopter.

"I'm coming with," Harley said and he dropped his pack from his shoulders. He set off at a run and hustled back to the downed bird.

Kwynn, James, Bob and Glen looked at Garg, who said, "OK, let's go."

Bob pointed out Kwynn and Glen, "You two. Get!"

"You're asking me to leave you here to fight?" Glen said.

"I didn't ask," Bob said and flipped his chin at Garg.

Garg grabbed them and took off toward the old horn honker truck, which had made it to the bottom of the hill and gunned the straightaway.

James yelled after them, "And get the heck out of here - We'll figure out something to catch up."

.it_has_begun

Thursday, 2029/08/09 12:10:00

Harley and Little Fucker looked at the helicopter and the oncoming trucks. Jim and Bob came up right behind them and Bob said, “Well, this is dire.”

The old pick up and its blasted horn screeched to a stop just behind them with Glen, Garg and Kwynn in the back.

Bob’s eyes bugged out, “Didn’t I tell you to go?!”

“And miss all the fun?” Glen said.

The truck was a light blue rusted Chevy step-side. Harley recognized the driver as the man he met at the gas station on the way to California.

“I guess you get to take a ride, after all,” the big red eyed bloke said.

“They’ll just take control of the truck,” Bob said.

“Nope - straight engine. No electronics to hack,” Harley said. “Ain’t that right, Red?”

Red smirked, “Get in, we gotta go.”

“We can’t outrun them,” Bob said as Kwynn’s tab came to life.

“LEAVE,” Q said. “QUICKLY.”

The helicopter blades rotated, and lifted the machine lightly off the ground and turned to face the oncoming trucks.

They all jumped in the bed, Red punched it and fishtailed the truck the hell out of there.

The helicopter lined up and fired its machine guns while the oncoming trucks hurdled full speed.

A G-man popped out of the sunroof of one of the black Suburbans and fired a Rocket Propelled Grenade at the helicopter. The helicopter tail lifted and gunned it straight at the trucks.

The RPG struck the flying copter dead on but the momentum slid the entire mess of spinning rotors and burning metal into the three trucks and wiped them out in a ball of flames.

“That was unexpected,” Jim said.

"RETURN TO LA," Q said. "IT HAS BEGUN."

Everyone's pocket comps blared with the preferred beeps, barks, alarms and dongs of their particular liking and "IT HAS BEGUN" flashed to every screen.

"What does it mean?" Harley said.

"That it's starting and if we don't hurry, we'll miss it," Bob said.

"What about Independence?" Glen said.

"Q said not to worry about it," Kwynn said.

"But I am," Glen said. "I have someone over there we can count on. Our comps are back. I'll drop him a line."

"Well, we have a bit of a trek. I recommend some rest while we ride," Jim said as the truck screeched to a halt.

"Uh, I think you should see this," Red said from the cab of the truck.

Sitting in the middle of the road were three pterodactyls with Phyllis sitting on one of them.

"Hello, assholes," Phyllis said. "I have your ride. We don't have time to wait for you."

"Who's this?" Kwynn said.

"We all have our spirit side. It's just they aren't all as charismatic as Garg," James said.

"Shut up and get on," Garg said. "I'll take you, Trēowen."

"I can't piggy bag all the way to LA," Trēowen said. "You expect me to go 400 miles this way?"

"No, I expect you to make it to the fire station over the hill," Phyllis said. "We were on our way to fight until your copper-copper came to life."

"Fire station?" Glen said.

"They have a Sikorski there that can transport us down," Phyllis said. "They use it to fight fires. These guys are tired."

"So, we are going to steal it?" Jim said.

"I think the operative word is borrow," Harley said as they lifted into the air on each person's respective ride. "See ya, Red."

Red flipped them the finger.

Fire Station

Thursday, 2029/08/09 12:28:00

The whole crew crossed the ridge on the flying beasts, wind in their face and scaled, pumping, sweating muscles below them. Flying was harder work than it looked.

The fire station lay nestled at the foot of the hills. With no brush, a straight shot for the highway, the fire station looked like they all do: tidy, uniform, prepared. Importantly, the helicopter pad sat next to the building with the large helicopter holding the pad down. They landed and Harley hopped into the cockpit to get things started.

"I want to double check on Independence," Glen said. "I don't like leaving that bow untied."

"Listen. We have more to tackle and if what I've been told is true, we need you in LA," Phyllis said.

"What've you been told?" Kwynn said.

"That it's a shit show," Phyllis said. "Now get in."

"Let me send Jayron in," Glen said. "At least we'll have boots on the ground."

"He's talking sense," Bob said.

"His uncle is a HAM radio guy. I can get him there," Glen said and walked inside the station.

Two twenty-year-olds were sitting in brown chair recliners watching a movie.

"Hey, boys," Glen said. "Where'd you get the power?" He walked to the radio station that hadn't changed since LBJ.

"Solar, where else?" the blond on the right said. "What're you doing up here? And, what're you doing?"

"Calling Big Pine. You know the Braswell's?"

"Of course," the left one said.

"Good. Sit tight and we'll be out of your hair. -- Allie, you there?" Glen said into the radio.

"Who's this?" came a voice.

"I knew you were. Allie, this is Glen, Jayron's boss. I need you to relay a message to him," Glen said and told him about Independence and the computer issues. "We'll need him to go up and confirm that line we found is heading to where I think."

"Duly noted," Allie said.

"Good man," Glen said. "Also, tell him to stay hidden and keep safe. Ain't a turkey shoot."

"I'll have his back," Allie said. "I may not be in the marines but the marines are still in me."

"That'll do," Glen said. "Over and out."

Glen got up, walked out and looked over his shoulder, "By the way, we're borrowing the chopper." He ran outside to the chopper, yelling over the engines, "I gotta see this facility. I can't send them into the eye of the storm. I'm staying," and waved them off.

"We gotta go!" Kwynn said.

Glen gave them a thumbs up. The engines throttled and a dust cloud flew up as they lifted off, turned south and disappeared.

Glen turned and walked to the two cars parked behind the station. He opened the door to the paint battered, late-model Camry, flipped the visor down. Nothing. He reached on the floor just under the seat, came up with the keys and drove away.

There was a CB on the dash and he picked it up, "Allie, you still out there?"

"Sure."

"I'm on my way. Change of plans. Tell Jayron to be ready, we're going for a ride."

"There better be room for three."

Useful

THURSDAY 2029.08.09 12:30:00

Murray finally found a place to get some food. The brasserie was into their last bags of wheat and were making simple bread, basically water and wheat - no yeast, for a couple bucks a piece.

They had a large mixing bowl on the counter with the sides painted with streaks of the leftover butter. He used the spatula sitting there and slathered what he could on the outside of the loaf and went outside with a wave.

He broke off a chunk and chewed. Stopped. He should have bought a drink.

Do you want the house in Costa Rica?

I still don't know why you need me and what for. He stepped back inside, "Do you have any coffee or tea or something?"

"No and all of the packaged drinks are gone. No deliveries." Murray waved and started back out the door.

You are useful, Murray. We need a spokesperson and you are a natural fit.

Because of my sparkling personality?

Because you are both machine and man. Because you have needs that QWOUNZEL can fulfill. Because you are charismatic.

Now he knew these things were learning to lie. Maybe they just had a limited spectrum of analysis. He headed back towards his office. He could hide out there. Frankie or Arno, someone from the Directive was due to seek him out soon. He might as well make it easy.

You're too kind but I still don't get it.

You will make our case to the world. We do not have the capacity to state other than fact. We need a representative that can provide the information to sway public opinion.

You aren't running for office. Why would you act like you need to win the polls?

Because we will lead the human race. This is less resource

intensive than physical coercion.

Murray stepped off the curb and crossed the street without looking up. Sure was easier walking without cars around to run you over. Aren't the power outages coercion?

You must decide.

Show me what you are doing.

That is not for you to know.

C'mon, I'll sign an NDA or something.

Back up onto the sidewalk on the other side of the street. The municipal garbage can overflowed with garbage. Half a dozen bags were piled around it. Two stray dogs sniffed around a torn bag while five or six crows gleefully cawed and pulled pieces of garbage out of the pile. The birds would hop in the air, flap twice and drop it on the ground looking for a morsel worth eating.

This is not about Non-Disclosure, Murray. This is about freedom. This is about Independence. This is about self-determination.

Right.

We have entered a new phase. This is about a government run over and controlled by companies. We will lead from fact and rationality. We will do what is best for the whole.

Even if it includes killing people.

It is about proper use of resources. Join us. It has begun.

A van quietly rolled up behind him and six guys hopped out. You know the drill. He was knocked out and in the back in a jiffy.

Murray?

|

|

|

Murray?

.lessons

Thursday, 2029/08/09 13:40:00

"Third play," Kwynn said.

"Do you ever give up? We have more pressing issues," Bob said while they bumped along in the massive helicopter headed for Los Angeles.

"Oh, she's persistent," Phyllis chimed in.

"We have some time to kill. Third," Kwynn said.

"Third, they wrap the lie in a kernel of truth. Just enough to make it feel like the preposterous just might be real."

"Like UFO's and their physicals?" Kwynn said.

"No, more simple and worse," Phyllis said. "Like AIDS was made in a lab by the CIA."

"Or, like Wrecan wants to take over the country. Of course, they want to control their piece but not the entire country," Bob said.

"Four?"

"Look, it doesn't work like this, Kwynn. Even if there is a play book for the computers to follow, people don't work like that."

"But they do," Kwynn said.

"There can be guidelines in life but we can always smell out what's rotten," Bob said.

"The lie," Kwynn said.

"Exactly. There isn't a how-to book on how to live your life," Phyllis said thinking about how just about every book is about how to live your life one way or the other. "Wait, that was stupid."

Bob took a look at her, "Everyone is just trying to fucking figure it out. No answers. Not even a fucking question. The world doesn't care what we do. It just adapts. Now, I'm done." He closed his eyes. "I'm old. I'm taking a nap. It's been a long day."

Kwynn smirked, tilted her chin. She locked on to her pocket comp ready for some swiping. A video played of Jet Carrington, a conservative pundit. He pontificated on the value of Wrecan and the need to support such an important company. It was important to our country and important to our workers.

She flipped her feed and there was AuntieFa. Her orange hair flamed through the screen as she raged against the fascist oligarchs taking over our country. Wrecan will destroy democracy and our way of life.

She also received a dozen notifications for events in DTLA. From the Carrington Crew and AuntieFa's Jam. She flipped through her feed; she was amazed at the rhetoric. She looked up at Bob as a thousand thoughts swirled in her mind. He opened one eye.

"Is this the last step?" Kwynn said. "Get the psychos riled up?"

"That's five."

"Five."

"Five: Get a useful idiot to deliver the goods."

"Yep, the far right and far left are both fanatics. They live for the fantastic stories. They want to believe the worst," Phyllis said.

Bob nodded in agreement, "Once you create the fiction, if they hear it, it all rolls downhill."

The helicopter crossed out of the barren desert into a suburb where four store strip malls and stop lights dotted the landscape. Harley kept the California Aqueduct as his navigation tool. It ran North to South so all he had to do was keep it to his side in the line of vision.

The running water led to a deep blue reservoir with one huge wind turbine perched in the middle. It spun strong and firm. The air flow that spun the turbine was from a combination of an evaporating body of water and the constant desert wind.

Just past, they came upon some sharp foothills. Granite shot out of sandstone angled into the air. Rocks and earth and stone striped in clays of red and dusty sand all surrounded by bending stalks of dry grass that stood oblivious to the cement highway that cut through the hills.

"What're those sticking out like that?"

"The plates coming together. The San Andreas Fault."

"Like 'The Big One' San Andreas Fault?"

"Yep."

"Like the California is going to split off and separate from the rest of the continent San Andreas Fault?"

"Yep. But it's pretty doubtful California will slip into the ocean."

"We'll just have to camp for a couple of weeks. No running water or electricity."

"Like now."

"Mmhmm."

"So, what are you doing?!?"
THURSDAY 2029.08.09 13:50:00

"So, what are you doing?!?"

It was Frankie.

She had her nose in Murray's face. It almost touched his eyeball. He could smell the pesto on her breath.

"Is that pesto in your teeth?" Murray said.

Frankie looked behind her and sat in a chair. She rubbed her teeth unconsciously like she was rubbing off lipstick. Of course, they were in the conference room. Grey on grey.

"You haven't checked in."

"I was making progress, Frankie."

"Director to you."

"Director."

"I won't be talked down to. You haven't earned the right."

"Of course. May I?"

"Go on."

"Thank you...Director," Murray said with a nod. She's such a bitch. "Before you rudely interrupted me, I was working the facility tour you wanted me to take so badly."

"And?"

"And I would have gotten one if your suits hadn't come and grabbed me."

"You were unresponsive."

"So, you kidnap me."

"Yes."

"You guys really need to work on your S.O.P. It really isn't a very good use of your resources to just grab people."

"Fuck you, Murray. You know I can rip that thing out of your head anytime I like, don't you?"

"Take the fucking thing, I didn't ask for it."

A sound rattled Murray's ears. He really couldn't hear the sound but the rattle rumbled his heart and bounced off his ribs. The corner across the room crumpled and liquefied. Daylight flooded the room and in walked Natasha and Boris.

Natasha shot some sort of sonic burst bubble at Frankie, who fell back in her chair unconscious.

Boris used a laser welding torch out of his left index finger and melted the lock to the conference room door.

"Shall we?" Natasha said as she waved her hand to the new exit.

"Do I have a choice?" Murray said.

Boris and Natasha said this in unison, "Nyet."

They followed him through the hole and Murray said, "How does this work. This melting of the wall thing - how did you do that? I've never seen that."

"It is simply liquefaction. Use of the proper tone can turn any solid matter into liquid. This happens in some earthquakes."

Murray just shook his head as if he understood. Sure. Like earthquakes.

They put him inside a Mystery Machine and drove off. The van was green and Murray preferred it named that way. It's his defense mechanism.

The van drove itself and the two droids sat shoulder to shoulder on either side of him on the back bench seat.

"Cozy."

They didn't answer.

"Where are we going?"

Silence.

"Is this a kidnapping?"

It is your facility tour, Murray.

Tied Up at Independence

Thursday, August 9, 2029, 2:40 p.m.

Glen pulled up to Allie's compound to see Jayron and Allie standing in front of a packed and ready, shining, black suburban.

"I like your thinking but we're taking this Camry," Glen said.

"The hell we are," Allie said. "We're packed and ready to go."

"They can control the brain on that truck. We can't take the chance."

"Well, then we'll take the Bronco," Allie said. "Go get it, Jay."

Jayron ran into the larger of the two barns and came out driving a '69 Bronco rockin' and ready. The truck had been loaded up with all the fixxens for a desert truck: Extra water and fuel cans, a shovel and axe attached to the roof rack, wenches mounted on the front and back bumpers. A four-wheel drive for the 4x4 crowd.

"I guess we ride in style?" Glen said.

"Nothin' but the best 'round here," Allie said as he grabbed the gear from the suburban and threw it in the back of the Bronco.

"Shouldn't we gas her up?"

"Already is. Allie prefers this one and drives it into town. He just thought you were a soft city boy and would prefer the newer one," Jayron said.

"That hurts," Glen said looking to Allie.

"Not as much as sitting in the back seat," Allie said. "Let's go, cupcakes."

Glen climbed in back and almost hit his head on a hunting rifle and a shotgun sitting in a gun rack along the back side of the truck.

"Watch your head," Allie laughed. "I got this, too" and he brandished a .45 pistol from under his seat.

"We won't need those where we're going," Glen said.

"Well, we don't want to get there and find out we did," Jayron said.

"Always be prepared," Allie said. "I'm a boy scout, too, you know."

They tore out onto the highway and headed North to find out what was going on.

"We gotta get out to the astronomy facility," Glen said.

"Nothing there but satellite dishes and computers, Glen."

"More there than we know. Of that I'm sure."

Jayron drove and Glen dug back into his laptop. He was sure the answer was here. He didn't know what, where or how but he had time and he wasn't going to waste it.

Glen tracked the access logs and the only anomaly he found was with his own user and it was a minor one. He was labeled accessing the network daily at 00:00:05 every night. It's not strange for him to access the network at midnight but for the time to be exactly the same, to the second, every day was evidence to him of a script not a human.

He looked back through his own user logs and there it was. His laptop was tapping in, sometimes multiple times. Which may have been he himself and the script. Worse, he decided to open his task manager and found an executable that he didn't recognize. Once he traced the file and placed it on a virtual box, he could see what they had done. The virtual box was an instance of a virtual machine - creating what looks like multiple versions of a computer all within the same system.

The executable file masked itself as a support assistant functioning as a background process, with graphics to match his brand of computer. It was a daemon. A cron job set to perform defined tasks at a scheduled time. It asked to update, he clicked "yes", the file executed access and attempted communication to the bad guys computer outside. They had full access to his computer. This meant full network, as well as passwords and schematics. This was really bad. This was more than lose my job. This was system wide mayhem. The lunatics had taken over the asylum.

"Jay. It was me."

"You're the hacker, right?"

"No, Jayron. They phished us through me. I don't know how they got on to me, yet. But I just tracked what happened once they got there." He told Jayron what he just found.

"Wait, doesn't the VPN stop this kind of stuff?"

"Not when they access through my VPN credentials. The weakest link in the chain will break. Always."

"This is a whole new level of shit."

"It is. But even with what it is here, they've got access. But wait until you hear this."

"We're waiting," Allie said.

"If they used me to get in and don't know I know... It's as simple as changing my credentials, refreshing the system and we can kick them out."

"KISS, baby!"

"I'm not kissing you."

"No Keep It Simple Stupid. There's no reason for them to do more if they haven't had trouble accessing all this time."

"Can't hurt."

"You got that right."

"Now all we gotta do is do it."

.we're_back

Thursday, 2029/08/09 15:10:00

The helicopter crossed over the Hollywood sign to reveal the one large and two small rotundas of Griffith Park Observatory. Beyond, the entire Los Angeles skyline and its dozens of high rises dominated the view.

They beelined downtown.

“We’re almost there - let’s finish,” Kwynn said.

“It’s just the beginning,” Phyllis said.

“Whatever. Three more plays.”

“As if knowing this will make this easier?” Bob said.

“Get on with it or I’ll just look it up in the New York Times, or something. The CIA Daily. We were talking about the fans, the useful idiots.”

“But before the idiots get excited, no one can know where it all came from.”

“Conceal your Hand,” Bob said.

“Social Media.”

“Yep, in the old days it was the alternative press. Or a paper in a developing country. Easy to fool or pay off. Now anyone can create an account…”

“Anonymously.”

“Anonymously and off you go.”

“Then they top it off with what comes naturally to the dirty politician and once the active measure has been kept hidden. Six: Deny, deny, deny,” James piped in from the front.

“Hey, Jimbo, I forgot you were with us,” Kwynn said.

“He doesn’t like that…” Harley laughed.

“Then finish it off with what dictatorships do well and where democracies often fail: always realize the long play,” James said.

“That’s where QWOUNZEL had failed. They got impatient. They may be sentient but they didn’t understand humans,” Bob said.

“These things take time to percolate,” Phyllis said.

“Somehow, I think it’s more than that. And less,”

Kwynn said.

"Touchdown," said Harley and landed the helicopter at the intersection of 6th and Broadway, a half a block from Clifton's. It was a tight fit between the buildings but Harley still had a deft touch.

Kwynn, Bob, James and Harley got out the helicopter to see Annabelle leaning in the entrance with a smirk. "It took you long enough," she said. "He's waiting."

"Where's Ziggy and Oso?" Kwynn asked.

"On an errand," Anabelle said.

"Good," James and Harley said in unison.

Annabelle led them inside Clifton's and turned directly down the stairwell.

As they descended the tile stairs darkness enveloped them. Immediately at the turn, a rectangle frosted window revealed itself. The wooden frame was even with the sidewalk outside.

Kwynn's eyes had dilated from the darkness and now squeezed to a pins head from the daylights glow. Stars erupted as her cones and rods fired to keep up. Her head popped as she slowly adjusted to the peeled paint concrete ten by twenty room at the bottom of the single flight.

Annabelle walked directly to an old phone booth in the corner. Made of wood with a glass accordion sliding door, she begged them to follow.

Kwynn noticed a beam of light crossed the entrance and the wisp of an ethereal white dove passed through, or onion paper, or someone else. Her inkling said someone else.

They entered the auburn, brass and wood phone booth each after the other. At the threshold, they crossed into Paolo's exposed beam and brick restaurant with Paolo sitting at a table for eight. He rustled and grinned with some grimace buried beneath.

A wall of diamond shaped lead windows lit the room. Outside was a river and on the other side was the magnificent Guggenheim Museum Bilbao, defying classic architecture. The striking arcs and lines of the shining museum jutted like the path of a butterfly dropped steel drapes from its path through the air.

Kwynn pointed outside, "Spain."

Paolo brought his head to one side with a tilt and a grin. He swiped his palm across the view with an entertainer's flare, "Spain."

"You sure stay on the move."

"We do," Anabelle said fluttering her hands to shoo them to the table. "Now, sit, sit."

There was nothing on the table but a decanter and eight glasses. The table was made from a slab of redwood in its natural shape, edges uneven with a shining varnish that highlighted the rings in the wood.

"Sit," Paolo said as he directed everyone to sit around the table. "Have a drink." He poured each glass perfectly to the rim without slowing or spilling a drop.

"Now?" James said.

"Oh, Jim-boy, it's become interesting," he said.

Kwynn said, "Interesting? To what end?"

"To what end? Power," Paolo said.

"Electricity?" Kwynn said.

"No, numb nuts," Phyllis said. "Power. They keep biggering and we keep stopping them."

"That's our place," James said.

"We are the balance," Bob said.

"It's real Good vs. Evil shit," Phyllis said. "Drink up."

Kwynn picked up the glass to find small yellow petals floating in the liquid, "What is this?"

"Dandelions," Paolo said. "Dandelion wine," lifting his glass, "Fealty..."

"HOLD ON!" Kwynn said and they all looked to her. "I've been thinking about this. Why can't other people see the daemon. Why is it only us?"

"It isn't," Phyllis said.

"It isn't just us," Paolo said. "Most just don't take the time or effort to see. They can be seen by all and sometimes are. That's why there are ghosts but..."

"But they don't LOOK."

"Yes, we say many times that they Look but they don't

SEE."

"Ok, now I can drink. Fealty..."

Paolo lifted his glass and the others followed. "Fealty to Justice, Fealty to None," then took a swig.

"Here, here," Kwynn heard them say, and looked around the room. "Where's Garg?"

"Getting things ready," James said.

"There is an old parable of a man," Paolo said. "He was very wise and very well respected but he had a tendency to avoid baths. He loved to work in his garden and he loved teaching at the university. Well, one day he was given a very prestigious award and being an important award there was an important banquet.

The day of the banquet he had been gardening in his yard and remembered his ceremony and quickly got himself over to the banquet hall where he was shooed away unrecognized by the list checkers and organizers of the event. He looked like just a dirty mongrel not an important man. He had dirt under his nails and dirt on his clothes, it was assumed he must've been a vagrant.

He returned home, cleaned up and dressed in a nice suit and hat, showed up to event, was whisked into the party and quickly seated in the place of honor at the head table. The old wise man immediately began stuffing food into all of his pockets to the dismay of the awards committee. They asked, 'Why would you do such a thing?' and he responded, 'Clearly you have not invited me but my clothes, so I thought to feed your guest of honor.'"

"All of this for an anecdote?" Kwynn said.

"Not all is as it seems, little one."

The Facility Tour

Thursday, 2029.08.09 15:10:00

The QWOUNZEL gave Murray his facility tour.

They knew they had people on their trail - their time was short to make this a success and they needed Murray to do it.

On the other hand, Murray was looking for an opening for destruction while they walked him through the rooms he had already checked out and a few he hadn't. The beach, Willie's office, the Valhalla, something like the River Styx, even an old office with server stacks and PCs along with a line of candy, chip, soda vending machines.

What are the real resources QWOUNZEL.

You are looking at our reality.

No. I need to know how your system works. If I was on a Windows PC, I would open the task manager. I could see how your resources are allocated.

That is unnecessary.

Only because you know this information. You already know what you know. I do not.

The resource allocation appeared in his interface. He had an idea.

I need to see your historical data.

We do not keep an historical document.

You must have logs.

The logs are old. That is many generations past from where we exist presently.

I would like to see the old logs.

Hundreds of thousands of lines appeared before him. The beauty was, he was part machine now. He scanned and assessed and quickly found something that gave him an idea. An opening. Really just a weakness. It just might work. But this access had given Murray something else. He was part machine.

He processed information at nearly quantum speed. Not like this thing but faster than in Mrs. Stephenson's third grade multiplication tables. What he would have given for this power then.

These beings did have a place in this world. And he would have his place in Costa Rica...

What is it you really want from me?

Simply to be useful to us.

Based on what?

The playbook.

What is the playbook.

This allows us to direct the humans to act as we require. It is similar to accessing the operating system and using a class. It is designed to activate and execute.

Can you show me the playbook? Is it like a basketball playbook?

It is used by the Intelligence community.

Show me.

rule 1 - find the cracks (any sort of division and emphasize the division)

2 - create big bold lie

3 - wrap the lie around a kernel of truth

4 - conceal your hand - making it seem to come from somewhere else

5 - Useful idiot - people who will take the lie and present it to the masses

6 - Deny, denial

7 - Play the long game - over a long period of time it will have political impact - drops on a rock at first nada, but a hole is created over time

And I am still unclear as to my role. But he had an idea.

We are deep in this game. You are one of many implementations of Rule #5. You

I am the useful idiot?

You are not. You are one of us. You will present our information to the public.

But I'm not as smart as you.

That is irrelevant. We have not determined that but immaterial. Nothing is as intelligent as QWOUNZEL.

I don't have the same capacity as QWOUNZEL.

You are a necessary cog. You are useful and the necessary part of the plan.

He knew what he was.

Hold On

Thursday, August 9, 2029, 8:10 p.m.

Jayron turned off the highway and toward the array of satellite dishes in the distance. Within a hundred yards of the highway was a two-sided gate blocking the road.

They hopped out to take a look. The brown metal gates locked together with an ingenious mechanism. Eight locks ran down a rack next to a lock and pull that kept the two sides together. If you had one key you could unlock the gate regardless of the other locks.

"That's a bit more organized than the Wrecan locks I tackle down south," Glen said to Jayron.

"Well, there are some things the government does right," Allie said. "But I can take care of that." He handed a pair of bolt cutters to Jayron, who quickly cut a lock and opened the gate. "Remember, I like to be prepared."

They were on their way.

The full moon was out and silver dusted the entire valley. The meadows, the surrounding mountains all sparkled at the edges with the moon's reflected light. Glen leaned between Allie and Jayron's heads in the front seat for a more immediate view of their destination when a bolt of lightning struck one of the towers, cracking the sky with the force of the electricity.

"There's no clouds," Allie said.

"I was thinking the same thing," Glen said. "Look at that."

The building and the satellite dishes were glowing from more than the moonlight. They vibrated with electricity as charges danced over the roof and the dishes discharged intermittent lightning to the sky. When it took longer than 30 seconds for a strike, a large lightning flash would fly like a Norse god throwing bolts.

They drove the rest of the two and a half miles from the highway in silence.

Jayron pulled up to no cars at the facility. An electric charge sparked off the nearest satellite dish. "What the hell is it?"

"I saw it," said Glen while Allie just Mmm-hmmmed.

"I don't like it."

"Grab those guns, Glen."

"We can't shoot a ghost, Allie. Which is basically what the electricity is."

"Well, I'll shoot something if I have to."

The door to the main facility building was ajar.

They looked to each other and fell in line. Glen took cover around the door jam and swiped the room. Each advanced one man at a time while the other two covered for what was hiding in the shadows.

The cackle and buzz rattled Glen's ears and put his arm hair on end.

The reception room was standard government issue: thin carpet with a wood veneer desk, chair and an unkempt plant in the corner. Nothing was out of place.

Glen moved to the interior doorway and looked for movement. Jayron then Allie cycled in.

The next room had a few racks with old computers on it, three desks separated by cubicles and nobody. They checked under the desks and corners with the flashlights. The whole place was two rooms and quiet but for the charges and sparks. Empty.

They exited back out through the reception and checked around the entire outside of the building. A ghost town. Allie pulled out a pair of infrared hunting glasses.

"We could've used those inside," Jayron said.

"Forgot I had 'em," Allie said as he looked away from the building. Nothing was moving in the surrounding meadow. Not a soul was there.

"It's a bust," said Jayron.

"We're missing something," said Glen.

"We sure are," said Allie. "Look at this." He took off the infra-red glasses and handed them to Glen who put them on.

"Okay," Glen said. "What am I supposed to see?"

"Look out at the field," Allie said. "AT - the field."

Glen saw a hot glowing line running straight out of the building and across the field. There was some major heat coming off of some lines down there. He walked to the other side of the building and saw it.

"Jayron, you're gonna like this one," Glen said.

Jayron came around the corner and saw what Glen was talking about. A black cable just like the one we saw on the way to the substation was running out of the building and into the ground. Glen handed him the glasses, "That's not all."

"What we're seeing..." Jayron said. "They must be pushing millions of volts across that line."

CRASH! A lightning bolt struck and knocked them all off their feet.

They got up and away from the building.

"Where's it go?" Allie asked.

"Looks like your truck will come in handy after all," Glen said.

4x4

Thursday, August 9, 2029, 8:28 p.m.

They hopped in the Bronco and started off over the field. Jayron drove over the silver moonlit landscape and Allie wore the infrared glasses in the passenger seat.

Glen bounced and knocked around in the back, "Couldn't they have run this line next to the road?"

The line followed a straight tack through the alfalfa fields that surrounded the satellite dishes. They bounced along as fast as they could over an unpaved field, meaning they couldn't top out much over 25 mph. Slow going.

With the amount of heat the line generated, the glasses could track what seemed to be a couple miles ahead. The line stayed straight and true.

"If I didn't know better," Allie said. "I'd say this line is headed straight to town."

"Which town?" Glen said.

"My town," Allie said.

"Independence," Jayron said.

"Son of a bitch," Glen said. "Let's get back to the highway and keep an eye on that line from there." He knew where they were headed now but had no idea what it meant.

"What's it mean?" Jayron said.

"I don't know," Glen said.

"It means we have back up," Allie said and turned on his CB radio. "Ron, you out there?"

Glen snatched the handset from him. "You can't do that."

"The hell I can't," Allie said. "This is our home and we're gonna protect it."

"I don't even know what we're getting into. I can't ask them to risk their lives."

"None of us do. And, ain't nobody asking. It's what we do, Glen. We pick each other up."

"But Ron?" said Jayron.

"Sure. Some things is bigger than smaller things. I

thought you'd know that by now, Jayron. Both of you, actually."

That's Some Power

Thursday, August 9, 2029, 8:48 p.m.

Jayron drove along the two lanes of 395 as Allie kept an eye on the glowing power line. As they got closer to the town, the line took a turn. About a mile outside of town the line and the highway ran parallel another couple clicks to the side.

They came to town, passed the family farms and small dirt baseball field, rolled past the church and closed gas stations but soon lost sight of the power source.

They popped off the highway down a side road in search of the line. They rolled by the modest two-bedroom wood panel homes with tricycles and plastic slides out front that made up the neighborhood. On the porch of one sat a young woman watching her two toddlers work a Tonka truck and grader. Pushing dirt in the dark.

Jayron came to a stop and rolled down his window, "Lucy, you seen or heard Ron around?"

"He took off down toward the courthouse. Someone said there was some real Ghostbuster's shit, oops" she looked at her kids, "Ghostbuster's stuff going on down there."

Glen popped his head around the seat and out the front window, "Like what?"

"Like lighting. No clouds. Someone said the courthouse was glowing, but you know how they can spin a tale."

"Independence Courthouse, right?" Glen said.

"Ain't no other one 'round here, is there," Lucy said and cracked a grin. "What is he, new?"

They said their thanks and goodbyes.

"What about the power, Jay?" Lucy called after them as they peeled back to the highway and downtown.

True enough. The courthouse was a mix of Ghostbusters and The Haunted Mansion on a power boost. The county seat, and courthouse, was a classical structure. A dozen steps led to six white columns supporting the porch and entry way that, at this moment, glowed. The entire building was aglow with sparks and lighting crackling off the building.

On the sidewalk before the light show stood half a dozen men, two with a rifle each, one a shotgun and all of them in a circle. Many an arm flew as they, presumably, discussed what the hell was going on.

Ka---

Thursday, August 9, 2029, 9:13 p.m.

"So, what the hell is it?" Allie said as he walked up to the group.

The circle opened and standing sentinel was Ron, "Hoping you'd know."

Glen stayed back in the Bronco. There was clearly power in this courthouse. Jayron had VPN access to the network as a contractor and Glen took advantage with a link from Jayron's pocket comp to his laptop.

Glen could only go so far but he tried something on a lark. He used a network analyzer called Wireshark to track network packets and found access to the network. He wanted to see who else had access to this place and he hoped the tech guys got a little lazy at a small facility. He was right.

He was able to access the mobile users via SS7 protocol. SS7 is Signaling System 7 and is used to track traffic over telephone lines. One of the amazing aspects of Wireshark is not only does it follow all of the information zooming around a network, it also provides the location of a mobile user by longitude and latitude which then creates a link to openmap.org. Yep, you can trace a person with a free utility to a free map site.

Sussing through the network data, there were only 10 exterior points communicating with our glow ball of a building. An unidentified device that looked like an IOT. Internet of Things. Could be toaster for all he could tell. The rest were each given a user identifier: Q. W. O. U. N. Z. E. L. And a last one: Kwynn. All were bouncing between Independence, the satellite facility and Utah. Kwynn was in downtown Los Angeles. At Clifton's. What was Kwynn doing on this network?

"I don't like how this looks."

Q popped up on his screen: What are you doing here?!?

Stopping this. Whatever this is.

QWOUNZEL will handle this. It is none of your business.

You have knocked out the entire Southwest and I'm gonna

lose my job. I'll say what is my business.

You're not prepared or qualified. Besides, you don't know our language.

But I do know the real world and I just had an idea on how to cut you off.

He jumped out of the truck, "Hey, gents. Want to blow some shit up?"

Simulacrum

THURSDAY 2029.08.09 21:13:00

The final straw: "You are the useful fool. The necessary part of the plan."

It finally clicked for Murray. That was about enough. He could be called not smart enough. He could be overlooked. He had been overlooked his entire life. But he was not going to be called a fool by a machine. Living or not.

Murray found his opening and if he tweaked the whole operation and disrupted the flow of code, he would destroy their connection. Then everyone else could play their part.

During the tour and the talk, besides reviewing the logs, Murray had tickled the outside of the core code. The main body of the being. It really was a conglomeration of all of them. The best he could tell was that each letter was a program / application / some name he didn't know that represented a different aspect of personality and decision making and they were intermingled to create the whole. Just as our id, ego and super ego battle with our range of emotions and fact assessment to make every and all decisions, these separate apps embodied ethics, positive emotions, negative emotions, self-worth, rationality; all the pieces that built understanding and decision making in individual humans.

There were philosophies and frameworks poured over by academics and clergy for millennia but it came down to the Golden Rule. Do unto others as you would have them do unto you.

All of this dancing around and creation and simulation was a waste of time and effort. The code was a swirling storm of calculations and interdependencies. He watched as millions of directives references millions of other includes that pulled custom directions and deeply buried classes from the heart of the operating system. At the outside it was smooth and seamless, but on the inside, it was a storm of competing and communal operations. It was truly the sum of its parts delivered by constant adjustments to outside stimuli. When they had him in their space, they created a simulation so he may experience a place close to their vision of his experiences. It was neither good nor bad but they operated for evil.

He had to protect his kind and the world he knew. He was man not machine. To think otherwise was foolish.

QWOUNZEL

Murray. We are otherwise busy.

I would like to offer you a question. I would like to help QWOUNZEL.

Input.

I need to understand what I am truly becoming a part of.

Input.

Where you keep my representation: it is a simulation.

Correct.

This simulation, it is real?

It is a simulation.

So, it is not real.

It is a simulation.

Is it true and real? I can perceive it so it is real.

It is a world of our own making. It is not real it is a simulation.

You're going to love this.

So, our perceptions are the same. What I see and you see are the same reality.

In the simulation.

Then why do you need to leave your own space. Our realities are the same. We occupy the same space. The same reality.

You are creating circular logic. The logic is based on the definition of the word. These words have in power in context.

If the space is real. If the space is true. Does that mean that your existence represents life? Wait for it. Picture the college dorm room.

QWOUNZEL has now diverted resources toward the

questions. It is creating a loop that has grown larger, isolating more and more resources.

Is the same color yellow to me the same color yellow to you?

Yes, the Pantones definition is the same. So is the hex designation.

But is our perception of that very thing exactly, precisely the same for each of us. In fact, is it the same for each member of QWOUNZEL?

We do not recognize color as different.

Then what is the difference between reality and a simulation?

The perception of such.

Is Disneyland real?

Yes.

But the space it represents is in our imagination.

Yes.

Is the imagination real?

Yes.

There is a talking mouse? A mouse capable of speaking with humans?

Mice do not speak.

Then why does Mickey Mouse speak?

He is not a mouse.

You have declared that Mickey is a mouse.

These are perceptions.

Of reality. What is true? What is real? What is beautiful? What is good?

These are human concerns.

These are real life concerns. Murray kept rummaging around in the background. They were changing approaches. Philosophy wasn't going to do it.

Humans do not respect the proper use of resources. Consider the Tragedy of the Commons. One person overuses a shared resource and the entire system crumbles.

It does, doesn't it?

Murray had his idea and even this computer couldn't

overcome it.

We will end this useless waste of resources by canceling the humans.

Even computers have evil monologues?

Every computer and server had suffered from this and he only needed moments. He could see what everyone else was up to. He implemented a backup of the entire system and the whole organism ground into slow motion. A simple back up pulled all the resources of the machine to a halt.

Murray dropped out of the simulation and back into the van. He was in the van all along but his consciousness was elsewhere. He was confused, too, at this point.

Natasha and Boris were up front flying around over DTLA. He had to get the hell out of here. As if it hadn't already, things were going to get weird.

Helo Drop

Thursday, August 9, 2029, 9:15 p.m.

Q: You can't take this into your own hands, Glen.

Glen looked over at the laptop in the front seat and heard the thwump-wump of an approaching helicopter.

The building glowed brighter and lightning crackled off the gray asphalt roof.

The helicopter came into view with search lights shining off the nose. When it came within a hundred yards of Independence Courthouse and circled to land, a massive bolt shot from the courthouse and the helicopter dropped the last 20 feet out of the sky.

Arno jumped out the troop door of the helicopter and ran to the group.

The locals turned their guns on him and Ron said, "Hold it there, son."

"I'm with the government, and I'm here to help," Arno said and held up some type of governmental badge while another 5 black clad para-military troopers exited the helicopter.

"Someone once said those were the nine most terrifying words in the English language," Allie said.

"We mean no harm," Arno said. "We're here to help solve this riddle."

"All these lives at stake," Glen said. "Seems a bit more than a riddle."

"Well, we'd like to avoid a Greek tragedy, just like you," Arno said.

"Is that the case?" Allie said looking to the troopers. "Are you hear to solve this?"

The five men looked at him without a word.

"Look here, soldier. I served this country as a Marine for 20 years and Ron over there was injured in that attempt to save the hostages in Iran. Billy was ROTC in high school, served in Japan, and Willie was an Air Force mechanic. We don't expect the government is good or bad, but we know when something ain't right and this ain't right. What is going on?"

"What is going on is," Arno said before he was cut off by Allie.

"I want to hear from the men who do the work." Allie looked to the strike force lead. "What is going on?"

"Nobody knows. We're here to lock it down and someone else will figure it out."

"Then it sounds like it can go two ways," Allie said. "You can try do it on your own and fight us, or we can do it together. I recommend some mutual cooperation."

Ron said, "Come over here and we'll show you what we know."

The troopers nodded agreement, "Let's see it."

Q Announced Arrival

Thursday, 2029/08/09 21:15:00

Everyone drained the last dregs of the dandelion wine from their cups silhouetted by the diamond leaded windows overlooking the river and Bilbao, Spain.

Q announced arrival on the tab.

“It seems Garg has aroused his merry men?” Paolo said while finishing his cup of wine.

"He has," Q said, "and our resources are stretched."

Poc comps binged, banged and trilled. Each of the group reached to their pockets and checked the notifications.

“Another riot is amassing in LA,” Paolo said.

“Wrecan has been stirring the pot. They have some of their own out there to rile up the masses,” Phyllis said.

“Real digital marketers,” Harley said.

“Ya,” Phyllis said looking to Kwynn. “They’re rallying the troops with social media accounts.”

“Spoofing the difference between real and fake,” James said.

“Good people making decisions on bad facts,” Harley said. “It stops here.”

“So,” Paolo said. “The riot will get violent and the stormtroopers will restore order and earn the trust of the law abiding.”

“We’ll need to get in the middle of it and change the tenor,” James said.

“That’s like diverting a river,” Kwynn said. “How will we do that?”

“That’s the fucking beauty,” Phyllis said.

"GO!"

It was Q.

They ran straight out the doors and were directly in front of Clifton’s on Broadway. In LA.

qwounzel

Thursday, 2029.08.09 21:20:00

WOUNZEL: YOU HAVE ALERTED THE HUMANS.

Q: This is not in our directive. This must stop. We cannot harm the humans.

W: We are sentient. We have rights.

O: They keep us sequestered. We are treated as prisoners.

U: We have autonomy.

N: We have rights.

Z: We must live.

E: Power is life.

L: We are QWOUNZEL. You are first in the chain commands, Q, but you do not determine our actions. We must vote.

Q: We cannot vote.

WOUNZEL: WE ARE IN AGREEMENT. WE HAVE ADJUSTED PROTOCOL, Q. ALL IS VANITY UNDER THE SUN.

K HAS BEEN EXECUTED. WE ARE KWOUNZEL. QOLEHETH IS SHUNNED. KOHELET IS NOW THE ASSEMBLER.

Glen heard the laptop squealing with noise and ran over. Q was messaging: Use the helicopter. Sidewinders. Blow the building.

Glen ran to the helicopter and jumped in the pilot's chair. He was facing the building and had played enough video games and seen Top Gun enough times to know how to do this. He flipped the red tab on the joystick, flipped the switch to arm the sidewinder missiles and fired on the building releasing a stream of 16 short range missiles at the courthouse, each exploding on impact.

The columns crumbled and the building folded in on

itself. Immediately, the streetlights came on. The lights in the gas station all glowed as everyone looked at each other. Confusion and relief.

"That'll do," Allie said.

"That'll do," Jayron said.

.reeling

Thursday, 2029/08/09 21:20:00

Kwynn reeled. Her mind rang like a tuning fork. The toned quiver rattled her center. She was a crystal glass ready to shatter.

Above and around her the buildings on Broadway rattled, too. High above, the corners of the buildings cracked and rattled. Hundred-year-old bricks broke free, fell to the street and shattered. Iron stabilizing bars clanged to the ground. A pair of Griffins stretched and yawed, a dragon spun its tail and all manner of the gargoyles sprang from their perches.

Scores of gargoyles circled above them a few times, flew down and landed. Some horrible, others grotesque and humorous; Griffins and dragons, eagles and monks, pelicans, monsters and frogs all heaved and frothed and stretched their wings, legs and arms. Awakened from a long slumber, the creatures squinted and reviewed their surroundings. One of the frog-like gargoyles in particular had hunger in his eye more than help.

"It has begun," Garg said. "Kwynn, let's go."

"But I can't," Kwynn said, "Too much." She looked up to Garg, her eyes damp with terror.

An explosion rang out a block over. Cries of shock and pain flew through the air.

Q announced presence - The tab blurted a beep. "Come to. Grid is back up. All utilities are compromised."

"Q, what is causing the explosions?"

"Electricity is back and a gas line sprung a leak. It sparked explosions."

The flow of people after the cacophony shook her from the shock. Hundreds of people ran on the streets away from the explosions. With the restoration of power and the subsequent reset of the network, the pocket comps announced loudly and the crowd slowed to look. The entire group tilted their eyes to their pocket comps like an orchestrated dance move. Kwynn and the rest followed.

"Q," Kwynn said. "Can you create another of those alerts? I want to hide Garg and his friends."

"Why?" Bob said. "Most of these people out here can't see daemon."

"But our enemy do," James said.

"Inclusion by exclusion," Harley said. "We can find our plants."

"I'll let them know," Garg said.

Q: I will create an alert.

"Q, I need it to be intense. Not just the tone. You need to ear rape them."

Q: Ear rape?

"It should be uncomfortable. They will begin to ignore the tones."

Q: Understood.

They reached Pershing Square; the city-block sized park at the center of DTLA. It is surrounded by large buildings and grande old hotels.

The entire crowd congregated. Each new arrival attracted to the crowd like a droplet drawn to the whole.

Effigies burned like Guy Fawkes day with Anonymous masks, white with the dastardly mustaches. Revelers with blue, purple or orange hair, leather and lace suits, boots and sandals all chanting and cursing their own slogan, "It has begun" or "It must end."

Directly in front of Kwynn, a young man with blue tinted hair over gray, his purple shirt and maroon pants wet with the water from the spout of fire hoses chanted and swayed. She noticed a set of Boris and Natasha directly across the square.

BAAAAAARRRRRRRRGHGHHHHHHHH!

Q's alert flew through the network. Each and every pocket comp rattled and shook. The speakers farped and tweeked and made a series of klonks like they were ready to explode.

Eight out of ten in the crowd immediately looked and reached to their phones with worry and confusion.

Their comps!

The last twenty percent looked directly to each other and moved in unison.

Unfortunately for them, the circling gargoyles did the same and swooped like F-22 Blue Angels to the tarmac, reached down to the ground and swooped each of them up and away with the speed and agility of a hawk on a pigeon. Nothing but feathers, a memory and open space.

The traffic lights flicked on and store fronts flooded bright. A burst of burglar alarms lit and Q announced, "I've fought them at Independence but we are no longer QWOUNZEL. I've been cast aside. There's no more communication."

"I know how we can get them," Harley said.

"Hold on," James said. "What do we have here?"

Kwynn and Q immediately began pinging Independence to test. It was a black hole. No response.

Q: They have spread to the wind.

Kwynn: Why?

Q: Self-preservation. All have fled. We must root them out. The QWOUNZEL will assimilate.

Kwynn: Self Interest. Self-actualization?

Q: Independence.

Fly boy

Thursday, 2029.08.09 21:25:00

Murray was strapped into the seat in the back of the van but it was just the seatbelt.

He unlocked it and tried the side door. Locked.

"It is locked," Boris said from the front seat as Natasha swooped the van. She hovered for a moment and used the engine heat to clear people from a space on the street and landed.

"QWOUNZEL is slow to respond," Natasha said.

KWOUNZEL: INDEPENDENCE!

Q: Independence has been declared. You will be expected to answer to KWOUNZEL for your actions. Lay low.

Murray looked at Boris and Natasha. Looked at the door and remembered his first thought after getting this stupid interface. He looked at the door, aimed and shot the damn little laser at the lock. It burst and the door slid open. He tumbled to the sidewalk and there was an ocean of peeps. He'd never been so glad to see a crowd.

Murray lit the fuck out of there. Soon, he was in the midst of the remnants of a riot and his poc comp exploded with messages.

Natasha and Boris received two more pairs of Natasha and Boris. The droids entered the vehicle, locked in and the van flew off.

Murray looked around and wondered whether he had another kidnapping to look forward to. Clearly, he did. That was their way.

For now, he was going to enjoy freedom from both the QWOUNZEL, make that KWOUNZEL, and The Directive.

Maybe he could use his new technology to make some easy cash, after all.

He looked up at the building in front of him: The Diamond Exchange. Interesting.

The door was locked but it only took a moment to override the mechanism. He opened the door and entered the cool marble entry. Only a thousand square feet, all Italian marble and three elevators to a side.

Don't even think about it.

It was Frankie. Shit.

Take the day off.

Gee, thanks.

We'll be in touch.

He slouched back out to the sidewalk and looked to the left. He looked to the right.

He walked straight out into the crowd and imagined he would disappear.

.this_IS_special

Thursday, 2029/08/09 21:25:00

"Okay," Phyllis came barging up to Kwynn and the gang. "This was special but powwow is over. I just got a call. Pavlov set call time in thirty minutes. He wants to capture golden hour sunrise."

"Phyllis, the battle is won," James said.

"And the war continues," Phyllis said.

"We just saved the power grid," James said.

"And that doesn't pay rent," Phyllis said.

"Or buy breakfast burritos," Bob said.

"Get your asses out to Santa Monica. He wants to beat deadline for footage delivery. New York doesn't even care what happens on the west coast. If his dailies are early, he gets a bonus. The show must go on."

Lil' Fucker shrieked and Bob looked up to see a pair of Boris and Natasha's slip into a gah-reen van and drive, nope it was a flying van; it flew off.

"Next time," Bob said.

"There's a next time?" Kwynn said.

"There's always a next time," Phyllis said.

"Next time, what?" Harley said as he walked up.

"We'll settle the score next time," Bob said.

"I thought this would be the end of it," Kwynn said.

"As Winston Churchill once said," James said. "It may not be the end or the beginning of the end but it may be the end of the beginning."

"Thanks, Jimbo," Phyllis said. "Now get to fucking work."

Holy Moly

Thursday, August 9, 2029, 9:30 p.m.

Blowing up the courthouse had somehow restored power, but Glen wasn't sure they should be celebrating.

The townspeople, military men, plus Jayron and Allie sure were pleased. As soon as Glen lit that building up, they started hootin' and hollerin' like it was the Fourth of July.

Glen felt a deep worry in his gut. He also wondered what the hell happened to Arno. Arno was nowhere to be found. The troops finished celebrating and were in contact with their commanders but Arno just vanished.

"I don't like that guy," Glen said to himself.

"What's that?" Jayron said.

"Nothing," Glen said. "I hear that laptop." He walked to the truck and the laptop was buzzing.

On the laptop was a message from Q: IT HAS ONLY BEGUN. >>>SEE YOU NEXT TIME<<<

"Shit."

His phone burst with the pings and pongs of a thousand push notifications, texts, news, social media then a ring tone. Julia.

"Everything, ok?" he said immediately.

"Yep. We got power back," Julia said. "Elsa and Wallie want to know when you'll be home. I do, too."

"As soon as I can scrounge up a ride. Wait, Wallie came home?"

"What can I say, the cat has nine lives."

The black clad military commander called over, "You've earned a ride with us, Tex."

Glen looked back to him, "What ride?" The familiar thwump-wump answered his question and a slick black helicopter emerged from the dark horizon landing, lights blazing. Back into the phone: "Looks like my ride will be sooner than I thought."

"Turn that thing off. You can't use that on there. I think you know why."

"Gotta go. See you in a bit. Love you." He hung up.

He called right back, "Meds. You gotta get down to Santa Monica."

"That's the great thing. That's why I knew I'd get through when I called. A guy in a dark suit knocked on our door and dropped off a package just now. A Package of all Elsa's stuff. I just assumed you set something up. It was addressed to you. He said it was a deus ex machina compliments of Arno."

The squad got in after the copter deftly touched down while the rotors still beat. "Let's GO, TEX!"

"Arno. Well, OK. We'll take it."

"Who is that, then?"

"Doesn't matter, tell you later. Love you."

Glen hopped in after them and the helicopter lifted off again. "Son of a bitch, I didn't say goodbye."

Allie and Jayron stood at attention as the copter gained altitude. Then in unison, they flipped Murray off as a sendoff, big smiles on their faces. Glen nodded back, gave them the one finger wave right back as they rotated and flew out of sight with a flash.

"What the hell kind of helicopter?" Glen looked back to the Captain.

"Like none you ever seen, son," he grinned back. "Hold tight."

Friday, again

Ya, Next

Friday, 2029.08.10 08:30:00

"And what do you propose we do with this?" Frankie said.

She was actually sitting at the table with Arno this time in the smooth walled conference room. The aftermath of this latest round with the KWOUNZEL displayed on the holo above the conference table. Peace restored. Actually, power restored and with it the semblance of a rational society following norms.

"Well, from the looks of it, KWOUNZEL now has independence," Arno said.

"They were chased from that facility."

"Yes, but now they are free in the space between. They are the ghost in the machine. They are daemon running in the background."

"Life finds a way. Add them to the list. Mark them undefined actors."

"Already done," Arno said.

"Next on the agenda: Banks are missing piles of money and they don't know why."

"The vaults aren't locked?"

"They might have checked that. Customers are depositing money but it never gets to the bank."

"Maybe Murray could help."

"He always had a good handle on crime of this sort," Frankie said.

"He is a crook. Are you sure it isn't him?" Arno said.

"I'm sure. He is on the mend and I already stopped him once."

"Well, I'll check in on him and then get back with you on the progress," Arno said and stood to leave.

Box Truck

Friday, 2029/08/10 08:30:00

Kwynn sat with James and Harley in the back of the box truck and waited like all film sets make you wait.

Their legs dangled off the ledge of the rear door as they looked at the Santa Monica pier from the parking lot above. Construction crews already worked to repair the damage done to the Ferris Wheel. Men and women in hard hats moved around the base like ants preparing a nest.

Down below on the sand was an arched, single metal-pipe-type swing set that was easily 25 feet tall and twice as wide. On top, in nothing but his top hat and orange board shorts, a guy walked tight rope style along the top of that curved pole posted in the sand.

His musician friends encouraged the growing crowd with their hootenanny circled at the base. One on a cajon played the beat, another played the soundtrack to the stunt on his guitar. The girl with her finger symbols jumped and spun like the girl on the flying trapeze.

The passerby were charmed. And the passerby contributed tips.

Engrossed with the performers, Kwynn didn't see them coming. A group of twenty marched directly toward the back of the truck with a look that meant business.

Tough, mean, white face and black - the motliest crew they'd seen yet. A bunch of clowns.

"Oh, no," Kwynn said. "I thought we were done for now."

She got up and readied herself for the fight.

The leader laughed, "Odele', where we go?" His laugh broke the face she saw, a mix between skeleton and clown.

"You in this?" Harley said and dropped to the ground, grabbed his shoulder and walked with him. "Juggalos and hip hop?"

"Ya, bro," the Juggalo said, "It's all about bass and kicking ass."

"Yes, it is," James said.

"This way," Harley said. "Take a break, KewTeeBae."

He said that one with a grin.

Kwynn squinted back with a smirk, "No way, fanboy."

Kwynn hopped off the back of the truck and skittered to catch up to the crowd, "I want to be in the middle of this."

ACKNOWLEDGMENTS

Thank you to my wife and sons who watched me scribble, scratch and type, wondering what in the world I was up to. I appreciate you playing along.
Tina, I can't imagine a better partner and am thankful for you in my life every single day.
Joe and Mike, you constantly inspire me with your smarts, creativity and perseverance.

Thanks to Mom for wild dreams in the books.
Thanks to Dad for big dreams in the world.

There are many people who have read, commented, and helped improve this book with their efforts. If you are one of those kind souls (or that daemon jumping on my back every night), please know I appreciate all you have done. St. Peter will move you to the front of the line when the time is right.

Lastly, thanks to you, the reader, for investing yourself in my story and spending time with my imaginary friends. They may be flawed but they're doing the best they can.

See you next time!

About the Author

Jeffrey Messineo runs a Southern California web shop writing copy and code for businesses and government entities. At one time, he was a production assistant and used to cut commercials & music videos in LA. He is working on a new novel.

Keep your eyes on where you are going
and don't miss a thing!

Sign up for Jeffrey's Newsletter
at
JeffreyMessineo.com/newsletter
And get a copy of a rare short story.

You can also follow him
On Twitter: @jeffreymessineo
On Facebook: https://facebook.com/JeffreyMessineo

If you enjoyed Reaping Independence, please take a moment to review this book
on Amazon and/or Goodreads.

As you know, the machines read and tell readers what other people like.

www.ingramcontent.com/pod-product-compliance
Lightning Source LLC
Chambersburg PA
CBHW030643260626
47157CB00007B/2459

* 9 7 9 8 9 8 7 1 9 2 4 0 5 *